Cinnamon Girl

A **VILLAGE COOKS** MYSTERY

Cinnamon Girl

A VILLAGE COOKS MYSTERY

VALERIE HOROWITZ

Annabel
PUBLISHING
Mendham, NJ

ISBN 978-0-9899110-1-6

Annabel PUBLISHING
PO Box 285 Mendham, NJ 07945

www.villagecooks.com

Find the author on Facebook:
www.facebook.com/ValerieHorowitzAuthorPage

Chicken and Coconut Milk Soup recipe from *The Original Thai Cookbook* by Jennifer
Brennan by permission of G.P. Putnam's Sons/Penguin. Roast Beef with Herbs recipe
from *The Pleasure of Herbs* by Phyllis Shaudys by permission of Storey Communications.
Banana Nut Bread recipe from *A Treasury of Great Recipes* by Vincent Price by
permission of Victoria Price. Riviera Fish Soup recipe from *Around my French Table*
by Dorie Greenspan by permission of Houghton Mifflin Harcourrt.

Printed on acid-free paper in the United States of America

For my mother, Sally Murphy

So many people have inhabited and inspired my book-filled and cookbook-filled life in all its intense chapters. I have been lucky to have been involved in many aspects of the book world. My life has been warmed by the friendship and professional relationships with those whom I read, wrote, argued, discussed, edited, published, and sold books to over the years. There are too many to name and thank, but I know you know who you are, and I thank you.

For *Cinnamon Girl*, I am indebted to those who encouraged me in moments of glory and panic as I moved through the process of bringing the book to print. I would especially like to thank my brother, Michael Lentz for his support. I am beholden to the beta-readers who have given me crucial feedback and a thumbs up: Nancy Creighton, Helen Ferrara, SuhAn Grupposo, Carol Johnson, Wendy Merron and Tina Samios. Thank you ladies! I deeply appreciate Danielle Alexander's expert editorial guidance and long friendship, and Carol L. Wright's detailed edits, encouragement and friendship. Peter Lo Ricco's design genius and skill brought Village Cooks to life on the cover.

My writing life has been informed by the example and kindness of Lea Wait and others in the Mystery Writers of America and Sisters in Crime writing community. I am grateful to them.

This book would not have been possible without the love and support of my husband, Ben, and son, Ian. Above all I want to thank them.

Characters

There are lots of characters in the Village Cooks community. Some appear briefly, some stay for longer. Because this is your first visit, I thought I'd introduce them:

Abby Alexander, Bonnie's best friend, a pastry chef at St. Cloud's Restaurant
Abigail Frost, owner of Abigail's English Tea Room
Andy Emerson, Bonnie's husband, a News-Journal newspaper reporter
Anna Maloney, manager of Mayfield Manor
Ben Lannigan, Kay's son, a New York attorney
Bill Billings, ex-United States President, Bonnie's father
Bill Fritz, an associate at Baker Security
Bob Lee, Abby's boyfriend, a county social worker
Bonnie Emerson, owner of Village Cooks
Carol Emerson, Andy's mother
Charlie Campbell, an associate at Baker Security
Danielle Schacht, a doctor
David, a waiter at St. Cloud's Restaurant
Dennis Russo, the Wilmington Middle School principal
Dianne, Jack and Max Barrett, the Emersons' neighbors
Elaine Billings, Bonnie's mother
Elizabeth Crisp, author of *Holiday Delights*
Ella Scott, owner of Willow Lane Inn
Evan Powers, co-owner of Wilmington Books
George Lemoine, chef at St. Cloud's Restaurant
Ginger Harrison, Tony Moran's girlfriend
Greg Baker, owner of Baker Security
Gulliver and Honey, Jeffrey Sloane's horses
Helen and Tom White, owners of the Peacock Inn
Ian Wright, the Emersons' next door neighbor
Janet Wald, Wilmington Middle School front office assistant
Jeanette Creighton, television reporter at WHBC
Jeffrey Sloane, owner of St. Cloud's Restaurant
Jim Leonard, co-owner of Wilmington Books
Karen O'Keefe, a Village Cooks customer
Kathy Post, a News-Journal photographer

Kay Lannigan, owner of Lannigan Antiques
Lauren Ruskin, a doctor
Liam Stone, Andy's boss, the News-Journal managing editor
Lisa Rounds, owner of Vintage Ladybug
Maggie Murphy, owner of Maggie's Irish Imports
Mark Lennon, director of Lennon Funeral Home
Michael Quinn, Wilmington Police detective
Miche Lombardi, manager of St. Cloud's Restaurant
Molly and Steve Schramm, owners of Schramm's Hardware
Mrs. Beeton, Village Cooks store cat
Nicole, David and Maxim Rue, Miche's neighbors
Paul Emerson, Andy's father
Pete Cannavale, snack bar attendant at Citizens Bank Park
Peter Kimball, a psychologist
Royal Jefferson, Elizabeth Crisp's publicist
Sally Harvey, employee at Village Cooks
Sam Birch, a News-Journal newspaper reporter
Steven O'Neill, Wilmington Police officer
Susan ("Sue") Russo, Dennis' wife, a social worker
Terry Ferrara, associate at Baker Security
Tony Moran, a prep chef at St. Cloud's Restaurant
Tracy Brown, knitwear designer at Heath Wear, London
William Emerson, Bonnie and Andy's thirteen-year-old son
Zoe Harrison, nine-year-old daughter of Ginger Harrison
Zuzu Rubin, owner of Zuzu's Travels

And then, of course, there are the special agents from the
United States Secret Service:

Adam Swift
David Jorgensen
Louie Nicholas
Michal Ann Wilson
Rachel Johnson
Rick Harris
Ron Miller
Ruth Cohen

Chapter 1

Chicken and Coconut Milk Soup
Gaeng Dom Yam Gai

6 to 8 servings

A lovely lemony, creamy soup, Don Yam Gai calls for chicken pieces cut through the bone with a heavy cleaver, Chinese style.* If you find gnawing on chicken pieces and delicately trying to remove the bone, vainly searching for a place to deposit it inhibiting your dinner conversation, you may debone the bird and substitute chicken pieces. In either case, use both dark and light meats for color and nutrition.

> 6 cups "thin" coconut milk
> 1 small chicken, sectioned and cut into bite-sized pieces (bone in)*
> 3 stalks lemon grass, bruised and cut into 1" lengths
> 2 teaspoons Laos powder (Ka)
> 3 green onions, finely chopped
> 2 tablespoons, coriander leaves, chopped
> 4 to 6 fresh Serrano chillies, seeded and choppedJuice of 2 limes
> 3 tablespoons fish sauce (Nam Pla)

In a saucepan, bring the "Thin" coconut milk to a boil. Add the chicken pieces, lemon grass and Laos powder. Reduce heat and simmer until the chicken is tender, about 15 minutes. Do not cover as this will tend to curdle coconut milk. When the chicken is tender, add the green onions, coriander leaves and chillies. Bring the heat up just below boiling. Remove the pan from heat, stir in lime juice, fish sauce and serve.

Beef, cut into thin strips or firm white fish pieces may be substituted for chicken.

*A whole breast, for instance, should yield 12 pieces when chopped.

Jennifer Brennan, *The Original Thai Cookbook* (1981)

I read cookbooks in bed. I read cookbooks on the couch, with and without the television on. I read cookbooks in the kitchen while I am cooking something on the stove, or stealing a few minutes to myself with a cup of tea. There's an overflow pile on my kitchen table next to the bookshelf crammed with them. I love to cook, but I love to read cookbooks more. Especially ones with head-notes: the author's anecdotes above the recipe instructions. This is where authors describe what the recipe means to them — usually an important memory that shaped them in some way. Sometimes they're funny, sometimes they're heartbreaking. If a cookbook doesn't have them, I'm disappointed. I'll still flip through the recipes and pictures, but without my usual gusto.

On the day it all started I was bruising lemon grass for my favorite fall indulgence, Chicken and Coconut Milk Soup, which has an amusing head-note (from *The Original Thai Cookbook*), when the doorbell rang.

Some people slice their lemon grass stalks and put them in the food processor. I find that it's better to "bruise" them, that is, gently pound the pieces with a mortar and pestle. I wish I could say I do it this way because I prefer a close visceral and Zen relationship with the food I am preparing. Nope, nothing that cosmic. I find that it tastes better, because bruising by hand is gentler, and the juices remain intact. And it's faster. And there's less to clean up.

So when the doorbell rang I ambled out of the kitchen, mortar and pestle in hand, and peered out my living room window. An African-American girl in sloppy pig tails, maybe nine years old, was standing on my front steps. *She's probably selling Girl Scout cookies*, I thought, as I went to open the door. *Should I buy some, or stick to my diet?*

"Hi! Can you give us some money?"

She grinned, but her eyes traveled away from mine.

Our front lawn is about one-third of an acre, and she had walked up the long brick path to the front door of our house. Down at the bottom of the driveway, a woman who looked to be in her thirties with long, curly, black hair, wearing a navy sweatshirt that said PENN in large red letters, waited with her hand on her hip. The girl's mother, I assumed.

"The teachers at our school told us to ask for money to buy science textbooks," the girl announced, a bit of taunt in her voice.

What? Science books? In Wilmington, where the school budget always passed? My son William goes to Wilmington Middle School, and hadn't brought home a flyer or said anything about a collection.

"Do you have anything in writing?" I asked, thinking as I said it that I sounded foolish, not sure exactly what I was getting at.

She wasn't carrying a brochure or a clipboard with something I was supposed to sign. Her hands were empty. One was on her right hip. She wore a vague smile. I motioned to the mother with a raised arm in a questioning gesture. The mother saw me, fidgeted, and looked away.

Pig tails glanced back at the woman, and then faced me again, twirling her leg forward into a coquettish Shirley Temple pose. I half expected her to put her finger on her cheek and purse her lips.

My puzzled expression must have told her I wasn't buying it.

"No, I don't," she uttered, then turned and ran toward the woman.

Not giggling anymore. I didn't know why, but I felt embarrassed.

"Most people don't donate money without getting a receipt, something in writing!" I hollered after her as they sped toward my neighbor Ian Wright's yard.

"I never heard anything about this, and my son goes to Wilmington Middle School!" I shouted, but they ignored me. As I closed the door my ash blond hair fell out of the messy semi-ponytail I had put it in while cooking.

Maybe I should have just given the little girl some money. But she had taken me completely by surprise, and I'm a control freak. Even at the store I lock my purse in the safe.

I own a cookbook and cookware store, Village Cooks, right in the heart of tiny Wilmington, New Jersey. My name is Bonnie Emerson, and when I'm not at the store I'm either running errands or chauffeuring my thirteen-year old son, William.

As I said, I'm a control freak, for a lot of reasons I won't delve into now. You hardly know me. You're interested in my Chicken and Coconut Milk Soup and knowing what the little girl really wanted.

When I have free time, I like to putter with all of my crazy kitchen tools and cook. I don't know which I like more, the gadgets or the food. That's why I have a cooking store.

I'm obsessed with the idea of being the perfect relaxed hostess, and that takes the right tools. If you want to serve escargot for Bastille Day, come to me and I will sell you not only the loveliest snail platters and the April Cornell Provence-patterned placemats and napkins to serve them on, but also a French cookbook with the perfect recipe for them — and not just the old reliable *Joy of Cooking*. (Not that I don't swear by dear *Joy*.) And I'll tell you where to go to get the freshest snails and the finest fresh seasonings. I have a terrific and steady clientele of Martha wannabees who rely on the quality of my goods and my advice.

Wilmington is a small town of about 2,500 in northwest New Jersey. I like to call it a "village." Everyone thinks of the industrial panorama in the Newark Airport–New York City corridor when they envision New Jersey, but that's just a small part of the state. People forget that it is the "Garden State," and once you get past the suburbs, it has incredibly beautiful countryside. Wilmington is in a woodsy area peppered with horse farms. Jackie Kennedy Onassis kept hers nearby. In the eighties and nineties a fair portion of the farmland was turned into McMansions, and our town has its share. Thanks to the historic houses sprinkled through town, they haven't ruined the village's character.

Village Cooks is one of about a dozen shops on Willow Lane, the main thoroughfare in Wilmington. At the west end, a county road cuts through marking the edge of town. On the corner, Finley Farms draws tourists from the suburbs close to New York on day trips with pumpkin and apple picking in the fall, strawberry and peach picking in the spring and summer, a perpetual giant hay pile for children to climb on, a farm-animal petting zoo, and of course a huge store filled with fresh fruits and vegetables, jams and pies made by locals. I myself cannot leave there without a cider donut. They just smell too darn good when you walk in.

Weekends are busy at Finley Farms and on Willow Lane. The Willow Lane Inn, a B&B in a white Federal-style house, bookends the other end of our strip of shops as it sits trimly behind its white picket fence, its staid appearance contradicted by its bright purple door and an array of purple hydrangeas in the front garden.

In between lay a beguiling array of food and shopping possibilities. And one empty storefront, directly across the street from Village Cooks, in which I hope someone will open a business very soon. It's an eyesore, and bad for business.

Before I started my Chicken and Coconut Milk Soup, I spent some of the afternoon making a to-do list for Village Cook's annual Cookbooktoberfest event, which was coming up in two weeks, on October sixteenth. In October, everyone is in the mood to cook. And every household needs a cookbook — or ten.

So I invented Cookbooktoberfest.

The main event at Cookbooktoberfest is a contest in which the public prepares a recipe from the featured cookbook and brings it to the book signing. The author samples the results, and the author and all of the participants then vote on a favorite. Customers love it because they get more than a book-signing interaction with the author. If I'm lucky, and I often am, the author talks with the contestants about their preparations and offers suggestions. The customers love the opportunity not only to have the author taste their cooking, but also to engage in true conversation with them. Contestants bring their already-used cookbooks in for signatures; often the authors add a personal comment about the recipe they made. "Your take on my lemon chicken was the juiciest!"

And there are those who don't participate in the cooking contest but come for the signing, and they buy books, too. Everyone shares the food, and the event turns into a party. I also have a sale table featuring "gently used" cookbooks — those that have been fingered a bit too much in the shop during the year. A local photographer takes pictures, and I put them up on our website, send the best to the newspaper, and hang the rest on the bulletin board in the store.

This would be our seventh annual Cookbooktoberfest. Elizabeth Crisp will be our featured author; she's promoting her new cookbook, *Holiday Delights*, which covers holidays throughout the year. I already had the book in stock, and it had generated quite a bit of interest before I even announced it as the selection.

The event takes quite a bit of planning. The author has to agree to do it. Usually they are flattered by the prospect of being the star author at an annual event, and intrigued by the contest idea. Then the publicity starts: I place an ad in the newspaper, post it on our store website, Facebook and

Twitter, send e-mails and postcards to customers, and make signs to hang in shop windows to promote the event. Usually there is a six to eight-week lag, and that gives me enough time to get the books in the store, have the customers come in to buy them, decide on what they are going to make, and allow word-of-mouth momentum to build.

This time, however, I'd been having trouble nailing down the author, and with only two weeks to go, I needed to get a commitment or find another cookbook author ASAP. I'd been playing telephone tag with Elizabeth Crisp's publicist, Royal Jefferson. Now living in New York, he is originally from New Orleans and was there visiting his family. He told me that since Hurricane Katrina happened, he went back as often as he could. His elderly mother still lives in the Garden District. Last Wednesday I'd called him there.

"Puts things in perspective, you know, darlin.' Otherwise life in New York just seems too crazy."

"We're only an hour away from New York. And I can't wait to meet you. You didn't come last year. I know it wasn't one of your authors, but…" I chided him.

"Darlin', I know, I know." He laughed heartily. "I can't get out of it this time." He chuckled. "This year I'll be Elizabeth's escort, don't you worry."

"Does that mean she's definitely coming?"

"Yes, ma'am, it does. And I'll be with her. With bells on."

On Thursday I had emailed him PDFs of three ideas for the poster for Elizabeth's approval. Now it was Saturday, and I had exactly two weeks until October 16 to get the word out, so I really needed Royal to call me back with his approval. I e-mailed him the PDFs a second time, left another urgent message on his cell phone, and had just gone into the kitchen and started to bruise the lemon grass when the doorbell rang. And this story begins.

The next morning, Sunday, we stayed in. I did laundry and puttered around in the kitchen as William caught up on television shows we'd DVR'd all week. My husband, Andy, a newspaper reporter at the News-Journal, was off on alternating Sundays. I could hear the theme music to "The Big Bang Theory" from the kitchen, then the rustle of papers that signaled that Andy was reading the Sunday paper while watching the show with William. Then their laughter as I heard Sheldon Cooper knock and utter his ubiquitous "Penny" / knock / "Penny" / knock / "Penny." Even though he's seen Sheldon knock a thousand times, William always finds that hysterically funny. Later, when William had moved on to a re-broadcast of Fringe and it seemed as if Andy was finally finished reading the Sunday paper, I said, "Andy, why don't you come upstairs and talk to me while I fold laundry?"

"What's up, babe?" he said as he settled on the bed and helped me fold washcloths.

"Something, uh, strange happened yesterday while you guys were out," I ventured, my voice quivering just a little.

"What happened? Are you okay?" I saw concern on his face as he stopped folding, and reached over and patted my arm. I put down the washcloth and lightly held his hand. So much larger than mine. Andy is a pretty big guy. He's not quite six feet but has a mop of somewhat unruly curly brown hair that sticks up and makes him look taller. He wears wire-rim glasses, just like his son.

"Yesterday a little girl came to the door and asked for money while you and William were out hiking at Bayer Preserve and I was working and making soup."

"What? Money for what?" he asked.

"She said she was collecting for science books for the school."

"Really? Our school? Wilmington Middle School wouldn't do that, " he said. " They don't need money for books." He paused, considered, and went on. "That's weird, honey. Are you sure that's what she said?"

"Yes," I replied, running my fingers up his arm, back and forth. I couldn't look at him. "I asked her if she had anything in writing."

"In writing?"

"You know, a brochure, a form on a clipboard, something official, like those Girl Scout cookie order forms," I said. "When I asked her, she looked up at me and twirled her pig tails and bent her leg like she was flirting.... It was weird. She reminded me of Shirley Temple."

"Shirley Temple in pig tails? I thought she had curly hair." Andy said in mock astonishment.

But I didn't laugh. "Yeah, she had two pig tails. She was black. And a woman was standing down on the sidewalk. I assumed it was her mother. I motioned to her, but then the little girl ran off, and she followed her. It was very strange, and over before I knew it had happened."

"Well, we'll certainly have to report this security breach to your father's office," he joked.

I glared at him. He was still not taking me seriously.

"Right," I said, and went back to my laundry folding.

My father was once the President of the United States. That's right, POTUS himself, Bill Billings. Our son William is named after him: William Billings Emerson. I am a "First Daughter." I was grown when Mom and Dad lived in the White House, so I was only there on holidays and special occasions. The most wonderful of which was my wedding, on New Year's Day, when the White House was at its most cheerful in full Christmas regalia. I loved planning my White House wedding, especially the menu and the table settings and flowers. Even before the wedding, I sometimes helped Mom and her staff brainstorm ideas for special events. But this part of it — the "security issue" — was some-thing I hated. Because something terrible once happened to our family.

Nineteen years ago, when my father was making his acceptance speech for nomination as candidate for governor of New Jersey, as we — Mom, my sister Brooke, and me — stood proudly beside him on a stage at the New Brunswick Hilton, an attempt was made on his life. One shot. It missed him. It got Brooke.

It shouldn't have happened. Assassination attempts on governors are virtually unheard of. The assassin was caught. He was a 27-year-old schizophrenic, off his meds, who had lived on our block as a child, and had known our family. In his troubled state, he apparently confused my father with his, his inner demons driving him to attempt to destroy his father.

I was 25, living in Manhattan and working as a cookbook editor for a major New York publisher, enjoying every minute of my career and friends, on top of the world. Andy covered the campaign for the state's largest newspaper, and we met when he interviewed our family for an early background piece on Dad.

Brooke was 32, already a professor of international relations at Columbia. We all thought she would follow in Dad's footsteps as the next politician in the family. Who knew, maybe she'd become the first woman President.

Instead the greatest tragedy of our lives made Dad's a household name. Later, we all knew but would never admit outwardly, it got him started on his path to the White House.

Being a natural control freak whose sister was killed in her father's assassination attempt adds up to some heavy baggage. After my sister's death Andy and I continued to date, but we were in no hurry. I was a mess for a long time. We were both so busy with our jobs; we only saw each other on weekends. That worked for us. Dad somehow made it through his term as Governor, but instead of running for re-election afterward, he took some time off.

Dad and Mom traveled to the Far East and India for a few months. Many thought he hadn't run again because he was considering a Presidential bid. That was partly true. I know that every morning that he woke up as Governor he was struck by the cold harsh truth that his desire for that office led to Brooke's death. He loved public service, and was a committed environmentalist who was able to use that to cross party lines. But being the Governor of New Jersey was hard on him.

When they got home from India they told us they had decided that Dad would run for President. And he did, with Mom at his side every step of the way. Losing Brooke had made them closer. Some couples split after they lose a child, but not William and Elaine Billings. We all needed to keep busy. We needed to go on. So we did. We're just a little more paranoid than everyone else.

"Have you ever seen either of them before?" Andy asked gently, because he knew I was annoyed that he wasn't taking me seriously. Good husbands have radar for that, and know when to try to repair the damage.

"Do you know where they live? Did they have a car? What state was on the license plate?" Andy was going into full reporter mode now, peppering me with questions.

I softened. "No, I've never seen them. And I didn't notice a car. But maybe there was one. It all happened so fast. And then they walked next door to Ian's."

"Ian's in Brookline, remember? We're feeding Bertie for him." Ian Wright was our beloved next door neighbor. Tall and gangly, he reminded me of Jimmy Stewart but his manners and accent were pure British aristocrat. We never knew why he and his wife, Mary, moved to our town when he retired from the Royal Navy; they came to the states to be near their son, who lived in Brookline, Massachusetts. Why didn't they move to Boston? It was five hours away. We never asked, and they never offered. Mary died of a heart attack three years ago. The next thing we knew Ian had gotten himself a parrot. Bertie.

And I had forgotten all about her today. My cue to run over there. Andy insisted on going with me. We told William we'd be right back.

Nothing was amiss. Nothing different on his stoop. No note from the pig-tailed girl on his front door. I was spooked, and was glad Andy was there. I rested my forehead on his back for a moment as he unlocked the door. He reached behind and patted my hair.

"It's okay, honey. Everything's okay." He opened the door and we went in. I rushed to the sunroom where Ian kept Bertie's cage. She was happy to see us and sang "My bonnie lies over the ocean," as she often did while her food and water were being filled. Ian had taught her that song in my honor. I was touched, and never tired of hearing it.

"Funny, I thought I left the light on in here last night," I said as I carefully brought Bertie out on my arm and closed the cage.

"Guess you didn't." Andy called as he went off to check the rest of the house. He went upstairs into all three bedrooms and the bathroom, while I stayed in the sunroom and held Bertie on my arm and petted his emerald feathers. Bertie was fine. He didn't seem to have noticed that I was late today. I usually went over right after breakfast, and now it was almost lunch time. Each night I also freshened up his water and gave him a good-night treat. I vaguely remembered thinking last night that he might be lonely because Ian had been gone all week, and I could have sworn I left the light on for him.

Andy came back. "All clear." He grinned. "They always say 'if only animals could talk,' and this one can, but still can't tell us if he's seen anything," I said, giggling. I put Bertie back in his cage. All three of us cheerfully called "See you later!" in unison.

"He may be a witness!" Andy laughed as we locked the door and headed back to our house. We both knew that the sunroom faced the backyard and the most that Bertie would have heard was the doorbell ringing, and maybe the little girl's footsteps as she gave up and walked away.

Around 11:30 we donned slickers and picked up our umbrellas and walked down the road a few houses to go to a birthday party. It had been clear and bright earlier, but storm clouds quickly rolled in mid-morning. Now it was raining hard. Max, one of the sons of our dear friends and neighbors, the Barretts, was celebrating his tenth birthday, and Andy and I had said we would help out. Over the years we were always at all our kids' birthday parties. William was a grade ahead of their older son, Josh. William came along with the proviso that if he got bored he would go upstairs and play Xbox with Josh. But we all knew that birthdays in both families were a tradition none of us would miss, and with the older boys too old for good old-fashioned birthday parties, we all enjoyed the prospect of one, while we still could.

Ten children were expected at noon. We helped with the final balloon-blowing before the onslaught of happy faces bearing presents for Max. Later, between cupcakes and Bionicle building, I matter-of-factly asked Max's parents, Dianne and Jack, if a strange girl had come to their door on Saturday afternoon collecting for science textbooks for Wilmington Middle School. But Dianne and Jack had been at Max and Josh's respective soccer games. Just my luck that they hadn't been home. I'd have to think of a casual way to ask our other neighbors.

The party ended at three. I offered to help clean up, but Dianne shook her head and said, "What's to clean up? Pizza plates and cupcake wrappers? Piece of cake." She giggled at her pun. "Go home, and thanks."

"Looks like none of them saw the little girl and her mother. So, what do you think?" Andy asked afterward as we said our good-byes and strolled home, under umbrellas once again, even though it was only drizzling. William ran on ahead of us.

He was picking up the conversation we'd had earlier while folding laundry, but with some seriousness this time.

"I don't know. I wish one of them had been home. I can't believe that I'm the only one who saw them. I think I'll call the school on Monday and check it out with them."

"Maybe you should just forget about it. Since ours was probably the only house where anyone was home, I don't think you should bother reporting it," Andy said.

I looked ahead and saw that William had found a wet stick he was banging on the pavement as he walked. If it were dry, it would have made a good walking stick. We were still on the road.

"Just try to forget about it. If we lived in the suburbs, this kind of stuff would happen all the time. You wouldn't give it a second thought. You're only freaked out because we live in a small town in the country and you know everyone in town," Andy went on.

"Maybe you're right," I agreed, considering it. I was probably over-reacting. "I shouldn't make such a big deal of it."

William's banging grew louder. "Put that down, honey," I said, "You'll get your hands all wet."

"I'm okay, Mom," William muttered as he gave it another whack.

"Oh, no. No." Andy raced ahead of me and stood, arms folded, at the top of our driveway. William ran over to him shouting, "What's wrong, Daddy? What is it?"

At the base of the driveway, down the incline, eight inches of water stood at the bottom of the barn door.

"Oh my God!" I cried when I saw it. Andy had scooted down and was pulling open the barn doors. Inside the barn was covered with about six inches of water surrounding both of our cars.

"I'll get my keys and get the cars out," he called to me.

"I'll get the wet vac." We sprung into action. "William, come with me into the house. It's too wet for you. Come inside. Now." He knew I meant business. We went inside.

While inside I got a hat and pulled the wet vac from its closet. By the time I got back outside, Andy was standing by the barn door, lost in thought.

The wet vac worked like a charm on the old concrete floor, like it always did. It only took Andy a few minutes to clear up the water.

"We're going to have to get a new drain put in." He shook his head. "And build some kind of a concrete berm in front of the doors so the water can't get into the garage."

"We'll have to dig up the side of the back yard about half a foot wide and drain the water down into the stream, maybe bury a PVC pipe," he continued, referring to the stream that passed behind and through our property and continued down, eventually feeding into the Cold Hill River. A bridle path had been laid alongside it years ago. Andy stomped around through the grass behind the barn to show me what he meant, and I followed. We were in that husband-and-wife-dealing-with-a-problem-head-on mode. Those private moments of truth-telling, facing reality. Facing a huge expense we knew we couldn't put off any longer. This wasn't the first time the barn had flooded after a big rain. We didn't say any more as we made our way back toward the gulley that bordered our house and Ian's, silently pacing out the length of the yard and the extent of the job we faced.

"Andy!" I uttered a startled cry as we reached the stream.

"What?" Andy's voice trailed off as he grabbed me and, as he saw what I saw, hugged me to his side.

The woman who had accompanied the little girl to our door the day before — the mysterious "Mom" — was lying face-down a couple of feet from the stream. Her left leg was smashed over a crumpled bush, and her boot was covered with mud. She was soaking wet, and her hair was matted. Two fallen leaves lay on top of her hair, and one on her neck. I couldn't see her arms. They must be scrunched under her torso. It looked like she was still wearing the PENN sweatshirt. It looked like she was dead.

What was she doing there? How did she die? How did she get into our backyard? And where was the little girl? I guessed I hadn't imagined the whole strange visit from yesterday after all. Nor had I blown it out of proportion, as it had started to seem that afternoon when I told Jack and Dianne about it at the birthday party.

I guessed we'd be calling the police after all.

Chapter 2

If I were forced to give up every fruit in the world but one I absolutely would have no trouble choosing. The lemon wins, hands down.

Laurie Colwin, *More Home Cooking* (2000)

When the police arrived, Andy took them down to see the body. I stayed in the house with William and called my friend, Abby Alexander. Abby is my rock, a level-headed, soft-spoken angel. She must own a hundred pairs of clogs, in every imaginable color, some with hand-painted patterns, which she needs for the long hours she spends on her feet as a pastry chef. She keeps her wavy chocolate brown hair short and close to her head, which gives her a pixie look that works with her large brown eyes.

Thank God she was home. When I told her the news she came right over. Today she was wearing black clogs, but with red jeans and a black turtleneck under her jean jacket.

When Abby arrived, she met Andy and the two police officers who were on their way into our house. Two others were putting police tape around the area surrounding the woman, and the medical examiner was on his knees next to the woman's body. As expected, the officers' faces were grim.

Abby took one look at them, and instead of greeting me with "hello" said quietly "I'll take William to my house. Call us later." She went into the living room to get him.

"Mom, if I go to Abby's I'll miss all the excitement," William pleaded. At thirteen, the age between childhood and teen, he wavered in his maturity. He had seen enough; I didn't want him to see any more.

Before I could reply, Andy spoke up. "No, you won't," Andy said, "we're all leaving. Mom and I have to go down to the police station to make a statement."

The officers nodded.

"Okay, all right, I'll go."

Abby smiled at William. "I made some lemon squares this morning. I know they're not your number one favorite, but they're up there, right?"

He chuckled, and nodded. Minor battle won. "They're not chocolate, but I'll take them."

I hugged Abby. "Thanks," I said into her shoulder, and felt myself begin to choke up. I was shaking. She squeezed me hard, and I composed myself again.

Off we all went, Abby and William to her house. Andy and I followed the officers in Andy's black Prius.

Our ride to the police station was silent except for the drizzle pattering the windshield. Andy pulled his cell phone out of his pocket and put it on speaker.

"Who are you calling?"

"The paper. I've got to report it. A dead body is news. And if the dead body is found on the property of the daughter of a former president who is married to a reporter, it's uh, news the paper wants to get right. And I'd rather the story came directly from me."

I grimaced. Good Lord, now everyone would know. We'd have to call my father.

Andy got straight through to his boss. "Stone? It's Andy Emerson." His editor's name was Liam Stone, but everyone called him "Stone," especially at the News-Journal, where shorthand and speed were the order of things.

I hugged my shoulders while I listened to Andy describe what happened.

After he finished a shorthand version of the events, Stone's craggy voice croaked "Call me after you get home from the police station."

"Will do." He signed off, and turned to me, as if I hadn't heard their exchange. "He'll send a reporter over after we get home."

"Jeez, I can hardly wait," I quipped. Andy didn't laugh. In fact, he gave me a dirty look and said sternly, "I told you, this is news. Big news."

"I know, I know. And I better call my father."

"Not now, because we're here." Andy motioned to the brick police station we had pulled up in front of.

"Okay, I'll call him when we get home," I said. We got out of the car and rushed up the steps in the blinding rain.

When we got inside the station, an officer offered us coffee. Just like in the movies. We accepted it, and then were "escorted" from the large open main room to one of the doors on the left.

We went inside, and found a conference table in a drab yellow room. Andy and I sat down and sipped our coffee. Surprisingly good. It tasted like real milk too, not the powdered stuff. "Not bad. Guess they drink so much of it here they know how to make it," Andy said.

The detective who took our statement was someone on Andy's running team. Their team came in second in a race last month. I had met him at the after-party. A familiar face. That made it a bit easier.

His name was Michael Quinn, a tall, well-built man, with thick brown hair, not unlike Andy's, but much shorter, stopping the curls. He had a clean-shaven face and serious brown eyes. Like Andy, he seemed to be in his early fifties. Michael explained to us that he was going to ask us questions and that we would be videotaped. Afterward we would have to sign a paper stating that our statements were true. We nodded. The whole thing took not much more than a half-hour. Had we just found the body, it probably would have taken ten minutes, but I told him (and the videotape) my weird story of the woman and her little girl coming to our house the day before. The event was so strange that it was hard to tell it so that it made sense. In the re-telling it seemed like a mind-game had been played on me. Michael — should I call him that? Or "Detective Quinn"? Better go with the latter, here in the station — asked me a lot of questions and I tried to make my story as clear as possible.

No, I had not seen either one of them before. No, I had not seen either one of them since. I told him that I suspected that Andy thought I was over-reacting, but I had been perplexed by the event ever since it happened, and had asked my neighbors about it at the birthday party earlier. Now I was even more confused. Did the woman persuade the little girl to ask for the money? Was it her daughter? And where was the little girl now? It felt like some kind of surreal Oliver Twist movie gone badly. Except now Fagin was dead.

"All right, then, we're finished for now," Michael finally announced. "I may have more questions for you in the future, but that's it for today." Michael stood up quickly and slid his chair back under the table. We followed.

As we were gathering our raincoats and heading out the door of what I guess was the interrogation room we heard a commotion in the large main room of the police station. We heard a man's voice yell "You can't bring me in here without a lawyer! I want a lawyer!" Then we saw a man being ushered in, apparently the source of the noise. Mid-thirties, medium height, his head a mass of wavy black hair just this side of wiry, handsome in a Heathcliff way. He was not handcuffed, but was being shuffled in with officers on either side, clearly for questioning. His eyes were red, fierce.

"Leave me the f#$% alone!" he shouted as one of the policemen must have gotten too close. Could they have found the killer that quickly, I wondered? Andy always said the police work fast. But I doubted they were this fast. DUI? Drugs? Maybe. Right age, could be a dealer. Too healthy-looking to be a serious user. Michael noticed that Andy and I were checking him out, and he motioned us out via a different aisle, and walked us quickly to the front door of the station, and opened it.

"This way, folks, we're all through here. We'll let you know if we have any more questions." He held the door.

"Please keep us posted with any developments," Andy said.

"That's a little touchy," Michael replied, "since you're the press." He stopped. "I don't know if I can do that," he finished as we all stepped toward the door. It was still raining outside.

"Off the record?" Andy grinned and put out his hand to shake Michael's.

"Technically, I don't have to tell you anything. But if I don't keep you posted, I might hear about it from your father, right?" He smiled at me.

After shaking Andy's hand Michael reached over and opened the door. We rushed through, down the steps to our car. I knew Michael would be calling the Secret Service. He was required to. I'd better hurry up and call my father.

When we got home, Andy immediately called Stone.

"Great," Andy said after hanging up.

"What?"

"The Prosecutor's office has already emailed a press release, so word is getting around. And the paper's sending a photographer too. But it's Kathy Post. So we don't have to worry."

I knew her, because she photographed Cookbooktoberfest for me every year, but I still groaned. "And which reporter are they sending?" I asked.

"Sam Birch."

"Good, at least he's funny. I could use a laugh about now."

"Stone sent his best, under the circumstances."

"Ha!" I snickered. "Under the circumstances…"

I shouldn't take it out on Andy, but this whole thing was making me cranky. And I still had to call my father.

I got his voicemail and left him a message, downplaying the whole thing.

I quickly freshened up. I ran a brush through my hair but didn't bother about lipstick. Then I scrubbed the kitchen sink while Andy read the paper. He must not have finished it all earlier. And I hadn't read any of it yet, thinking I would pick it up this afternoon, after the party. But I knew I wouldn't be able to concentrate now. I couldn't get the image of that poor woman lying in the mud out of my mind.

Sam and Kathy arrived fifteen tense minutes later. Kathy was a knock-out, tall and slim with wavy shoulder-length blonde hair. Sam carried one of her camera cases. Nice guy, I thought. He had thin graying hair and a beard, and was taller and skinnier than Kathy.

"Sorry, man, so sorry," said Sam as he shook Andy's hand. "Tough break."

"I know, I know. Sam, you know Bonnie." We nodded.

"Bonnie, you know Kathy."

We smiled at each other.

"Come on in." I said, and ushered them into the living room. "Would you like some coffee?"

They all looked surprised. Oops. This was not a social visit.

"No, thanks," said Kathy, brightly. "Can you show me outside? It stopped raining, thank God, but it'll be dark soon. I'd like to get a few pictures right away."

We all knew we wanted Andy's newspaper to get the scoop ahead of the rest of the media.

"We'll all go," offered Andy, and led the way out and around to the side of our house.

The medical examiner's van was just driving away with the body. We all stared at it for a moment. The police had taken down the tarp but had wrapped a yellow tape around a rhododendron bush on the side of our house and strung it over to where they had wrapped it around a tree on the far side of the stream, sealing off the area. Other than that, it looked like it always did after a rain: the stream edges muddied, low brush and a few rocks opening to the woods and the bridle path that ran through it.

"Not much of a picture," I muttered. No one replied. Sam and Andy were talking, but I couldn't hear what they were saying, and Kathy was busy getting out her equipment and setting up.

After a few minutes of kicking around not knowing what to do, and feeling more anxious looking at the spot, I said, "I'm going inside."

Andy looked up, a bit startled. "Okay, hon, we'll be in in a few minutes." And went back to his conversation with Sam.

Kathy was still doing whatever it is photographers do to set up their shots when I left and walked around and back into the house.

I didn't make coffee, but I did make myself a cup of tea. Sleepytime, with honey. To calm me down. I had just stirred the honey in when the door opened and they all clunked back in.

Kathy came right over to me. "Thank you, Bonnie. So sorry that this happened — on your property."

I nodded and tried to smile. She said her goodbyes to Sam and Andy and left.

Andy and Sam settled into facing paisley wing chairs in the living room. I curled up on the big gold velvet couch with my tea.

"Andy already told me quite a bit, but now I'm going to take notes, and may quote what you say in the article. All right?" Sam looked at me.

"Sure."

He proceeded to ask us about the circumstances surrounding finding the body. We told him, but neither of us mentioned the woman and the little girl's "visit" the day before. We didn't embroider anything, in fact, just simply and clearly told him what happened. We were on our way home from Max Barrett's birthday party down the road. The party had ended at two. It had been beautiful early, then in the late morning there was a sudden heavy downpour. When we got near our house, we saw water by the barn door, and got out the wet-vac and cleaned it up. This had happened before when there was a lot of rain in a short period of time. Then Andy and I went outside and were walking around, talking about putting in a drainage pipe, when I saw a woman lying face down right next to the stream, a few feet from the bridle path from the woods. She wasn't moving. Then Andy called the police.

Afterward Sam smiled at me then turned toward Andy and said, "I'll try to quote you both as little as possible."

"Thanks, man."

We walked him to the door. I was anxious to head over to Abby's to get William and bring him home. When we opened the door we saw a television truck pulled up outside. A pretty dark-haired reporter was heading toward our door.

"Oh no," the three of us groaned in unison.

"Let the games begin," I said, to no one in particular. Sam nodded, and slipped out.

"Hi, I'm Jeanette Creighton from WHBC and I'm here about the woman who was found here."

We nodded. At least she was polite. She could have said "the dead body you found" or something more gruesome.

Two more vans pulled up.

Andy told Jeanette, "We found her around over there, by the stream."

He pointed, and led the way, once again. It was dark now, and you couldn't see much beyond the yellow police tape and the woods. You could hear the stream tinkling over the rocks, and a few birds. I hoped Jeanette Creighton would get discouraged and leave. But she didn't. Sam was still sitting in his car, typing into his laptop, no doubt putting the story online.

Andy knew how to handle things. I was impressed as I listened to him say, "Listen, I'm press too, I'm a reporter, I work for the Post. So I get it. I'll tell you what happened, and I'll tell you everything I know. You'll have to trust that."

"Got it," she said. "Can I film you?"

"Me, but not my wife. I'll make a brief statement in fifteen minutes."

I guessed he was waiting to see if any other television crews arrived, then he could handle them all at once.

"Got it," Jeannette quipped again. Then, "I understand that she's—" she looked over at me, "—President Billing's daughter, Bonnie Billings?"

Her voice went up with excitement as she said my name. All children of Presidents become minor celebrities, and I had, too. "You have to share something the press can hang their hat on," my father had advised. My White House New Year's Day wedding had provided plenty.

After I met and married Andy I traded my New York life for a quiet one with my family and Village Cooks. My parents visited fairly often now that Dad was out of office, and we had holidays at the big old Tudor house in Montclair I had grown up in, about forty minutes away. They had kept the house and returned to it after Dad left the White House. They loved the old charmer with its four fireplaces. Back when Dad was Governor of New Jersey they chose to stay in their house on Upper Mountain Avenue rather than live at Drumthwacket, the official governor's home in Princeton. It made them feel closer to Brooke. No one questioned their decision. They weren't the first and wouldn't be the last Governor's family to do so.

We went back inside.

"I'm not going to mention the girl coming to the house yesterday. I'm going to keep it private, at least for now." Andy said, and wrote down a few notes on a pad. I paced. And puttered.

Sure enough, fifteen minutes later there were a total of four television vans parked out front. Jeanette Creighton must have told the others that a statement was forthcoming, because none of them approached our door.

At precisely 4:45 Andy stepped out the front door. I stayed inside in the hallway, and peered through the edge of the window drapes, close enough to hear him.

"Good evening," he began, and actually smiled at the reporters and camera people who had set up lights and equipment on our lawn. The bright lights made the scene seem surreal, like a movie set.

"At about 2:15 this afternoon my family — my wife, Bonnie Emerson, my son, William Emerson, and I — were walking down the road from a neighbor's toward our house. It was raining. We noticed some water building up by our barn door. We sent our son inside. After we vacuumed up the water, my wife and I were returning to our house when she noticed a woman lying motionless on the ground face down near the stream. The woman was African-American and wore a navy blue sweatshirt, jeans, and black boots. She was soaking wet, there were a few wet leaves on her, and she was obviously dead. We immediately called the police."

He paused for a breath, and a few cameras flashed.

He smiled again. "I will not take questions, because there is nothing more to tell. The police are investigating. Please follow up with them. Thank you very much, ladies and gentlemen." He turned and easily ambled toward the house. *How could he be so calm?* I wondered.

Not only did Abby have lemon squares ready, but she had baked a goat cheese, fennel, and caramelized onion tart while William sat at her counter and entertained her with Guitar Hero on his DS. They looked relaxed, like they had enjoyed keeping each other company. Certainly they were in better shape than Andy and me. I was a wreck. On the way to Abby's house, it occurred to me that the killer knew my house. My family might be in danger. It brought back memories.

"They videotaped us as we gave our statement," Andy explained to Abby as he plopped down on a stool. "Then the paper sent over Sam Birch to do a story. Then the TV people showed up, so I made a statement."

I groaned. Abby sized us up. "I'll make some tea," she said, and proceeded to put the kettle on. Her kitchen counter was made of stainless steel and her stove and double oven was top of the line. What you would expect of a serious pastry chef. Otherwise her kitchen was traditional suburban country in a suburban town house: window over sink, herbs on windowsill, cabinets painted light blue, oak round table and chairs in the breakfast nook, light blue calico curtains, oak stools at the counter. But she sure managed to make something special in that oven.

Abby reached for the remote to her kitchen TV.

Andy warned her off. "Don't bother, I don't think they'll have it this fast. We'll probably be on the eleven o'clock news."

But he was wrong.

"Mom, Dad, come quick!" hollered William from the other room. "Dad is on the news!" And so he was. They featured Andy's entire statement, which had been less than two minutes long. But we knew the next day's newspaper would have a photo of the crime scene and not him, since Kathy Post hadn't taken any pictures of him. And Sam's story, probably already online, would also be in print, and would be written and edited properly. We'd have some dignity in print, at least. Thank God for the print press. After it was over, we returned to the kitchen and Andy and I plopped on the stools while Abby headed to check the oven.

As she did so, Abby asked, "What was it like at the police station?"

Andy answered. "It wasn't so bad. Michael Quinn was on duty. He was on my running team last year. He questioned us. He made it pretty quick. I thought he did a good job."

"You could tell that he was careful with his questions, they were very clear and direct, like he was breaking down the facts of the story," I put in. "It was actually pretty interesting," I added. "The process." I smiled.

"Do they know who the woman is? Or where her daughter is?" Abby asked as she handed us our mugs of Lemon Zinger and passed the honey jar over to us.

"I don't think so." I cupped my hands around the hot mug and took a sip. "But they did bring in a man just as we were leaving. He was upset, and cursing, but he was kind of handsome, too."

I flashed a look at Abby, who was single, but she didn't blush or respond. She had a boyfriend, Bob Lee, and this was not the time for lightness. This was a tragedy.

"Probably a drug dealer," I added, causing William's eyes to light up. I winked at him, then put my nose to my mug to take in the full aroma of the Lemon Zinger, one of my favorite teas.

Then we all moved over to the table. We were all pretty quiet as we wolfed down Abby's tart and the salad of baby greens and mustard dressing she made to go with it. It was delicious. I was glad it was a light dinner, after the pizza and cake we had eaten at the birthday party. Afterward William and Andy each ate two of the lemon squares while I picked at one.

We had finished eating and had moved into Abby's living room, and were chatting about William's botany project when Andy's iPhone rang. Because he was a reporter, his iPhone rang a lot.

It was Michael Quinn. So soon? It hadn't been two hours since we left the police station. After a series of "no kiddings," "no's" and "uh-huhs," he finally clicked off.

His news was quite interesting. It turned out that the man they had brought in was the boyfriend of the woman we found. He had been stopped for speeding out on Old Chesterfield Road and had a drugged demeanor, so they brought him in for questioning. During their interview, they made the connection between the guy and the dead woman — that part wasn't clear, but they had done so, somehow. The morgue was in the building, so they brought him down there to see her. The boyfriend's name was Tony Moran, and he identified the woman as Ginger Harrison. He said she had been in drug rehab down near Princeton, and that she moved to Wilmington a few months ago to be near him.

He said she had a daughter. The little girl? I thought. He said he didn't know what had happened to her. Michael said they believed Tony was telling the truth, because he had an alibi. They verified that he had been at work at St. Cloud's Restaurant.

"My restaurant?" Abby exclaimed, then paused, her face stricken.

"Our Tony? Oh my God, it can't be Tony from St. Cloud?" She continued, and pronounced it the French way, "san cloo." Everyone else pronounced it Saint Cloud, except for Abby, the owner Jeffrey Sloane, and Miche Lombardi, the restaurant manager.

"He is the sweetest guy," she went on, and kicked absently at her chair leg. "He did have something bad happen in the past, now that I think about it. Drugs. Cocaine, I think, nothing worse."

"Cocaine's pretty bad," I said, eyeing William, who was now feigning interest in Super Mario Brothers on his iPad. But I knew he was listening, and fascinated. I knew I had to get him home soon too; it was getting late, and it was a school night.

"He's from Philadelphia. I don't think he went to cooking school. Doesn't talk much about his past. Loves movies. Film noir, thrillers, and old black-and-white classics with dark themes. Like 'Rebecca' and 'The Thirty-Nine Steps.'"

"Those are great movies. He's got excellent taste," Andy began.

"What does he do at the restaurant?" William broke in, accustomed to interrupting his dad.

Abby explained. "He's a prep chef. And very good at it. Has a lot of promise, according to Jeffrey and Chef Lemoine."

Jeffrey Sloane bought the Cobblestone Inn five years ago and turned it into St. Cloud, switching the menu from steaks and American grill fare to French-Asian fusion. Andy and I had eaten there often.

Jeffrey, who looked like a textbook California beach-boy-turned-man with his naturally blonde hair, blue eyes, and handsome features, was better at charming the customers than he was a chef, so he had hired one, George Lemoine. And Tony Moran was his prep chef.

It was no secret in town that Jeffrey was gay. I liked him, and found myself wishing he would settle down with someone, or if he had indeed done so, let it be known, and introduce the man, so I could stop worrying about his happiness. I often wondered if he knew that everyone knew that he was gay, and didn't care, because he never mentioned his personal life. Maybe the restaurant was his personal life. It certainly took up his evenings.

When we got home, William went upstairs to take his shower and Andy mixed a gin and tonic for each of us. I guessed we'd be checking out the ten o'clock and the eleven o'clock television news. Dad still hadn't called back. Lord.

We were running only about half an hour behind our usual Sunday night schedule, so William would be fine. Kids need their routines, their schedule. I wondered what kind of Sunday night routine that little pig-tailed girl had, and knew that whatever it involved, it had been destroyed by Ginger Harrison's death.

Chapter 3

Roast Beef with Herbs

For many years we had roast beef at least twice a month on Sundays. I was then working six days a week, so I devised ways to make cooking easier, especially since Sunday was my only free day for gardening.

I would put the roast in the oven at 325 degrees around 2:00. One of my daughters would peel the carrots and onions while I scrubbed the baking potatoes. Then out to the gardens...

Around 4:00 I'd come in, bringing chives for the sour cream, and put 2 t. of the herb mix on the roast, add the onions to the meat pan, put the pierced and oiled potatoes in the oven and the carrots on the stove on low, and go back outside again.

At 5:00 I'd come in and turn the potatoes over (they baked on an old aluminum cookie pan), stir up the onions so they'd brown on all sides, add the carrots to the meat pan, and go back outside.

We were usually starving and ready to enjoy our gourmet "banquet" by 5:30 or 6:00, even though the "chef" had been gardening all afternoon!

Roast Beef Seasoning

3 t. parsley, 2 t. rosemary and chives, 1 t. each summer savory, dried minced garlic, and thyme. Mix well and store in covered jar. Use 2 t. per roast, the last hour or so of cooking.

Phyllis Shaudys, *The Pleasure of Herbs* (1986)

I decided against calling the school to officially verify the child's solicitation that had started this nightmare. On Monday morning, I drove William to school, and helped him carry in his botany project, a sprouted onion that he had planted. It was now four feet tall, and sported a lovely white flower on the top. My store is closed on Mondays, so I had plenty of time. I stopped and chatted with Janet Wald, the very pleasant woman in the front office who, after squealing "I saw your husband on the news!

How awful!" — assured me that no such fundraising effort was under way.

"They just increased our taxes when we voted on the school gym addition. Of course we don't need money for science books." She twirled her rimless glasses and glanced back at her computer.

The novelty was over. I was keeping her from her work. And there was no class trip to Washington, DC, or anywhere distant planned that required fundraising. I don't know what I had been thinking.

She asked, "Did you tell the police about it?"

"I just wanted to check with you, and I'm checking with some of the other neighbors too, to see if the girl had gone to any of their houses," I said, not answering her question. She didn't seem to notice.

I also hadn't told Abby about the strange "incident," as I was now calling it in my mind. "Incident" is a better word to muse over than "solicitation." And I couldn't get my mind around it, no matter how many times I replayed the details of the event in my head. I didn't want to talk about the little girl in pig tails coming to our door in front of William, so Abby only knew that a woman's body had been found in our yard, and that Michael Quinn had called to tell us her name and her relationship to Tony Moran, the man who worked at St. Cloud's Restaurant with Abby.

After I left the school I decided to stop by St. Cloud's, even though I had never been there before when they weren't open. They were closed on Mondays, too, but I knew Abby had baking to do for an afternoon tea party they were catering. Miche, the elegant manager with jet black hair pulled back in a tight ballerina bun, handled the catering end of the business. I parked and walked to the back door, where Jeffrey stood outside, having a puff. He was dressed in a pumpkin-colored button down Ralph Lauren shirt, well-tailored brown corduroy pants and tassel loafers. I wondered if he knew about Tony Moran and Ginger Harrison.

"You caught me!" He smiled his charming Beach Boys smile and, with a quick head movement, flipped his blond bangs out of his eyes. "Yes, I still have the dirty habit. Started in college and never able to quit. But I'm cutting down."

I nodded understandingly. "Hi, Jeffrey, how are things?"

He stamped out his cigarette, picked up the butt and placed it in a tissue he removed from his pocket.

"Fine, fine. Come in. What a nice surprise on this beautiful fall day," he said grandly as he escorted me in the kitchen door.

"Is Abby here?"

She must have heard me. "Over here. I'm over here!" She called from the rear of the kitchen, so I followed her voice. Which wasn't easy over Springsteen's voice singing "Everybody's got a hu-u-ungry heart" from her CD boombox.

I didn't want to get Abby in trouble. I hollered, "I thought I'd stop in and see if you wanted to go riding later." I came up with this quickly, wanting an excuse in front of Jeffrey. I just wanted to see my friend, and hash over my feelings about finding Ginger Harrison's body, now that the shock was wearing off. I wanted to tell her about the strange little girl who had been with Ginger. I would have been happy to sit in the car in the parking lot and talk. I didn't really want to go riding.

"I forgot my cell when I drove William to school, so I figured I'd just stop in and ask you," I added. Not bad, on the spot.

"Sounds great. But it'll take me at least another hour to finish up here. I have to finish these scones and pack them for Miche to bring to the tea. Can I meet you around 11–11:30?" Abby's eyes barely left the dough she was working on, but I gathered she knew I wanted to — needed — to talk.

"Why don't you two take my horses out today?" Jeffrey piped in. "I won't be able to exercise them today because I'm helping Miche do the county historic society tea out in Arlington, so I'll be gone all afternoon. It's a big group. We have four helpers." His eyes trailed over to the St. Cloud's Restaurant and Caterers van parked in the driveway.

"You'd be doing me a favor," he added with that twinkle in his eyes that I guessed probably made everyone in his path melt. "If you take them out I won't have to pay to have them exercised."

I liked him, despite his excessive charm. He sure seemed calm for someone who would be catering a large afternoon tea in a few hours. Then again, Abby was doing the baking, and Miche was getting everything else ready. He would just go along and probably be the one to pour the tea while charming the guests. Abby never went out on catering gigs. She was a behind-the-scenes kind of gal.

"We usually go to Garrity's and rent horses for an hour," Abby said. She looked at me, and I nodded.

"But it would be a nice change to go to Morris Farms. We'd love to, and thanks!" she added.

"Good. I'll call them and let them know to expect you after 11," he said, and turned toward the restaurant's office. "Bye, ladies, have fun!" he called as he walked down the hall.

"Is there any news?" Abby asked once we were alone.

"No, not that I've heard. I just need to talk to you," I answered. "I was hoping to talk to you here while you worked, but this will be better. I didn't know what to expect, I thought maybe you could talk. But I see that you can't, since Jeffrey and Miche are around. Don't worry, it's fine, the store's closed today. It looks like you have a lot to do still, so I'll meet you at Morris Farms at 11:30."

I tried to smile brightly as I left. She did too.

I had two hours to kill. So I went to the store, made myself a cappuccino in our mini-kitchen in the back, and finally reached Royal Jefferson on the phone.

He apologized. "I was just getting ready to call you. I was on a fly-fishing trip up in the Catskills. Got back late last night. Sorry, darlin.' Elizabeth is excited about the event. It'll be a highlight of her book tour, since it's more than the usual book signing. But she wants you to use a different picture."

Royal Jefferson went on to say that he would email me a new photo of Elizabeth to replace the dated one I had used on my spec design. Other than that she liked my designs, and chose the one I too favored of the three. Elizabeth is a gorgeous woman, with a sensuous face and long, thick ginger-colored hair with just the right amount of wave. And absolutely no frizz. My mop could never look that smooth and elegant. But I have to admit I like being blond and blue-eyed, because I can get away with only lipstick and still look cheerful, even when my mood is not, or when I'm feeling fat. I should lose about 25 pounds, but since I turned

40 a few years ago, it's not easy. Especially since I love to cook. So I try to exercise every day.

I guess you could call horseback riding exercise, since it uses some leg muscles, but it never helps my weight. Even so, Abby and I try to go riding every few weeks or so, when we can. It's nice to have a friend who rides too, because Andy and William are not interested in horses at all.

Abby and I didn't meet over riding. We met over *Little Women*. I am probably one of the biggest Louisa May Alcott fans ever, and was thrilled when I learned that a musical based on *Little Women* was coming to Broadway. I went to see it by myself, one Wednesday matinee. None of my friends were interested enough to go with me, but I didn't care. I ordered myself a ticket online and arranged for Sally Harvey, my one employee, to work the whole day at Village Cooks and for Andy to get off early to meet William after school.

I rather enjoyed the indulgence of seeing the play by myself. On the crowded train ride home, a woman sat down next to me whom I recognized from the audience. She had been in the row in front of me, one person over. I mentioned this to her after she smiled at me as she sat down, and we struck up a conversation. It was Abby.

Neither of us liked the songs, but we loved the set, and of course, the story. She had gone with a friend from culinary school who lived in the city. We had a heated discussion about which parts of the book we would and wouldn't have put in the musical, and compared it to the various film versions. We agreed that we liked Katherine Hepburn's Jo the best. Abby told me she was the pastry chef at St. Cloud's Restaurant and I told her about my shop. That weekend she dropped in to Village Cooks, and we've been friends ever since.

When I got to the parking lot at Morris Farms I was glad to see Abby's navy Forester already parked. She was just getting out of the car, and we hugged and walked in together. The stable master, Steve, was expecting us, and brought us around to the rear where Jeffrey's horses, Gulliver and Honey, were waiting. I climbed up onto Gulliver, a large handsome chestnut male who I knew could handle my weight, while Abby got on Honey, a golden mare.

We cantered through the meadow behind the barn, and headed to the woods beyond. The horses naturally rode side by side down the trail, and we were able to talk. I told Abby about the little girl with the pig tails. Because she was my friend she was able to suspend disbelief about the strange incident, as Andy had. It was easy to tell her.

"I'll ask Bob if he knows anything about the little girl," she offered as I finished the story. Abby's boyfriend, Bob Lee, is a county social worker. He had been divorced for two years when they met last year. No children. I knew Abby wanted kids, so I hoped they were in the cards for her. But they were both in their late thirties, and she had mentioned the possibility of adoption more than once to me, in confidence. She was worried about her fertility.

We trotted back out of the woods and through the meadow back to the barn. We had been gone about an hour. Not quite a workout for Gulliver and Honey, but an outing and some exercise nonetheless. Gulliver, true to his name, was hulking but nimble and fast. Honey had been a little slow, distracted. Horses were like that sometimes, you never knew why. It could be anything. I loved riding on a cool crisp fall day, even when the clouds passed back and forth over the sun causing shadows, like they were today.

We said our goodbyes and as I got into my car I saw Abby settle into hers, and grab her cell phone to call Bob. It's nice to have such a good friend who believes your wacko stories without judgment. I wound my way back over to Wilmington Middle School, rehearsing in my head as I drove. Abby had convinced me to report the incident to the principal, because the school was involved indirectly.

I got there at 12:45. Some grades were at lunch and others at recess. Janet looked surprised to see me back at the school, but she did her job and checked. Mr. Russo was in his office and could see me for a few minutes. He greeted me with a predictable handshake as I walked in.

Mr. Russo had been a gym teacher for ten years before joining the administration, and he kept in shape. His shaved head and powerful physique made him look more like an Army sergeant than a principal. I guess that was the point. The kids were in awe of him, thanks to a rumor that he had been a Navy Seal. He probably knew about the rumor, but Mr. Russo didn't do anything to confirm or deny it. In fact, not much was known about Mr. Russo other than that he was married and had no children. His wife Susan was a social worker. They lived in the neighboring town of Stapleton.

I did my best, telling, once again, my tale of the pigtailed girl who rang my bell around five on Saturday afternoon looking for money for science textbooks. I hated answering "Yes" when Mr. Russo asked me if she was African-American. That was his only question. Other than that, he listened attentively to my story.

"I don't know anything about this. If we were going to ask for funds for school books, we would have done so through the usual channels," he said, after I'd finished. "But we wouldn't have done so. Textbooks are always fully funded without issue. We don't need to raise money for them."

He was so even in his speech that we could have been discussing the annual Science Expo. He did not seem to find my story strange at all. Or maybe he was used to crazy stories from parents, and was humoring me. He idly scratched his left forearm. I could see his muscles ripple.

"Do you think there's any connection to the woman's body you found on your property?" he asked. "Was the woman African-American too?" he added with authority, before I had a chance to answer his first question.

I hesitated. "Yes, she was. It may have been the woman who was with the little girl. She was down on the sidewalk waiting, and I didn't get a good look at her." Something told me not to tell him that I knew for certain that they were one and the same. His two questions about race disarmed me, and I felt unsettled. Again. This thing was so strange, from the girl with the pig tails to the body in the yard. My control-freak self was losing it.

With that, the one o'clock bell rang, signaling a period change, and we said polite goodbyes. Mr. Russo thanked me for coming in personally and letting him know about the incident. Once again, he said the school didn't need to ask residents for money that way, adding that no other parents had come forward with a similar story.

"Got it," I said, "Thanks for your time, Mr. Russo."

That was that, meeting over. I was dismissed from the principal's office feeling like he'd forget about me a moment later and move on to the next parental crisis. I skulked out into the hall feeling as if I had just avoided getting in trouble. I don't know why this crazy story made me feel guilty.

I got in my white Honda CRV. Not sure what to do next, I stopped at the butcher to pick up a roast. I figured I'd make Roast Beef with Herbs, since we hadn't had a nice roast in a while. The butcher shop was crowded with other mothers doing errands before rushing home to meet their children. Forty-five minutes later I was relieved to be home, although my mind was racing.

After he left the White House my father told me that even though I would not have the Secret Service with me anymore I would always have to keep my eyes open, always be a little more wary than everyone else. As we well knew, disturbed people and enemies of our nation were not immune to the idea of targeting relatives of our leaders. When I opened the door to that little girl I should have been more careful. I should not have opened the door to a stranger, even if it was a child.

Plus, I was cooking. That should be sacrosanct. And where was the little girl now, anyway? Was she Ginger Harrison's daughter? Was she dead, too? Somewhere else in my yard, or in the woods out back? Bayer Preserve? Had the police checked all around? I wasn't sure. They were still working when Andy had made his statement to the press, but by the time we got back from Abby's, they had gone. I shivered as I put the kettle on for a cup of tea, always the first thing I do when I walk in the door. Control freak and tea-lover that I am.

I love Mondays. If I schedule my errands well, I usually have a bit of time to myself before William gets home, unlike Tuesday through Friday when I rush home from the store and sometimes barely make it before the school bus arrives at 3:30. Sally starts at two, and I try to leave at three.

I admit I don't miss the nine-to-five world. I love being able to make my own schedule. When I opened up Village Cooks, it was a dream come true. My other dream was to become a mother. Thankfully I'd succeeded at both.

I put a tea bag in my cup and saw that I had plenty of time before the school bus arrived. I took the tea bag out of my cup and added a drop of milk. Perfect. Rooibos (roy-bosh) is a South African red tea that I have loved every since Abby brought it back from a trip there a few years ago. Now Twining's offers it in bags, so it is easy to get. I took a sip and opened the newspaper. I hadn't checked the online version.

The story was on page five, thank God. And there was only one photo. Sam Birch did a good job — just the facts. Kathy Post's photo showed the spot where I had found Ginger.

"How was your day?" I asked later as William jumped off the bottom step of the bus, blue backpack on his shoulder. "Great," he said. "I'm gonna make some popcorn."

We went inside and he made a bag of microwave popcorn and grabbed a bottle of Vitamin Water from the refrigerator. A second later he was gone, and our after school "conversation" was over. Oh well.

The phone rang. It was Abby. She got right to it. "I just talked to Bob and I have some news."

"Really?" I said. "Where are you?" I gulped my tea.

"I'm home. I'm fine," she said, "But Bob just called. They found the little girl. She is Ginger Harrison's daughter, and her name is Zoe." She sounded breathless.

"Go on," I said. I was getting excited too.

"They found her in a rooming house. You know, Mayfield Manor, on the edge of town?" I knew it. There were rumors that transient druggies lived there, but there had never been any arrests, and the place was well-kept on the outside. I had never been inside, but always noticed lights on in the upstairs windows when I drove by at night. I thought the place was mysterious, and had long been intrigued by it.

"I know the place. Where is she now?"

"Social services will find a family to keep her while things get sorted out."

"Oh my God. Will Bob get to speak to her first? Or the police? Isn't she what they'd call a material witness?" I had more questions, but I took a breath.

"She's with Bob now. He is supposed to come over for dinner at six. He thinks he'll be done by then. I'll find out all about it when I see him."

"Why don't you two come over here instead? I have a roast in the oven, and there's plenty. It'll be ready by six, but we can reheat it for you and Bob when you get here, if you can't get here by then."

"That sounds nice. As a matter of fact, I was just going to grill some steaks. I'm sure he'll like that idea. He loves your cooking," she said. "I'll call him. If it's a problem, I'll call you back. If not, we'll see you at six. Then he can tell all of us about it. Will Andy be home by then?"

"He said he'd be home by six, so it looks like we're copacetic."

"Great. Okay. See you later."

"Bye."

I went into the living room and told William that Abby and Bob would be coming over for dinner but that it might have to be a little later than usual. He was pleased.

"In the meantime, it's homework time, bud."

"I know, I know." He brought his backpack into the dining room and got to work while I worked in the kitchen making the salad for dinner. I wanted something light and sweet to balance the heavy roast and potatoes, so I made a simple mesclun salad, chopped up a few strawberries, and added some slivered almonds for crunch. I tossed it all with a light vinaigrette. William hated too much vinegar.

As I worked I couldn't help but think of the contrast between William's life and Zoe's. Now, she had no mother. Who knew if she had a father. And there was my son, whistling as he did his math calculations at the dining room table, while I merrily — did I say merrily? —unloaded the dishwasher after placing the salad in the refrigerator to rest until dinner time.

Ginger Harrison. That poor woman. I had been thinking so much about Zoe — after all, I had met her — that I hadn't thought too much about Ginger. I had only seen her twice. The second time was drilled into my memory: a dark figure splayed out on the ground on a dark, rainy day. She looked fairly tall, big-boned. I had never seen a dead body before. Those who have and who have seen the faces of the dead always describe them with horror. But I hadn't seen her face. Just the back of her. Black hair, navy sweatshirt, jeans. Her hair had looked choppy, as if it fell in segments, as wigs sometimes do. I wondered if it was a wig she was wearing, or hair extensions. Then of course there were the obvious questions — who killed her and why? How long had she been there? Was she there all night? Did it happen while we were home, unaware, inside? Or sleeping?

And I puzzled over her background. Where was she from? Did she live in town? What was her story?

Andy and Abby breezed in the back door, having arrived at the same time, Andy holding the door for Abby. My gentleman sweetheart.

"Hi!" Abby brushed my cheek and plopped a paper bag on the counter. Andy gave me a kiss, glanced at Abby's bag and then at his empty hands, and turned them up and down, grinning sheepishly. We all laughed.

"What did you bring?" I asked Abby.

"I'm sorry I'm late. I was nervous waiting to come over here, so I baked a loaf of bread, and then I had to wait for it to come out of the oven."

"Smells great," said William as he joined us in the kitchen. "What kind is it?"

"Honey wheat," she paused. "With some flax thrown in for the omega threes."

"Will I like it?" William asked sweetly.

"I sure hope so."

"Don't you always love Abby's baking?" I chimed in.

William thought a while. "Yes!" he pronounced and we all cheered at the honest innocence of children.

"Can I show you something in my game, Dad?"

"We'll wait for Bob. It should only be a few minutes. I'll call you when he gets here," I told them, nodding.

"Thanks, Mom." Andy and William traipsed off.

Abby grabbed the bread basket from the cabinet. She knew where I kept it. Then she opened the brown paper bag, drew out the golden loaf and put it in the bread basket.

"Looks awesome, Abbs," I said.

She got the butter out of the fridge while I finished setting the big old oak farm table. I set out thick Wedgwood blue homespun napkins and matching placemats, and white dinner and salad plates. I put blue candles in the pewter candlesticks, and lit them. Abby got out the water glasses and brought them in, just as we heard a knock and "Hi" from the back door as Bob entered. He kissed Abby with true emotion, but looked frazzled otherwise.

"I need to go slice the roast." I said and left them alone in the living room and went to put the food on the table. It took me a few minutes to do so. Just in time, Andy and William came back downstairs.

"Hi Bob," they said in unison, and everyone laughed and sat down.

"Like father, like son," said Bob, grinning. Then I caught his glance at Abby, but she was busy unwrapping the bread from the cloth and breaking off a piece.

"William?" she asked.

"Yes, a big piece, please."

"And why again is it that we break the bread rather than cutting it with a knife at dinner?" asked Andy as he settled at the head of the table and Bob and I brought in the plates of roast beef and potatoes and sat down.

"Because you're more connected to it if you break bread by hand," explained Abby. "I only slice it if I'm making sandwiches, or if I'm serving something that calls for slices, like bruschetta."

"Aha," said Andy.

Then William said grace and we all dug in.

After a few minutes of eating and some sprinkled compliments I readily accepted, I broached the subject.

"Bob, can you tell us about the little girl now? Or should we wait for after dinner?" I wondered if his news would be appropriate for William's young ears, and hoped he'd catch my drift.

"Let's wait till afterward. I need to decompress. And I also need to catch up on William's progress in Minecraft," Bob replied and all the grownups around the table took deep breaths and relaxed.

William hadn't noticed. He was eager to talk about his game and chattered on cheerfully as we all ate.

Then, the expected "May I please be excused?" followed by Andy's "Yes, you may." And William bounded back upstairs.

"One hour till your shower!" I called after him.

"Right, Mom," he called back. I got up and put on the kettle for tea.

Abby and I cleared and set out mugs while Andy and Bob caught up on the baseball scores. I filled the teapot with hot water to "hot the pot" so it would be hot when I poured the tea and boiling water into it. By the time we had loaded the dishwasher, the kettle was chirping and I dumped the hot water out and filled the teapot with loose jasmine tea and the boiling water.

Abby portioned blueberries and whipped cream into dessert bowls, and we went back to join the guys in the dining room.

"Well," Andy sighed. "Come on, Bob, tell us what's going on."

Bob had a lot to say.

"We picked up Zoe at Mayfield Manor. She was watching television with the super's wife and manager of the place, Mrs. Maloney. Anna Maloney. She's a retired bookkeeper. Nice lady, very kind. Apparently she watched Zoe a lot while her mother," he paused, "was out."

The tea was steeped now, so I poured. Abby passed around the honey.

He went on.

"Zoe went along with us without a problem. Seemed like she was used to going places with other adults. Didn't even ask for her Mom till we got her to the office. I got her an orange soda, and when I handed it to her she looked at it for a minute, like she was dreaming or something. Then she said, 'Where's my mother?'"

He choked a bit. "I had to tell her. What could I do? I didn't want to tell her right away, but she forced my hand by asking. Thank God Sue Russo was there. She was sitting next to her, and reached over and took her hand, so I told her the truth."

"Do you know Sue Russo?" he asked me.

"I know her as Susan," I answered.

"Either way, she uses both," he said. "Some people hate nicknames, but she doesn't mind."

He drank some tea, then toyed with his berries.

He went on. "Anyway, Zoe took it like a trooper. I think it was easier on her than it was on Sue and me. Sue was with her husband once a few years ago when a student died in a fire at home and Dennis Russo had to announce it to the kids at the school. He's a smart principal. He went class to class, with Sue at his side, and told each group individually and took their questions. Took the whole day…

"Anyway," he went on, "I was glad Sue was there. Zoe took one look at me, then looked at Sue and asked her 'Where do I go now?' and that was it."

"Maybe she wasn't close to her mother?" Andy ventured.

"You can say that again," Bob continued. "Apparently that poor kid has spent her life in foster care until a few months ago, when her mother got clean and was able to get Zoe back. I checked the records, and Zoe hadn't lived with her mother since she was 8 months old."

"Maybe it's a blessing then that Zoe never got to know her, considering…" Abby reached for Bob's hand. He let it stay a moment, then scooped more berries. We all followed suit for a few minutes, and the sadness of the situation hung over the room.

"We did ask Zoe what kinds of things she'd been doing with her Mom. She said they went for walks all the time, and that they liked to play imaginary games while they were walking. She told us that they would look in people's houses and try to imagine their lives, and make up stories about the people. In fact," he paused and looked at me with new excitement, "she said that once she went up to a lady's house and pretended she needed money for school. She said she wanted to pretend she was a Girl Scout selling cookies but since she didn't have a uniform on, or any cookies, she told the lady she was collecting for schoolbooks."

"Wow!" I said. "That explains it. Now I can stop yapping to Andy about the strange little girl. And I can sleep tonight." Then I remembered Ginger's body. "Well, no, actually, I can't."

I glanced at the yard and everyone followed my eyes, and knew what I was thinking. No one said anything for a minute. We finished our dessert.

It didn't quite make sense to me. "But you're saying that her mother let her go up to a strange house and pretend like that?" I asked. "That's hard to imagine, unless she was very high."

"She told her Mom she left a doll here, that a little girl she knew a long time ago lived here and she had come here for a play date, and she wanted to see if the doll was still here."

"That's a pretty astute lie, quick on the spot," said Abby.

"Kids in the system are quick on their feet," Bob told us. "Lying becomes second nature, I'm afraid."

We all stared at him.

"What's next, Bob? Where will she go?" asked Andy.

"Sue's taking her to a foster family right now. She'll be there until the court decides what next. Since she's already in the system, we already know there's no family she can go to."

"That is terribly sad," I said.

"Well, the police still have to solve the murder. And the coroner has the body now. It'll be interesting to learn whether there are drugs in her system, or she's clean."

"And then there's the issue of the boyfriend, Tony, the guy I work with," Abby chimed in.

"Yeah, it's a complicated situation." Bob sighed. "As you said, Abbs, maybe it's a good thing that she didn't know her mother very well."

"But she will have some memories of her, and let's hope they're good ones."

That seemed a good ending to our meal, so Abby and Bob said their goodbyes, hollered "Good night" up to William, and left.

"Your dad called," Andy told me as we cleared the dessert dishes and finished loading the dishwasher.

"Finally. Is he mad?"

"Mad? Why would he be mad? You didn't DO anything. You just found a dead body in your yard."

I sighed. "So what did he say?" I asked.

"He said that Michael Quinn had notified the Secret Service and that when he was informed he had called Michael himself, and was satisfied with the information Michael gave him."

"Do I have to call him back?"

"Not tonight. He's in Japan. He'll call you in a few days when he gets back to Boston. Your Mom is with him. I don't think he told her, because he didn't mention her at all."

"And if she knew, she'd be really upset, being so far away." I gave him a kiss. "Thanks for handling that for me."

"It was nothing. I love your dad."

Valerie Horowitz

"I know, you married me because I was slightly famous," I joked.

"I married you because I love all of those long holiday dinner-table conversations with your dad. And your mother's cooking." He tousled my hair and kissed me.

Then we headed upstairs to check on William, who was already asleep, before we turned in. *Until this is all over and we find the killer I better make sure he is always with an adult, and safe*, I thought. I had a feeling Andy was thinking the same thing.

I didn't sleep much. It had all seemed surreal, almost abstract, as the events of the day tumbled through my head. Now the reality of a killer on my property was sinking in. Michael Quinn had said it was probably a personal attack, someone who drove her there and left her. Someone who knew her. But I was still nervous. This was just too close to home. What if the killer looked in William's bedroom window? Or saw us from the back, in the living room, through the wall of windows? I tossed for a few hours, then went downstairs and made myself a gin and tonic. I plopped in a wing chair, put my feet up on the crewel footstool, and stared out at the black woods. I was not going to let the darkness get me. I was going to do something about this. I had to find the killer before he, or she, got closer to my family. I suspected that Andy felt the same way, but he was able to sleep. He had his "sources," and if I knew him, he was planning to make a few calls in the morning.

Chapter 4

1630. Devonshire Cream

The milk should stand 24 hours in the winter, half that time when the weather is very warm. The milkpan is then set on a stove, and should there remain until the milk is quite hot; but it must not boil, or there will be a thick skin on the surface. When it is sufficiently done, the undulations on the surface look thick, and small rings appear. The time required for scalding cream depends on the size of the pan and the heat of the fire; but the slower it is done, the better. The pan should be placed in the dairy when the cream is sufficiently scalded, and skimmed the following day. This cream is so much esteemed that it is sent to the London markets in small square tins, and is exceedingly delicious eaten with fresh fruit. In Devonshire, butter is made from this cream, and is usually very firm.

Mrs. Beeton's Book of Household Management (1861)

Sally Harvey was there when I opened the shop the next day. I was surprised to see her, because she wasn't due until 2. She's my only employee at Village Cooks, and she has been with me since I started the business five years ago. Sally is an English widow who came to the U.S. to be near her daughter and grandchildren when her husband died. She usually closes the shop, so I can be home for William after school. Today I was especially glad to see her because I had never gotten back to sleep; I'd been awake since 2:30 a.m. I wasn't even sure if I had really slept before then. Maybe I dozed a little. But I had fortified myself with coffee for caffeine and a breakfast burrito for protein, and I hoped that would suffice.

"What are you doing here so early?" I asked when I saw her. She was just closing the register drawer as I came in.

"Don't you remember? I have a doctor's appointment at 2, so I told you I'd come in early for two hours, then be back from 4 to 6. I'll try to get here before then, so you can be home for William." She had the prettiest smile, and her pearly white teeth matched her short white pageboy haircut. Her hair was thick, and always falling out from being tucked behind her ears. She probably needed a different hairstyle, one that didn't require tucking. But when it was loose it always reminded me of a white cloud, or a pillow. Porcelain skin and blue eyes completed the softness she portrayed. The type of woman who looked so friendly and trusting that you wanted to tell her everything. She would have made a great psychologist, but instead was a magnificent salesperson. Her British accent heightened her appeal and charmed everyone. I was lucky to have her.

But what to do if she was late? I guessed I'd have to hang up the "Back in Fifteen Minutes" sign we rarely used, and go home to meet William at 3:30.

"Now I remember." I smiled. "Which doctor is it?"

"Dr. Schacht, for my six-month checkup. I had the blood work done last week. I'm sure I'm fine."

"I'm sorry I forgot," I said, and sat down at the stool next to hers behind the counter.

"That's not like you, dear."

"I know," I smiled weakly, and told her about my very busy weekend.

"Good Lord, I need a drink!" she exclaimed as I finished up. "Coffee, that is. I'll go make a pot." She went in back to the small private kitchen. I followed and leaned on the counter while she rinsed out the pot and filled it with water, ground some fair trade Costa Rican coffee beans, put them in, and flipped the switch. I could have helped, but I just stood there.

Mrs. Beeton, our store cat, came over and rubbed up against me. I bent down and picked her up. She's a tuxedo cat who loves to be held. Sometimes, when no one else was in the store, I would put her on my shoulder and she would hang on my neck as I went about my business. She was a gift from my husband when I opened the store. "Every bookstore must have a store cat," he proclaimed as he plopped the large black and white ball of fur in my arms. To my surprise, the cat didn't flinch, just looked up at me with her beautiful pale green eyes. I was incredibly touched by his thoughtfulness, and am reminded of how much I love him every time I see Mrs. Beeton.

We named her after the English author of *Mrs Beeton's Book of Household Management*, one of the most famous cookbooks ever written. Or should I say compiled. It is probable that Isabella Beeton copied many of the recipes from others, but the book is still beloved as a guidebook to all aspects of Victorian home life. It was the first book to place the ingredients at the beginning of some of the newer recipes, an innovative format at the time, still used today. The recipes are illustrated by colored engravings. There are illustrations and descriptions of kitchen gadgets used in the era too, making the book fascinating for lovers of kitchen "stuff" like myself.

When I give customers who don't know who she is the quick explanation, I refer to her as "the Victorian Martha Stewart, author of the most famous English cookbook ever published." If they are interested I show them our facsimile copies of the book (still in print) and tell them that it contains 900 recipes. If they are really interested, I go on to tell them that she started writing articles for her husband's business, The Englishwoman's Domestic Magazine, when she was 21, two years later compiled them into a book, and died at 28 after giving birth to four children. The book describes the food of other countries in Europe, offers fashion tips, and offers advice on household topics such as child care, etiquette, holiday celebrations, household organization, laundry, the keeping of chickens and the management of servants. The book was such a popular success that her husband kept the brand alive and continued to publish it after her death, with updated prefaces suggesting that she was still alive.

"You look very tired," Sally uttered as we returned to the front. Since it was now ten, she unlocked the front door and turned over the "Closed. Gone Home to Cook Something Delicious!" sign to read "Open. Get Ready to Cook Something Delicious!"

I followed her around like a puppy. She glanced around to make sure that everything was okay with the products on the shelves. Nothing had fallen on the floor during the night, or been toppled by Mrs. Beeton. All the lights were on. Then she marched back into the kitchen and came back out with two steaming cups. We both liked it with Vanilla Silk creamer, and kept it in our refrigerator at all times. She had added a half packet of Splenda to hers.

"I like Dr. Schacht," she proclaimed, as she settled on the stool, as if the last few minutes of chores had been a mere interruption.

"I've never met her. What's she like?"

"Well, that's just brilliant," she exclaimed and stood up as a stunning raven-haired woman walked in, her shoulder-length curls falling in ringlets, the top pulled back with a hair clip. "It's Dr. Schacht."

She wore a red cashmere cowl neck sweater and hip-hugger black wool pants with a thick leather belt and a large golden buckle depicting a fleur de lis. About 5'7' or 8,' she carried herself like a dancer.

"Good morning, Sally." She smiled.

"We were just talking about you," Sally said, and stood. "This is my boss, Bonnie Emerson." I stood too, and we shook hands as Sally said, "Bonnie, this is Dr. Danielle Schacht."

"Why were you talking about me?" she asked.

"Because I have an appointment with you this afternoon, and we were discussing our schedule."

"Oh, right. Office hours are from two to eight today. So I'm doing a few errands beforehand. Actually, I'm looking for a gift for my sister Wendy's fortieth birthday. She's an amazing cook, and has taught me a lot, too, as a matter of fact."

"How nice," said Sally, and started walking around the shop. "Did you have anything particular in mind?"

"Well, I want it to be something substantial, since it's a big birthday. And I want it to be something special because," she stopped for a moment, "she's been very good to me since Bob died."

There was an awkward silence. "What kind of cooking does she like to do?" I piped up.

"Everyone knows she loves wine, so others will probably get her wine."

"Does she bake?"

"Yes, but she loves to do other things too — braised beef, paella, sauces, that sort of thing."

"What kind of pots and pans does she have?" asked Sally.

"I'm not sure. But she does have a copper frying pan that she adores." When she emphasized the word "adores," I knew we had the ticket.

"If she loves her copper frying pan, she'd probably love more copper pots. They're expensive, and most people think of them as an extravagance."

"Which means that would be something she wouldn't necessarily buy for herself, but would be the perfect gift," chimed in Sally. "Where did she get her frying pan? Do you know?"

"As a matter of fact, I remember now. Wendy told me she bought it for herself on her thirtieth birthday."

"Ah," I said, "she's probably been wishing for more all these years, but never got around to treating herself."

"That sounds like her. She's selfless."

""It also means she treasures the pan if she's kept it all these years. She probably knows how to take care of it."

"Wendy only uses silicon spatulas, and I've seen her stir sauce in it with a wooden spoon."

"I have a feeling that she would be thrilled by a new copper pot from you. It will show her that you are thoughtful enough to get her something she probably secretly desires deep inside." We all laughed at my words.

"Let me show you what we have." Sally led her over to the wall where the copper pots shone cheerfully. Although we had some hanging in the store windows, I had placed a full selection along the dark back wall intentionally, and they brightened the area. We had a good supply of copper pots from France.

I stood behind the counter and took another sip of my coffee.

"These are absolutely beautiful," said Dr. Schacht. "Why do some have linings and some are plain copper?"

"The lined ones are lined with tin," Sally explained. "The unlined ones are used primarily for food cooked quickly with high heat, like candy." She handled one.

"That's why it's small, too," offered Dr. Schacht.

"Yes, you don't make a three-quart pot of chocolate at home every day." They both laughed.

"Maybe I would," chuckled Dr. Schacht, "but that would be setting a poor example for my patients."

"Copper is acidic, too, that's why it's lined with either stainless or tin. Tin is most common, and perfectly acceptable."

"I see that some have brass handles and some have iron handles," the doctor observed. "Which is better?"

"It's a personal choice. There's no difference in the quality that I know of."

"I think she'd like the brass. It's pretty." She turned and looked at the expanse of pots on display. "Now, what to get her? Do you think I should get her another frying pan, in a different size?"

"I think a sauce pan would be more distinctive," Sally said as she brought out a three-quart beauty with a brass handle and a lid.

"Oh, I like that. She could make stew in that."

"Yes, or spaghetti sauce."

"I think I'd like to get her this one, and another. What's this?" Dr. Schacht pointed at a long oval copper pot.

"That's a fish poacher. Doe she make fish often?" Sally carefully brought it down from its perch.

"Hmm. Sometimes. It sure looks impressive, but I don't think she'd use it more than once a month or so."

"You said she likes to make sauces, so how about a smaller saucepan, then you'll have a set," Sally suggested.

"Good idea."

They settled on three saucepans, a one-quart, a two-quart, and a three-quart. Quite extravagant, but a lovely grouping that any chef would be delighted to use for years to come.

Sally packed the three boxes in one larger box, and wrapped the box with our signature blue toile paper and finished it off with a wide yellow ribbon and a large bow. She was a pro at making bows. I always struggled with them.

Dr. Schacht added a set of pretty blue ceramic measuring cups for herself, and paid.

"Thank you, Doctor. I'm sure she'll be thrilled with them." Sally carried the box, and they both went outside to her car. I watched as Dr. Schacht unlocked the trunk of her white Volvo wagon and Sally slipped the heavy box in. A strong woman for 70. A vital woman. I hoped her medical appointment went well.

When she came back in I said, "Please, sit down and rest."

"That was fun, wasn't it?" she offered perkily.

"Dr. Schacht seems very nice. And she's very stylish, for a doctor. When did her husband die?"

"Let's see, I guess it's about two, maybe three years ago now. Car accident. Drunk driver. What a tragedy. And they were getting ready to start a family."

"Really?" I said. Dr. Schacht was probably in her late thirties, early forties.

"I know what you're thinking. She's probably in her early forties now. They were going through the in-vitro fertilization process, unsuccessfully, and then the accident happened. They'd only been married for a year. Poor thing."

Our conversation was interrupted by the arrival of another customer, and then some more, who kept us busy until 1:30, when Sally left.

"Don't worry about a thing. I'm having a second wind." I shooed her out the door. "Good luck with your appointment. I'll see you later."

"I'll be back as soon as I can."

I went in back, pulled some ham and swiss out of the refrigerator, and placed it between two pieces of rye bread. While I waited for it to grill in our sandwich maker, which only took a minute or two, I popped open a Diet Coke.

The store was empty while I ate my lunch. I called Wilmington Printers, and they said my order was ready. Then the door opened and Miche Lombardi came in. She wore a black turtleneck, a blue pea coat, and jeans. I wondered why she wasn't at the restaurant now, during the lunch rush. I had met her several times, but I didn't know her well. Was she single? Married? Kids? I searched my memory, but I didn't know.

I loved being around Miche, and listening to her talk. She was very, very French. On her mother's side, from Quebec. On her father's side, she was Italian. That combination made her a force to be reckoned with. Opinionated. And bossy. A good quality in a restaurant manager.

"Hi, Bonnie" she said brightly. "I'm looking for a cookbook."

"Okay," I said, "Any particular kind? Something new?"

"I know someone who was just admitted to CIA, and I want to get him something special." CIA is the Culinary Institute of America, the prestigious cooking school in Hyde Park, New York. They also have a school in California. The students work in on-site restaurants. I had been there once, on my birthday. A wonderful occasion and an impressive place. I had "Julia Child's beef bourguignon" at the on-campus French restaurant and it was superb.

"That's fantastic," I smiled. "Now the challenge will be to find him something he doesn't already have." Chefs are notorious cookbook collectors.

"He doesn't have much," she said. "He doesn't have much money. I don't think he owns a cookbook at all. That's why I'd like to get him one. Something important, and useful. But I don't want to get him the *Joy of Cooking*, because he'll want me to think he already has that."

She paused. "Do you know what I mean?"

"I know exactly what you mean," and led her over to the basic cookbook section that held most of the classics.

"Well, you could get him something new, like the new Bobby Flay, or you could get him a classic by someone like Escoffier or Brillat-Savarin," I offered.

"Something classic would be better. But he won't know who they are — Brillat-Savarin and Escoffier. Although he should. That's why he's going to school. I don't want to embarrass him."

"How about *Mastering the Art of French Cooking* by Julia Child? It's a two-volume set so it makes a wonderful gift, it's the very definition of a classic cookbook, and I'm sure he knows who she is." I pulled a boxed set off the shelf.

"Parfait," she said, reverting to her native French in her excitement. "That would be perfect!" she exclaimed.

After she left, I wondered who the gift was for. She hadn't offered a name, but she had said "he," so I knew it was for a man. Jeffrey, her boss?

No, he already owned a restaurant, had probably been to cooking school years ago, and was no longer a chef. Tony Moran, the chef I saw at the police station? If the gift were meant for Tony, the investigation into Ginger's murder might affect his plans. But Michael Quinn probably expected him to stick around.

The rest of the afternoon flew by. But when Sally hadn't returned from her appointment with Dr. Schacht at 3:30, I put the "Back in 15 Minutes" sign on the door and went home in time to meet William's school bus.

I love my house. For so many reasons. A horse stable built at the turn of the twentieth century, it stands on the edge of the seven-acre property that had been in my husband's family for generations. We left the appearance of the front of the stables that faced the road as we found it. We gutted the rear wall and built a wall of windows and a pair of French doors near the kitchen end facing the fields and woods in back. We turned the main part of the building into a great room/dining room, with a separate kitchen and a small powder room. Because I couldn't imagine living without a fireplace (he wouldn't admit it, but Andy couldn't either), when we built the bedroom wing on the north side we installed a double fireplace, and put our master bedroom on the other side of it. The wing houses three other bedrooms (one belongs to William, another is Andy's study, and the third is a guest room).

We got married in our backyard, between an old barn which now serves as our garage and a row of fine old maples that sprawl out and mark the end of our property from the woods behind us. We held our reception on the brick patio that faced the wall of windows. There's a thick patch of bushes on the other side of the patio. It's a bit overgrown — butterfly bushes, forsythia and black-eyed Susans in happy disarray. William has seen a rabbit out there a few times. He must live in the underbrush.

"There he is. Shhh. Don't run after him. You'll scare him. He'll run away."

I say this every time, and every time my son chases him anyway. I don't mind. This is what I always dreamed of. The innocence of childhood and bunny rabbits, a life filled with Play-Doh and "Puff the Magic Dragon," and now the beginning teenage years with girls, proms, and driving lessons to come. Far from my single days in New York. Far from my days of bypassing druggies in Washington Square Park and stepping over the occasional drunk who had passed out on my corner. We're lucky. Our road is not a through road. Bayer Nature Preserve is adjacent to some of the properties. It is very quiet. We hear crickets at night, the occasional barking dog. There are horse and sheep farms within a half mile or so in each direction.

At seven o'clock the phone rang. Sally was breathless.

"I'm so sorry, Bonnie. My cell phone died. I never got back to the store. Dr. Schacht sent me for a CT scan, and I had to go all the way to the hospital radiology department, and I just got home."

"Don't worry about it, Sally," I said. "Take it easy. It's okay. Why did Dr. Schacht order tests?"

"I had them three months ago, remember? Then today when she was listening to my chest she thought she heard something. So she sent me right in for a follow-up. It was crowded, I had to wait."

Hmm, I thought. This could be bad. "When will you get the results?"

"She asked for what they call a 'wet read' so she'll have preliminary results tomorrow."

"Will you be all right tonight?"

"Oh, honey, you are sweet to ask. I'll be fine. I've been through worse. I won't lose a wink of sleep. Don't worry about me, I'll go to bed and curl up with a cookbook. I brought home that new Viennese one. You know me," she reassured me.

"Okay, then, see you tomorrow?" I asked, trying to match her tone but inside I was deeply worried about the urgency of the tests.

"Bright and early." She signed off.

Too cheerful? If it were me going through those tests, I would be up all night worrying, writing my will in my head, imagining William going to college and growing up without me to see it. But maybe I'm just neurotic, a worrier, and Sally has the better handle on things. Good for her.

Then I remembered the "Back in 15 Minutes" sign on the door. It was not a good idea to leave that up all night; it should be changed to "Closed. Gone Home to Cook Something Delicious!" If someone walking by after dark saw the "15 Minutes" sign they might think something was awry. And they might bang on the door and wake up Mrs. Beeton or set off the alarm.

I told Andy about Sally's call.

"You want to go back to the store to change the sign, is that what you're telling me?"

"I do. I know it sounds silly. But it's bothering me. It's just not right. Someone could walk by at midnight and see the sign. They might bang on the door and set off the alarm. I don't want to invite trouble. I'll be back in a few minutes."

"I think you're nuts." He kissed me on the cheek. "But go ahead, off with you."

He hollered upstairs to William "Your crazy mom is running to the store for a few minutes. But I'm down here watching Jeopardy. Want to join me?"

"Sure, Dad!" William leaped down the stairs.

And I left them with Alex Trebek.

All of the parking spaces on the block were taken. *Odd*, I thought, and wondered what was going on. Rather than going around to my parking space in the back, I parked in the driveway next to Lannigan Antiques, which is next door to Village Cooks. Kay, a good friend of Sally's, had owned the business, specializing in china, for over 20 years. I knew Kay wouldn't mind me using her driveway after hours while I ran into my shop to change the sign.

It only took a minute to unlock the door, grab the sign, put it on the shelf, reach for the correct sign and re-lock the door. As I did so, I saw movement out of the corner of my eye.

None of the stores were open this late; the town center was quiet. But there, walking toward a green Ford Explorer, were school principal Mr. Russo and Tony Moran. Mr. Russo and Tony Moran? How on earth did they know each other? I paused, and listened.

"Don't worry, Tony, everything will be all right," I heard Mr. Russo say before his door slammed. Tony was already in the passenger seat. They drove off, not seeing me.

What were they doing in town at this time of night? The only building that might possibly have life was the town hall two blocks down. Could they have been at a meeting at town hall, and parked the car this far away?

I got in my car and drove to the town hall parking lot to check it out. Something was indeed going on, the lot was almost full. But not full. What were Tony and Mr. Russo doing here? I resolved to check the town website when I got home to see what meetings were happening this Tuesday night.

I played my old "My Fair Lady" CD all the way home, and sang "Wouldn't it be loverly?" at the top of my lungs, harmonizing with Julie Andrews. It was kind of nice to be out in the evening by myself on this clear starry night.

When I got home, William was already in the shower, getting ready for bed. Andy was stretched out in one of the big paisley wing chairs in the living room, his laptop on his lap. I let them both be, and quietly went into the study where the desktop computer was already on. When I checked the town website, I found that the planning board had met that night. What interest did Mr. Russo and Tony Moran have in the town planning board? I checked the list of board members of the committee to see if there was anyone I knew on the committee. Bingo! Kay Lannigan was a member. Tomorrow I'd find a discreet way to ask her about what had transpired at the meeting.

I didn't have to. When I opened the store the next day, Kay rushed in. She was in her usual fall attire, a tweed skirt and brown twin set, today set off by a gold scarf. She was in her seventies, but looked a decade younger. With perfect posture, white hair pulled back in a French twist, small hazel eyes and a naturally kind expression, she was everyone's image of a regal grandmother. But she was not as staid as she seemed. She was a student and practitioner of the Japanese tea ceremony. Few in town knew that she had spent most of her adult life in Japan, spoke fluent Japanese, and had left her husband there sometime back in the eighties to raise her son, Ben, in a townhouse in Wilmington Commons.

Today she was miffed. "Bonnie, you will not believe what happened at the meeting last night," she exclaimed as she paced around my store. She followed me as I went around turning on lights, the coffee pot, and the air conditioner.

"What happened?" I asked.

"Dennis Russo submitted a plan to build a school for dyslexic kids on the old Donovan property next to Wilmington Commons."

"Really? I didn't know he was starting a school."

"Neither did I," she said, as I opened the cabinet and took out two mugs.

"It sounds like a good idea, though."

"He called it 'language-based learning difficulties.' He said there is a large percentage — I forget the number he gave — of children with this problem who feel singled out when they get pulled out of their classroom for reading help, or called on to read aloud."

"Interesting," I nodded. "Did you know anything about this?"

She reached for a cup of coffee, which by now had finished perking, while I got the Vanilla Silk out of the refrigerator in the back room. Then she answered me. "I don't think it's a bad idea; in fact, I think it's an excellent idea. I'm just surprised that I haven't heard anything about it until now." She turned and looked at me.

I shrugged.

"Did he have anyone else with him? A lawyer?" I wondered about Tony Moran.

"There was a young guy sitting next to him, and I saw them walk out together but that may have been coincidental; I don't know if they knew each other."

"Did you recognize the guy?"

"No, afraid not. The whole thing is strange. He should have had a lawyer and an architect with him. But it was just him and his plans, making his case." She sighed. "The young guy said nothing."

"I wonder where he's getting the financial backing. And he'll need to get a license to run the school, state and county approval, all that."

"He said the first step was to get approval to build the building. He showed us the plans, and they included a nature walk area on the west side. The building is going to be one story, made of stone and concrete, with a big arch around the front door. It looks pretty."

"How many kids would it hold?"

"He said it would hold 80 to 100 kids and about 30 teachers and staff."

"Hmm. It sounds like he truly wants to do this. Does he have a name for the school?"

"Moran Academy. I don't know who it's named after."

But I did. I decided not to say anything to Kay just yet. I needed to think. Did Tony Moran have money? Was he the financial backer? If he had that kind of money, why was he working as a prep chef at St. Cloud's Restaurant? And did this have anything to do with Ginger Harrison, Tony's murdered girlfriend?

Kay left, and went next door to open her shop. It was a quiet, rainy Wednesday morning. I puttered around and brought out some new cookbooks that had come in from the book supplier the day before. Cookbook season gets in full swing in October, but new books start arriving as early as September. These were crock pot and seafood cookbooks, the latest takes on each. Then I booted up the computer, and found Royal's e-mail with the new photo of Elizabeth Crisp. She was wearing a green sweater in the photo which complemented her auburn hair, so I changed the color of the border in the flyer to the same green, using the Photoshop dropper that allowed me to match the color exactly. I loved that feature. Now it looked great, very professional.

Pleased with myself, I e-mailed it to the printer with instructions for a rush order to print 50 in color on glossy paper, plus 300 postcards based on a reduced-size design I had created, and one on poster board enlarged to 18" x 20." That was for the store window.

I have e-mail addresses for many of my customers, and I used the time to create an e-mail "blast" with the flyer as an attachment, and had that ready to go, too. I called the printer, and learned that they got my e-mail and the job would be done by 5 p.m. the next day. Perfect. I would mail the postcards Thursday night, then send out the e-mails on Saturday, so that they would all arrive on the same day. I would also tweet the announcement and post the flyer on the store Facebook page. It would give participants a week to prepare. Not much time. I usually gave them at least two weeks. Maybe this would add to the excitement, I hoped. And I hoped that my customers would understand the announcement delay, having heard the news of the discovery of Ginger's Harrison's body on our property.

The store was empty of customers, as often happened on rainy days. While I worked I thought about the murder. How had Ginger gotten to our property? It just didn't make sense. Had she walked there, or gotten out of a car? She couldn't have been dumped out of a car, because the place she was found was about 150 feet from the road. She was wet. What was she doing out in the rain? Or had she gone there before the storm, and we hadn't noticed her? I decided that was the more likely scenario. Lost in thought, I sorted the display of serving spoons. Customers often put them back in the wrong place.

Finally the bell jangled, and Ian Wright wiped his feet and pulled off his hood.

"Hi, Bonnie." He saluted.

"Ian, you're back! Good to see you."

"I wanted to thank you for taking care of Bertie while I was away."

"You didn't have to come out in the rain to do that, Ian. You could have called."

"I know, but I wanted to. And I need to do a little shopping. I need a new frying pan. I got back from Boston last night, and when I got up to make breakfast this morning I took one look at that old Teflon pan and decided I could not stand using it for one more day."

"So what did you have for breakfast, instead of eggs?"

"Cereal, like a true American. Cheerios, in fact." He laughed. "Sally would be proud. Is she here?"

I grinned. "She will be soon." I showed him the full range of what we had in stock, and he settled on a mid-priced non-stick T-fal frying pan that I had started carrying only recently, after Consumer Reports gave it a good review.

As I was ringing up his sale, Sally came in.

"Is it that time already?" I couldn't believe it was two o'clock. Ian had been my only customer. But I had gotten a lot done.

"Are you going to the wake for Ginger Harrison tonight?" she asked as she put on her blue Village Cooks apron and joined me behind the counter.

"I didn't know anything about it. I thought she was here in town because of Tony, and assumed her family is somewhere else. Did he arrange the service?"

"Yes, and paid for it too, apparently. The wake is tonight from 7 to 9, and the funeral is tomorrow. I am going to the wake only," she said, and smiled at Ian.

"Do you think I should go? I didn't know her. But then again, she died on our property…"

"Would you like me to go with you ladies? I didn't know her either, but I'd like to pay my respects to her family," offered Ian.

"Let's all go," Sally said brightly.

I smiled in agreement and asked, "Does she have any family around here? Besides Zoe, that is?"

"Who knows?" said Sally, "We'll find out tonight, won't we?"

Chapter 5

"I'm bushed, I'll stay home with William."

Andy stretched as he finished his dinner. I had made tacos, one of William's favorites.

"You go ahead to the wake, Bonnie. If I can get some free time tomorrow morning I'll come to the funeral."

"Okay," I said. "Ian and Sally are meeting me there anyway."

"Ian and Sally?" Andy said, emphasizing "and." He grinned.

"Well, they'll be coming separately, I expect." I grinned. "But it's a start."

"Very nice," he said, and whirled me around and gave me a kiss.

"What's that for?" I asked.

"I hope we'll be as cute as they are when we're their age."

"But they're not even a couple — yet."

"They will be, soon enough." He kissed me again. "And besides, they're already cute." "And they have so much in common," I added. They were both British ex-pats, and widowed.

I left my purple silk blouse on, but changed into a black gabardine pantsuit. As I drove to the Lennon Funeral Home I wondered who would be there. I found myself a little bit nervous. I had a strange role in all of this. I was the one who found the body. I had started the action, set the ball rolling — I had made all of the drama public. Before me, Ginger had lain there quietly dead. I felt responsible for all the ruckus, and that I owed her something. I needed to figure out who did this to her. And I needed to do it for Zoe.

When I walked up the path I saw Ian and Sally waiting at the entrance. They were laughing and chatting easily, as if they had known each other forever. Cheered by the sight, I took a deep breath and greeted them.

"Hi, Ian, hi, Sally."

"It's good to see you." Ian made a small bow.

"Hello dear."

Sally gave me a quick kiss on the cheek, and I returned hers.

"Here we go," I said with what I hope sounded like firm resolve rather than the fear and discomfort that I felt.

Once inside, we were greeted by Bob and Abby. They were in the lobby, standing in front of a huge mahogany grandfather clock. They appeared to be deep in serious conversation, so I approached slowly. Ian and Sally were behind me, chatting quietly to each other.

I waited a moment, then went over. I kissed each of them on the cheek. "Hi guys, I'm so glad you're here."

"Bonnie, I didn't expect you to come, honey. I'm proud of you." Abby said in a low voice as she squeezed my hand.

I smiled bravely. "What's it like in there?"

Bob answered. "Well, Tony Moran is in there, with Zoe. A few others from the restaurant, Mr. and Mrs. Russo…"

I broke in. "Mr. Russo is here? Why would he be here?"

"Good question, now that I think of it. I don't know how he knew her."

"Was Zoe a student at his school?" Abby put in.

"Yes, of course, that's it," said Bob with some relief. "He's here in an official capacity."

"Well, I'm heading in," I said, as I saw that Ian and Sally had already done so. I followed right behind them. Tony and Zoe were standing on the side of the room, in a receiving line of sorts. A very small receiving line. I recognized everyone else in the room. Four or five teachers, the Russos, Miche and Jeffrey from the restaurant, Kay Lannigan, Michael Quinn and another detective I recognized but whose name I didn't know.

I waited my turn, and then said "I'm so sorry" to both Tony and Zoe. Zoe didn't seem to take extra notice of me. She seemed calmer than she had been that day she had knocked on my door, when she had seemed hopped up. She was certainly subdued now. And who wouldn't be, a nine-year-old girl with her mother in an open coffin ten feet away.

Then I approached the coffin, right behind Ian in line. I waited while he said a prayer, then put his arm around Sally's shoulders and walked her to some empty chairs in a row halfway back. Ginger was dressed in a black long-sleeved jersey wrap dress and wore a simple silver chain that held a single tear-shaped crystal. Her hair was sleeked back, and she wore red lipstick. The shade of red looked beautiful on her, not too bright, just right. Funny the things you notice when you're looking at a corpse. Her ears weren't pierced. She wore no jewelry other than the necklace. I reached in and put my hand on hers and spoke to her silently, "Ginger, I never knew you, but I will never forget you."

As I walked over to join Ian and Sally I saw Dr. Schacht come in. She was speaking to Tony and Zoe, and lingered with them for quite a while, conversing softly. It looked like she was reassuring them. What an angel.

We sat there quietly for a while. I didn't see anyone unfamiliar. Didn't Ginger have any family? It had been a few days since she died, certainly long enough for them to make the trip from Philadelphia. If that was really where she was from. Maybe it had just been the place where she lived last; maybe she was originally from somewhere else. But there weren't any friends either. I felt sorrier than ever for Tony and Zoe. Would Tony take Zoe in? Where was she living now? I'd have to ask Bob these questions later.

At nine Mark Lennon came in and addressed the mourners and told us that the service would continue at nine the next morning with a short final viewing and prayer service, and then the burial at Oxford Hills Cemetary. We filed out quietly. As we did, I noticed that Mr. Russo went over to Tony and put his arm around him and walked Tony and Zoe out, Mrs. Russo trailing behind, followed by Dr. Schacht.

When we got outside, we found Jeffrey and Miche standing by the door. Jeffrey was smoking a cigarette.

"Hello, all," Jeffrey hailed. "Why don't we all go for a drink and wash away all of this?"

I looked at Abby, who looked at Bob, who nodded.

"Sure," I said. "What about you?" I beckoned to Sally and Ian.

Ian stammered a bit.

"Why don't you go ahead, Bonnie, and Ian will drive me home. Won't you, Ian?" asked Sally.

"Of course, I'd be delighted."

And off they went, leaving me as the fifth wheel. But I didn't mind.

"Where to?" I turned to the others.

Abby answered. "The restaurant. Right, Jeffrey?"

"No, we're there all the time. Let's go some place different. How about the Peacock?"

The Peacock Inn was a local restaurant, bar, and music club that everyone called simply "The Peacock." It wasn't an inn at all, but it was inviting. Like St. Cloud, it was on Willow Lane, but about a mile down the road. National indie, folk bands and singer-songwriters stopped in on their circuit tours of smaller clubs. Andy and I saw Lucinda Williams there a year or so before she got famous. I loved the place. One wall featured a mural of a peacock and his magnificent feathers painted by an artist back in the sixties. It was done in the style of old Fillmore posters. I wondered if it was done by the same artist. A wall of windows opening out to the woods brought in wonderful views during the dinner hour, made more romantic by lights twinkling in the trees just outside. The woodwork was hand hewn, arts and crafts style, and the heavy tables and chairs were built in mission style as well. The owners, Helen and Tom White were a stylish couple with great taste. They had done a magnificent job, and loved collecting arts and crafts pieces so much that they had been inspired to open Grove Park, their furniture and housewares shop.

"I'm in," I ventured, and the others agreed.

We met there about ten minutes later and found a table halfway back from the stage. Tonight was karaoke night, and I was glad we weren't sitting too close. A woman in her mid-twenties was up there singing along to "The Edge of Glory" by Lady Gaga, and doing a decent job of a difficult song. She was pretty, with a blue streak in her long dark-hair. A group of five at a table over on the left was swaying and singing along with her. Must be her friends.

Jeffrey ordered the first round, and kindly paid for it.

"I'll get the next round," Bob put in.

When the drinks arrived, Miche took a sip of her wine and said "Whew, that was tough. I felt so sorry for that little girl, Zoe."

"What will happen to her now?" I asked Bob.

"I'm not her case manager, but I know her case manager well, and I've been asking about her, as a matter of fact."

Jeffrey wrapped his hands around his glass and took a deep breath. He exhaled and asked, "What did you learn?"

"Well, she's not going to stay with Tony Moran. We have to find a home for her after the funeral."

"Why not Tony?" Abby asked.

"I can't say, publicly."

"Publicly?" Jeffrey snorted. "But I'm his boss. And we all work with him." He gestured to Miche and Abby.

"Don't worry, it's not because he did something bad. It's a private matter. He wouldn't be able to keep her if he wanted to. That's all I can say. I'm sorry I can't say more. He isn't her father, and he's under no obligation."

Miche didn't seem surprised. "Hmm," she said softly. "I don't think he knew Zoe very well."

"Well, I hope she finds a loving family," I said. "And I hope it doesn't take too long. Will she go to a foster family in the meantime?"

"They're playing the Beach Boys!" Jeffrey popped up. "'Good Vibrations'! I'm going to go and sing too!" He raced up to join two young women who were dancing and singing to the tune. Within a few seconds, he was bopping along with them.

"Ha," uttered Bob, who stopped to watch the upheaval, and then answered, "She's in a foster family now for the short term, but they can't keep her permanently."

"And Ginger had no family?" I asked. "I didn't see anyone I didn't recognize at the funeral. I expected to see some of her relatives."

"Didn't seem to have any. None of her records show any next of kin. And we checked back to when she got into the system about fourteen years ago. "

"That's so sad." Abby snuggled closer to Bob.

"Yeah, she's been in and out of the system for a long time."

"I wish I could adopt her." Miche surprised the rest of us. "But I don't think motherhood is in the cards for me. Mr. Right hasn't come along yet, and now I work most evenings, my family is in Quebec, I wouldn't be able to offer a good home life — dinners, homework, all of that…." Her voice trickled off as she choked a little. Abby patted her hand, and Bob and I smiled at her, trying to convey our understanding.

"You would make a great mother." Abby went on, "Who knows? Maybe something will happen and your life will change. Don't think the door is closed. You're still in your early thirties, sweetie."

Miche winced, and smiled weakly.

Bob changed the subject. God bless him. "I don't think the police have any suspects," he paused, "but that's not important to me."

"Not important to you?" Miche was perturbed.

"Well, it is important to me, but it's not my priority. I want to help find a home for Zoe. I know I'm not her case manager, but her Mom was found at your house, Bonnie, so I feel connected."

Abby smiled.

"I do too," I said. "After all, I found Ginger. I feel responsible for finding her killer, for her sake, and Zoe's."

"I care too!" said Miche.

"So do I," piped in Abby.

"Well why don't we all try to pool our resources and information to find the killer? We can all find out what we can and compare notes."

"Oh I hate the sound of that — the 'killer,'" said Abby. "You know the killer is out there somewhere. The thought of it gives me the creeps."

With that Jeffrey bounced back into his seat.

"That was wicked!" he said. "Who's next?"

I joined him for "Eight Days a Week." I had never sung karaoke with someone before. And Jeffrey was a lot of fun to sing with. He put his arm around me and we shook our heads pretending we had Beatle mops. For a little while, I forgot about Ginger and Zoe.

The next morning Abby called me. "Did you mean what you said about pooling our resources to find the killer?"

"Yes, I did, but I don't know where to start."

"Bob and I talked about it on the way home last night and we think it's a good idea."

"Okay. I'm going to the funeral. Let's all keep our ears open and report to each other what we find."

"Deal!" she said and rang off.

I laughed at her sudden hang up. She probably had to get back to her baking. It sounded like she was at the restaurant.

The store didn't open until eleven, so I had time to go to the funeral home. I put on the same black nehru-style jacket I wore the previous night, but this time without a blouse, buttoned it up all the way, and this time matched it with the skirt that had come as part of the three-piece suit. I hoped Andy would join me. But you never know with reporters, the day could start out quiet and end up with all hell breaking loose. Or vice versa.

This time I saw Dennis Russo, his wife Sue, and Danielle Schacht standing in front of Lennon Funeral Home when I got there.

Danielle took my arm as I greeted them and said, "I'm glad you're here. Let's go in." And she steered me inside before I got a chance to say anything to Mr. Russo. Darn, I wanted to find out how Mr. Russo was connected to Tony Moran. Now I had lost my chance.

When we got inside Danielle steered me to a row in the back where there was no one near.

"Are you going up to the casket?" I stage whispered.

"No, I said goodbye to her last night."

"Did you know her?"

"She was my patient, briefly. Are you going up?"

"I don't think so, either."

"Then just sit here with me." She gripped my arm.

"Will do." I smiled.

"I was surprised to see Mr. Russo here," I ventured.

"He was Zoe's principal, and I think he knows Tony from the old neighborhood."

"Old neighborhood?"

"Yeah, South Philadelphia. Ginger was from Philly too, but not that part of town; she was from out west. Let's see if I can remember what she told me. I think she said she met Tony when they worked in the same restaurant in downtown Philly."

She nodded toward Zoe. "Such a sweet little girl." There was something extra in her voice. "I examined her for Social Services. Do you know what she did the whole time I was checking her out, after she knew that her mother was dead?"

"What?"

"She hummed."

"Hummed?"

"She hummed that song 'Cinnamon Girl' by Neil Young. Do you know it?"

"Sure I do." I remembered it from years back, and own the "Everybody Knows This is Nowhere" CD. "I love that song."

"So I asked her," she went on quietly, "why she was humming that song. I told her it was one of my favorites. She said it was her Mom's favorite, too, that her mother sang it to her a few times."

"Oh, wow." That was all I could muster. I pictured Ginger singing it to her, the two of them on a couch, Ginger running her fingers through her daughter's hair lovingly, singing to her. Her little cinnamon girl. Despite her demons, she must have been a loving mother in the limited time she spent with Zoe.

"So what did you do?" I stammered, finally.

"I helped her get dressed. And then I sang it to her." She squeezed my arm and nodded toward the little girl, standing up front by her mother's casket. She was wearing a navy dress with a white collar and bow. She was crying softly as she stood there, all by herself, the tears silently trickling down her brave cheeks.

Everyone in the room was transfixed, watching her, taking it all in. This little girl had finally had a brief chance to get to know her mother when she was taken from her by some terrible killer. And now here she was, all alone.

Tony was sitting in the front row, head down. He was sobbing. I wished someone would go up to Zoe and help her, comfort her.

Just as I thought it, Danielle got up and went toward her. She gently took Zoe's arm and brought her to an empty chair in the front row. She looked over at me. I nodded. It was the right thing to do.

Then Mark Lennon came in and said they were going to start the prayer service. I stayed in my seat in the back, closed my eyes, and prayed.

Later I joined in the row of cars with their lights and flashers on as the small funeral procession drove out of town to the cemetery. Ginger was to be buried in Oxford Hills Cemetery; about four miles west of Wilmington, where the ex-urban terrain started to become real country. It was a small cemetery, as they go. A white fence surrounded the expanse of the grass and gravestones. An old white farmhouse surrounded by a handful of maple trees had been turned into the cemetery office, and we filed past it, to the far southwestern end of the place. There were only about a dozen cars.

I got out, and took a breath. It was a magnificent crisp fall day and the leaves on the distant hillside were full of color. Danielle had taken her own car, and said she would meet me here. I knew they both had to work, but I wished Andy or Abby were here with me, so I didn't have to drive alone. Darn, I should have called Sally and asked her to join me. I didn't, I knew, because up to the last minute I wasn't sure I was going to attend.

Part of me felt I shouldn't have come, since I didn't know Ginger, and was intruding on the privacy of a sacred moment of those who did. Going to the wake last night would have been enough. On the other hand, I was the one who found her, on my own property, and I felt an invisible strand between us. I needed to see her through to her true resting place, and not the horrid spot near our stream where she had breathed her last.

So I pulled myself together and joined the others whose slamming car doors jolted the peaceful silence, and made the trek to the gravesite. There I joined Dennis and Susan Russo, Tony Moran, Danielle Schacht, Jeffrey Sloane and Miche Lombardi, Michael Quinn and what looked like a few others from the police force, and about half a dozen other people I didn't know. Zoe had arrived with Bob Lee and another social worker I didn't recognize, a woman. I saw Danielle wince with emotion as Zoe ran over to her and grab her hand. I choked up a bit too. Bob and the woman followed close behind, and stood behind them. I tried to get Bob's eye, but couldn't.

Someone touched my elbow. I turned and saw that it was Jim Leonard, the owner of Wilmington Books. I had never seen him in a suit before. He looked handsome. I was accustomed to seeing him in a shirt and jeans or chinos.

I leaned close and asked him, "Did you know Ginger?"

"She bought a book for Zoe once, a while ago" he answered, his mouth close to my ear. "I helped her choose the book. She didn't have any idea what an eight-year-old girl would read, and she wanted so badly to get the right book."

"What did she buy?" I stage-whispered.

"*Beezus and Ramona.*" He grinned.

"Perfect!" I said.

Then we were quiet as we saw Mark Lennon move forward. During an uncomfortable moment as we waited for him to get started I noted that only Tony displayed any grief, as his body heaved with dry sobs.

I looked around at the others. Somewhere I had heard or read that the killer is usually at the funeral, especially the graveside. Was there anyone there that I hadn't seen at the funeral home? I just wasn't sure. Could one of these people be Ginger's murderer? Was having sold a book to the deceased enough reason for Jim Leonard to be there? I wasn't sure of that either. But he seemed kind, maybe he was just that kind of guy.

Mr. Lennon led the basic Christian cemetery service. I was disappointed that there were no family members there to offer personal embellishments. There were no requests for her favorite childhood verse because no one there knew her as a child. No one there to sing her favorite song as a teenager because no one there knew her as a teenager. Except for Tony, they all looked so stoic, as if they were there only because duty called them to. It made me sad. And mad. I looked at Dennis and Sue. Dennis had his arms folded. Sue had her hands in her jacket pockets. She stared straight ahead. Neither of them was comforting Tony at all, as his shoulders continued to betray his sobs. He sure was a mess. And Zoe, well, she looked down at the bows on her black patent leather shoes and held tight to Danielle Schacht's hand. Danielle's jaw was tight. I could tell she was trying hard not to cry. I couldn't see Miche and Jeffrey from where I was standing, they were blocked by Tony and the Russos.

But afterward, as I turned to walk back over the long grassy way to my car, someone grabbed my shoulder. I looked around and saw that it was Miche.

"Hi Bonnie," she murmered.

"Oh, I didn't see you there."

"Jeffrey went on ahead. I think he needed a smoke. You know him. Can I walk with you?" she asked.

"Sure," I said. Then added, "So sad."

"I feel bad for little Zoe," she said, and I nodded. There was nothing more to say. Others had gone ahead; no one lingered at the grave. I could see Susan Russo and Tony Moran getting into the back seat of the green Ford Explorer I had seen that night.

We strolled in time together across the grass and finally reached the pathway that would lead us to our cars. We were the last of the small party of mourners. When we got there she broke the silence. "I see Jeffrey down there by the car." We continued down the path.

"So Abby stayed at the restaurant to help the chef get lunch prepped so that you and Jeffrey could come to the services?" I asked.

"Not exactly. The restaurant is closed today, for Tony, but some of the mourners are going there for lunch. Abby and Chef Lemoine were going to make some quiches and salad, nothing fancy. Why don't you come along?"

"Thanks for inviting me, but I've got to go open the store. I'm already late."

With that we reached Jeffrey's silver Audi and she popped in. He was already in the driver's seat and nodded at me.

"Are you coming over to the restaurant?" he called over to me as Miche was getting settled.

"Thanks, but I can't, I have to open the shop," I said.

"Ok, then, take care," he said.

Miche smiled a solemn goodbye.

"You too," I answered, and they drove away.

When I got to my car, which was parked about six cars down from theirs, I gasped. I couldn't believe what I saw. The tires on the grassy side of the car were both deflated. I walked around it on the gravel road and saw that the tires on the other side were flat also. Did all of my tires suddenly go bad? Or had someone done this? If so, who? And why?

I took a closer look. No, the air hadn't been let out. They'd been slashed. With a knife.

The violence of the act shook me. Then I reminded myself that this was not a normal funeral (if there was such a thing), that Ginger had in fact been murdered, by a violent person who was still out there. I started to shake, and reached for my cell phone to call AAA and Andy.

"Are you okay?" Danielle walked up toward me as I stood in the middle of the gravel roadway. She had her keys out.

"Look, someone's slashed my tires!" I shouted.

She came running over and grabbed my arm.

"What? That can't be." She let go and walked around the Honda, shaking her head.

"I can't believe it," she murmured as she came back to me. I began to splutter a little, but I didn't cry. From a distance anyone would have thought I was a distraught mourner. This was so much more. I was truly spooked now.

"Come." She steered me to her Volvo and opened the passenger door. I got in.

"Dial Andy's number and then give me your cell!" she commanded.

I obeyed, and handed her the phone.

"Andy, this is Dr. Danielle Schacht." She practically barked. "I am with Bonnie at the cemetery. The burial is over. Someone has slashed Bonnie's tires. I am taking her home."

She paused while he spoke, and then said "Okay, very wise." She hung up and turned to me. "He's calling AAA, and the police."

"I could have done that myself. He doesn't need to."

"Too late now, he's doing it. He said to open the car and leave the keys in the ignition. He said he's five minutes away."

"Okay," I agreed. We drove over to my car. I got out and put them in the ignition. Then I got back in her car. We drove back toward town, the silence broken only when I gave her my address and she answered, "I know where that is. Pretty street."

"Oh, no, the shop!" I remembered suddenly. Someone had to open Village Cooks.

"Andy said he'd call Sally and see if she could do it. If not, the store will just be closed. Nothing else we can do. You need to get home."

"I'm all right, I think."

"But you can't work under these circumstances."

"You're right. I need to pull myself together."

"And you probably shouldn't be alone. You could be in danger."

Dear Lord, she was right. Someone was after me, or at the least, trying to scare me. I felt like I was in a made-for-TV movie. And this was the part where the murderer torments the person who found the victim.

"But I didn't see anything," I cried out.

"What?" Danielle was distracted as she began to slow down.

"Why are you slowing down?" By the time I said it she had pulled over on the side of the road and was parking behind a silver Audi parked on the shoulder.

"Doesn't that look like the Russos' car? And behind them, Jeffrey's?"

There were people standing around outside the cars. The Russos and Jeffrey. They were in what seemed to be frantic conversation. When our doors slammed as Danielle and I got out of her car, no one looked up. As we got closer I saw Miche huddled over someone over near the bushes. Was that Tony? Maybe he had gotten sick and they had to pull over? Not an unreasonable assumption, considering he had just buried his girlfriend.

Yes, it was Tony. On someone's front lawn. There were no cars in the driveway, so the occupants were probably not home. He was huddled over with his arms crossed in front of him like he was shivering. Miche appeared to be speaking softly to him, and rubbing his arm.

"What's going on?" Danielle asked the Russos and Jeffrey when we got to them.

They were standing on the sidewalk. Jeffrey was smoking a cigarette. He looked uncomfortable.

"Oh, hi," Dennis said. Sue smiled weakly, and Jeffrey said nothing.

"Tony jumped out of the car. Don't worry, he's all right." Dennis told them.

"What? While it was moving?" Danielle turned to look over at Tony.

"Yes, but I was going slowly. I had just been stopped at a light, and had just started going again."

"How awful" was all I could muster. Jeffrey stared at me.

"Miche is talking to him. She'll calm him down." Sue rubbed her arm, unconsciously imitating what Miche was doing to comfort Tony. She looked worn, her face more sculpted and shadowy in her black pantsuit.

"We're trying to decide what to do with him." Jeffrey finally spoke. "I think we should still bring him to the restaurant for lunch, but afterward we're not sure he should be alone."

Dennis told us, "I just put in a call to a psychologist I know, Peter Kimball. I'm hoping he can meet us at the restaurant and figure out what to do."

With that his phone rang. He stepped away. It was probably Dr. Kimball calling back. We heard Dennis explain the situation, mutter a few "Okay's" and hang up quickly. "He's on his way."

Sue sighed in relief when her husband got off the phone. "I'll go tell Miche," she offered. She left Dennis there with us and headed over to Miche and Tony, now sitting on the grass.

"How long have you known Tony?" I asked Dennis. "You seem like such a good friend to him."

"I went to high school with his older brother. My best friend in the neighborhood. Back in Philly. So we go way back."

"Oh, that's interesting. Where is he now? I didn't see anyone who looked like a brother at the funeral."

"Bobby died in the Gulf War. Only a few hundred U.S. soldiers died, and he was one of the unlucky few. Tony's parents are gone, too. He doesn't have anyone other than some older cousins who moved to Florida. We're all he's got."

He motioned to Sue. "She's like a mother to him."

"And you're like a father, it seems," Danielle added and patted his shoulder.

We could see he was fighting back tears. We were all relieved when Miche and Tony joined us.

"I'm okay now, Dennis. Really," Tony's voice was a little shaky, but not out of control. He was eyeing Jeffrey as he said it.

"Let's go now," Sue said softly, and they all quickly got in their two cars and were gone. Off to the restaurant, and, we hoped, a session with Dr. Kimball.

Danielle and I stood there for a moment, trying to process what had just happened. We hadn't told any of them about my slashed tires, and no one had asked why we were driving together. Then again, people often went to funerals with other people.

"Let's go now," Danielle echoed Sue, softly, too.

We drove in silence. It wasn't far to my house, about ten minutes. When we got there she parked the car on the road, turned off the ignition, and turned to face me.

"Why would someone want to scare me?" I implored. "I found the body, but that's all. I didn't see anything. I am not a witness. I don't know who killed Ginger."

"I don't have any idea. Let's go inside, please."

We got out of the car, walked down the path and I shakily reached under the stone rabbit for the spare back door key, since my house key was on the keychain I had left in the ignition of my car. I let us in.

"It's lovely," Danielle said.

"Thank you. Put your coat in here." I led her to the coat closet. Then we went into the living room and I sat down. She was still standing. I noticed that she was looking at the view out the expanse of windows along the back of the house.

"I found her over there." I pointed toward Ian Wright's house, and the stream that ran eastward. Danielle found a red knitted throw I'd had for years on the back of a paisley wing chair, and came over and wrapped it around my shoulders. What a kind doctor she must be, I thought as she finally sat down across from me on the ottoman of the wing chair facing where I sat on the big gold velvet couch.

"Can I make you some tea?" she asked. She looked like she needed to do something, perched there on the edge, but I really didn't want any. I wanted someone to talk to.

"No thanks, unless you do." She shook her head. "Are you in a hurry? Do you have to be somewhere?" I asked.

"Not for about an hour," she answered and got up off the ottoman and plopped herself down in the other wing chair of the pair. To my surprise she put her feet up on the ottoman, despite the fact that she was wearing a black knitted knee-length skirt that matched her double-breasted jacket with pewter buttons. A St. John's suit, I thought. I couldn't place her shoes, but they looked like one-inch black pumps. Simple, elegant, no nonsense, like her. I smiled. I liked Dr. Danielle Schacht.

"Let's relax, then," I said. She nodded and put her head back. So did I. Once again, we were silent for a while.

Eventually the phone rang, as we knew it would. Andy said he was at the cemetery, and the police had examined the car and were dusting the tires for fingerprints before AAA would tow it to the garage.

"Is Michael Quinn there?" I asked.

"No, it's an officer named Steven O'Neill."

"Just one?"

"He's in charge, and there's another one with him. I didn't get the other guy's name. Should I be taking notes?" This was one of our in-jokes, since he was a reporter and took notes for a living. It had the desired effect of lightening my mood. And the fact that he made a joke made me hope that he wasn't as shaken by this as I was. Or that he was able to put a brave face on it.

"Are you okay? Is Danielle still there?" he asked.

"Yes, she is, and I'm fine. But she has to go soon."

"I figured as much, so I called Ian Wright. He'll be over in a few minutes. I hope you don't mind, Bonnie, but I've got to get back to work and I didn't want you to be alone."

"That's fine, great idea. Did you reach Sally? Can she go to the store?"

"Yes, she's there. She said to tell you not to worry about a thing."

"That's good. But I need to call her and ask her to close the store at five and run over to Wilmington Printers to get the postcards and stuff. And find the address list and stamps on my desk. The postcards have to be mailed right away."

He sighed, but didn't say anything.

"Andy, there's one more thing."

"What?" a little impatiently.

I told him about Tony Moran jumping out of the car. He took it all in, then said, "Poor guy. Bye." And hung up.

I told Danielle all of this. But she didn't jump up to leave. She said, dreamily, "I'm worried about Zoe."

"That little thing sure has taken to you."

"And I to her." I noticed the tears in her eye as the doorbell rang and Ian Wright came rushing into the room.

"Bonnie, are you all right?" He reached for me and I stood up and gave him a hug.

"Yes, Ian, I am, and thanks for coming over. Danielle drove me home but she has to get to the office."

"Yes, I have patients starting at two," she agreed, and got up and gave me a squeeze before she was off.

Ian took her place in the wing chair. "Well, you must tell me all about it," he said.

So I did.

"Tony has got to get hold of himself," he said when I had finished. "I certainly hope Russo's friend can help him."

"Me too." I hesitated, then went on, "Do you think it could have been a suicide attempt? Out of guilt?"

"Are you suggesting that he could have murdered his own girlfriend?"

"Maybe. Or her death was an accident he was involved in, and he can't bring himself to come forward with the truth."

"That's plausible. Or he could have been upset about burying his girlfriend and acted without thinking, crazed with grief. Maybe he's just unstable. The car wasn't going very fast, so I doubt that it was a legitimate suicide attempt." He paused and gave me a good hard look. "But it could be someone else who killed her, and that person could still be out there.

And the murderer is probably the person who slashed your tires." He recrossed his legs.

"All right then, let's review the list of suspects," he said, firmly. "Since we don't know who was here with Ginger, let's look at the people who were at the cemetery. Who exactly was there at the gravesite with you?"

"Let's see," I breathed. "Zoe was with Bob Lee and another social worker I don't know, a woman. Tony Moran came with the Russos, Jeffrey Sloane and Miche were there, Danielle of course, and about a half dozen other people I didn't know. Oh, and Michael Quinn and a couple of guys who looked like they might be detectives or officials too."

"Were all of them white?"

"Ian!"

"I'm just wondering if any of Ginger's relatives were there."

"Zoe was the only black person there." I paused and added, "I thought of that too. No family other than Zoe there. And Tony of course. Poor Ginger."

"Could you see your car from the gravesite?"

"You're thinking that maybe someone did it during the service?" I pondered. "Hmm. Could be. I couldn't see any of the cars from the gravesite, it was up a little hill and over to the west."

"So anyone could have driven up and slashed your tires while you were at the service with the other mourners."

"Yes, they could have." I sighed.

"Or," I put in, "since the other mourners sure skedaddled away from that grave pretty fast when the service was over, one of them could have done it to my car before I got there. First you walk across the grass, then you get to a small gravel road that leads to the main road where the cars parked along the side. It's a bit of a walk."

"Did you walk to your car alone?"

"I started to, and I was taking my time, and then Miche came over and walked with me."

"Miche?" He seemed surprised. "What about Jeffrey?"

"She said he had gone ahead to have a smoke."

"Anything else that you saw, or remember?"

"Well, I saw Tony and Sue get into a backseat of a car, but I didn't see Dennis."

"Hmm." He picked a piece of lint off of his flannel trouser leg.

"Dennis was probably already in the driver's seat when I saw the others."

"But why would they both get in the back? Why didn't Sue get in the front?"

"Maybe someone else was there, who got in the front seat?"

"That's highly unlikely." Ian's clipped British accent snapped formally. "A wife usually sits next to her husband in the front of a car. If there were a fourth person there, he or she would have gotten in the back with Tony."

"Especially at a time like this," I added.

"Especially," he agreed.

At that moment the phone rang. I picked it up.

"Hi, Sally. It's good to hear your voice," I told her, and it was.

"How are you, dear? I'm sorry I haven't called earlier but we had a few customers."

"I'm fine. Ian's here. Don't worry about me."

"I'm glad to hear that Ian's there. I'm sure he's taking good care of you, but I will worry about you nonetheless. I will be there at 6:15 and will bring dinner."

"Bring dinner? Thank you, but how are you going to do that while you are at the store working? And I'm sorry to ask this, but I need you to close early and go to the printer and pick up the postcards so we can get them in the mail tomorrow."

"Already thought of that. I've got it covered, don't worry. I already got the list and stamps from your desk. They're in my purse. Just stay safe. And ask Ian if he would like to stay to dinner."

I looked over at Ian, who was looking back at me inquisitively.

"Do you want to stay for dinner? Sally's coming over, and bringing it with her. She'll be here by 6:15."

"Of course, I'd be delighted." He sounded more gallant than usual. Maybe it was the prospect of seeing Sally. I hoped it was.

"Ok, then. Thank you, Sally. I'll tell Andy to be here by then."

"Then it's settled. See you then!" And she was gone.

"She's incredible," I said as I put the phone back in its cradle. "Sally Harvey is an amazing woman. I have no idea how she's going to run the store, pick up the posters and cards at the printer, and prepare dinner for five people at the same time."

"Yes, she is an amazing woman," he nodded, and blushed just a little. Ian insisted on making us tea.

"Don't you dare move. I've got it under control," he harrumphed as he ambled out of the room.

I sat back and relaxed while I listened to Ian fill the water in the kettle and the tea pot and then wrestle around to retrieve cups and saucers and spoons for us. Then I heard the back door opening and a "Be right back!" as it slammed behind him. He was gone for a few minutes. Just as the kettle was beginning to whistle, he came back in and set up the tray for us.

He brought the tray in and sat it down. While we waited for the tea to steep I asked him, "What were you doing outside?"

"I just wanted to take a look around the perimeter."

"The perimeter?" I laughed. "Of the house? Who are you, James Bond?"

"You may laugh, my dear, but I feel much better now that I have circled the house and ascertained your safety."

"I love you, Ian Wright." I gave him a warm smile, then "played Mother" and poured our tea.

"Do you have any biscuits?" he replied sheepishly.

"On the counter, under the glass dome." He went in and returned with a plate full of chocolate chip cookies that I had made that morning before the funeral. I hoped Ian wouldn't eat them all. But they were large, and very rich, so he probably wouldn't.

"Have you had lunch?" I asked.

"Yes, earlier." I wondered if that was true. He went on, "I was just feeling a bit peckish."

"There's some leftover lasagna in the refrigerator that would heat nicely in three minutes in the microwave, if you'd like a little more to eat."

"Not a bad idea. I'll save the cookies for dessert." And he was gone again.

Believe it or not, after all of the excitement of the funeral, having my tires slashed and Tony jumping out of the car, while Ian was in the kitchen heating the lasagna, I fell asleep. And Ian let me. When I woke up I found myself stretched out on the couch with the red afghan over me. Ian was seated in the armchair facing me, reading Cook's Illustrated magazine.

"Cook's Illustrated?" I chuckled.

"It was all I could find. I already read the newspaper this morning, and I didn't want to go through your books."

"Thank you for letting me rest."

No sooner had I gotten the words out when the back door opened and William appeared. Three-thirty on the dot.

"Hi Ian! What's going on, Mom? You look funny."

"Ian dropped by, and I just woke up from a nap."

"Okay, cool." He retreated to the kitchen, poured himself a glass of milk, and came back and joined us in the living room, where he grabbed a few cookies.

"How was school?" Ian asked.

"Pretty good. We started studying weather in science. Did you know that air pollution is really bad in southern California?"

I stifled a laugh. "Yes, I did."

"They never show it on TV, and lots of shows are set in LA." William grabbed a few more chocolate chips and his glass of milk, and headed toward the stairs. "I gotta go."

"Where's he going?" Ian asked me.

"Down time. He has an hour to do whatever he wants, within reason, after school. Then, he does his homework without complaint. It's our deal."

"Very interesting," mused Ian.

"Works for us," I said.

"Apparently."

"Ian?"

"Yes, Bonnie."

"Do you think someone's going to kill me?"

"Certainly not!" He straightened up. "Someone is trying to frighten you, that is all. My hope," he went on, "is that the examination of fingerprints on your car will lead to the apprehension of the killer."

"Do you think he, or she, left fingerprints?"

"I'm hoping that it was a spontaneous act, and the person who did it acted quickly and carelessly, out of anger."

"As opposed to planning to do it, and wearing gloves?"

"Exactly."

"Whatever their intent, I get the message."

"What message do you think they were sending?"

"That I should stay away from the whole situation. Maybe that I should not have gone to the funeral."

The phone rang. I picked it up. The unmistakable, powerful voice of my father boomed through the phone.

"Bonnie! Are you all right?" Yikes. A lot of people sure were asking me that.

"Hi, Dad."

I took a deep breath and said, "Yes, I'm fine. And yes, Ian is here with me. I'll put him on." I handed the phone to Ian. "He's flying back from Japan tomorrow. He wants to talk to you."

Ian took the cordless outside with him. He was back pretty quickly.

"Did he tell you to keep an eye on me?"

"He did. And he said that Andy had called him."

"Oh, boy. I'll bet the police are going over the car with a fine-toothed comb. They don't want to be answerable to President Billings."

"I'd wager that some of them served while he was Commander-in-Chief and they will not rest until they have examined every inch of your car."

"And the surrounding area, no doubt."

"That too. This is serious, my dear. You are the daughter of an ex-President, and while it was not an attempt at taking your life, it was a violent act against you. Not to be taken lightly."

"Wait a minute. How did Dad know you were here?"

"I have no idea." He picked up the tray and started into the kitchen. "Andy must have told him."

"Right," I said, but I wasn't so sure.

When he returned I said, "Did you know that federal drug laws were tightened significantly when my father was President? You were in England, so you probably didn't hear about that."

"I did know that."

"Do you think that could have something to do with all of this?"

"Drug laws? Because Ginger had used drugs? That's a stretch," he said, although he looked quizzical, like he was puzzling it out as an idea at the same time he was dismissing it.

"Maybe I'm grasping at straws. But I'm trying to find something that links me to the crime."

"Crimes," he corrected. "The vandalism to your car is sufficient to consider it a felony. Felony and murder, not a pretty picture."

"Dear Lord" was all I could say in response. Ian and I sat quietly for a few minutes, lost in our own thoughts. We were both relieved when the front door opened and Andy came in. He leaned over and kissed me, and shook Ian's hand as he got up. Then he sat down on the couch next to me. "Is William here?" he asked.

"Yes, and it's almost homework time."

"Are you done for the day?" asked Ian.

"Yes, I'm home. I filed my story and took off early. I put a call into Michael Quinn and am waiting for him to call me back."

"And you called my father, I gather?"

"Don't be mad, honey. I had to. It's part of the deal of being married to you. He made me promise a long time ago that I would alert him to even the smallest breach of your safety."

"Has he told my mother about Ginger yet?"

"He's going to tell her everything once they get on the plane from LA to Newark."

"She'll want to come right here," I said.

"So will he. But he knows better. If you're not safe, President Billings certainly isn't. *They* certainly aren't." He meant my mother. I froze.

"He's right," added Ian. "It's better if they go to Montclair. You can see them once this is all cleared up."

"Once they catch the killer, you mean. And the felon."

"They may be one and the same," Ian replied. Andy was silent. I felt like they knew something I didn't. But I didn't care. I just wanted this to be over with.

Andy grabbed my hand in his. "Honey," he began. I eyed him. What else was wrong?

He went on. "I called my parents. They'll be here in about an hour. I asked them to take William to stay with them for a few days. Just until all of this is cleared up."

"Oh, no, not William," I gurgled. Although I am a very strong woman, I wanted to cry. Not my baby.

But then my lioness instinct took over. I did not want any harm to come to my child, especially if I had a part in causing it.

So I said quietly, "Thank you, Andy, I'm glad you called them. I'll go pack his clothes."

I got up, walked out of the room, and started upstairs.

"Send him down and I'll tell him," Andy hollered after me.

"Okay."

"Dad wants to talk to you," I told William as I went into his room and found him playing Xbox.

"He's home early."

"Yeah, go see," I patted him on the head and he was gone.

An hour and ten minutes later Carol and Paul Emerson were in the living room, hugging their grandson — their grandson who was a bit confused, but glad he was excused from his homework for one night, and wouldn't have to go to school for a few days.

"Don't worry, fella, I'll call your teacher in the morning. She'll email what you're missing to Grandma. It'll be fun to have Grandma and Grandpa as your teachers for a few days."

"But they're not real teachers," William looked warily at me.

"No, but you'll get full credit for the work you do with them, don't worry, honey."

I hugged him. "Be a good boy for Mommy. Call me as soon as you get there."

Paul said, "We're going to stop and have dinner out somewhere on the way to Princeton."

"Friendly's?" William asked hopefully.

Paul responded with a huge grin, and wrapped his arm around his grandson's shoulder. "Sure. We haven't been to Friendly's since your last visit, and I miss it."

"I hope it hasn't been remodeled," I added. "I hate they way they redecorated the one in Northfield."

"But the clam chowder and the ice cream will still be the same!" Carol put in cheerily. Ever the optimist, she was such a nice woman. I was thankful that Carol and Paul had come right away when Andy called them, even though I was heartbroken at the idea of having William away from home. I knew it was for the best.

And I didn't cry until after they left, and Sally arrived promptly at 6:15, with a crockpot and a grocery bag, as promised, and a large envelope that said Wilmington Printers on it. Ian rushed to help her in.

"Oh, Sally!" I burst out, and hugged her. "William had to go and stay with Carol and Paul! This is just awful!"

"I know, dear, it's terrible. But it's for the best," she cooed.

We settled down next to each other at the kitchen table, still hugging, and Andy and Ian buzzed around us, unpacking what she brought and setting the table. She had brought a crockpot full of chili, some cornbread, a green salad, and a bottle of wine.

"How did you manage all of this?" I sputtered when I saw it all.

"Well, I did open the store fifteen minutes late," she grinned. "I had the cornbread in the freezer, and some chopped onions in there too, so I was able to brown the meat and onions in a jiff then mix everything together in the crockpot. I brought it to the store and it cooked in the back room all afternoon."

"And the salad?"

"That, I'm afraid, is left over from last night. Not sure how well the red onion and cranberries will go with the chili, but it'll have to do."

"It will *have to do*," Andy mimicked a posh English accent, laughing.

And we all settled down to a peaceful meal. The wine helped relax me, and the hot food did me good. I didn't realize that I was hungry until I ate my first mouthful of steaming chili. Sally's chili recipe was no nonsense, and could be made in twenty minutes on the skillet if need be, with ground turkey or beef. She called it an "Old Reliable" — one of the recipes that she had made for years and had come to rely on as an assured success. Most of them, like the chili, were no frills, but could be counted on for a predictable deliciousness.

We chatted about the food and the story Andy had filed that day. We lingered at the table for longer than usual after we had finished eating. Sally and Ian got up and cleared while Andy and I stayed ar the table. It really felt strange to have dinner without William, and it had been not much more than an hour since he left. I missed him already. I gave Andy a sad look, and knew he read my mind and shared my feelings.

Then Ian opened a second bottle of wine, and wordlessly poured some in each of our glasses.

I broke the silence. "Do you I think I should cancel Cookbooktoberfest? It's a week from Saturday. The postcards haven't been mailed yet."

"I was wondering about that myself," Sally said. "Actually, a customer asked." She paused. "People know that Ginger Harrison's body was found here, and they're legitimately concerned."

"Concerned or worried for themselves? Do you think that safety could be a problem at Cookbooktoberfest?" I looked at Sally, then Ian, then Andy, who nodded.

"It could be, honey. Let's give it a few more days."

"But I have to mail the postcards in the morning. What if Elizabeth Crisp hears about this and cancels? That would be terrible. This is just awful!" I cried.

Andy's tone was calm and firm. "I'll help you address the postcards. You can mail them in the morning. If it has to be canceled, so be it. In the meantime, you need to get them in the mail if it is going to happen."

"Andy's right," said Ian, and I saw that he was giving Sally a look that said it was time for them to go home.

"Yes, things will be brighter tomorrow, dear," she said. "Ian and I will be off now. I will see you tomorrow."

And with that they were gone, and Andy and I were alone in our kitchen, the dark woods outside the glass seeming ominous as they never had before.

Sally had brought the print-out of the names and addresses for the cards, and enough books of stamps to mail them. I set to work writing the names and addresses, and passed them to Andy, who put the stamps on them.

As we worked I said idly, "I should make labels next time."

Andy nodded.

"I have something else to tell you," he said, after a few minutes.

"What else could there be?"

"I ordered security. There is a car in front of the house with two guards in it who will take periodic surveillance walks around the house and property."

He went on. "They are waiting for me to tell you, and invite them in to meet you. I had to tell you about them, in case you saw one of them and freaked out."

"In case I saw someone?" I was stunned. "Oh, all right, I know, you are concerned for my welfare, I'm a President's daughter and someone enacted violence against me, in addition to murdering someone on our property, so we must have security guards patrolling around our house 24/7."

"Don't be angry."

"I'm not angry. I get it."

"Do you, really?"

"Yes. And I'm glad you called your parents and asked them to take William. It was the right thing to do. If anything happens to him, I'll die."

"Me too."

"Send them in."

So that's how I met Greg Baker, the owner of Baker Security, and Charlie Campbell, his associate. Once they had come in and we had all introduced ourselves, I asked them to sit down at the table with us.

Greg started right in with the business at hand. "I own the firm, and I'm taking the first shift. That way I can fully assess the situation and inform my people of the best way to protect you." Greg rubbed a hand over his shaved head as he spoke in clipped tones. I estimated him to be in his late fifities, and in excellent shape. He was medium height, compact, but muscular. He wore chinos, a button-down yellow shirt, and a green zippered fleece jacket that had "Baker Security" embroidered on it.

Charlie Campbell was taller, and younger, maybe 35, with black hair shorn close military-style, and the same clothing, except his button-down was light blue. Neither of them had pulled their chairs in, and they sat stiffly.

"How long are your shifts?"

Greg answered, "Three eight-hour shifts, groups of two. You'll be covered round the clock. We have a third person who will be your driver and stay with you when you leave the house. You need to let us know if you are going anywhere; we need an hour's notice."

Andy seemed impressed. "Sounds reasonable."

I nodded agreement.

Charlie Campbell hadn't said a word the whole time.

Greg stood up, and Charlie followed. Greg said, "Well, let us know if you need anything. I guess I'll let you folks turn in."

So we did, with the knowledge — comforting or unsettling? — that Baker Security was outside watching over us after this horrendous day.

Chapter 6

Friday dawned only a tiny bit brighter, despite Sally's promise. Andy and I both slept fitfully, and hated waking up to a house without William in it. The phone rang just as we were having our soft-boiled eggs, toast, and coffee. It was Michael Quinn. We put the phone on "speaker."

"Sorry to call so early, but I figured you'd be up."

"We are," Andy answered.

"We've got the results from the tests done on Bonnie's car. The tires were slashed with a Swiss Army knife. Since the blade was small, and when you got to the car the tires were flat, we think the tires were slashed right after you arrived, while you were at the gravesite. It would have taken that long for the tires to flatten after such small slits were made in the rubber. There were a lot of them, though."

Andy asked, "How many?"

"43 total on all four tires."

"What about fingerprints? Were there any on the car?"

"None. So either it was wiped clean, or the person was careful not to touch the car."

"That's bad news. I was hoping that prints would wrap up this whole mess, and William could come home," I said.

"I'm sorry he had to go to the Emersons, Bonnie, but we had to take precautions."

I glared at Andy. I asked with my eyes: Michael Quinn was in on the decision too? Before me?

Andy shrugged his shoulders. "So what's next?" he asked Michael.

"Honestly, we've got zip. There were no forensic remains around Ginger Harrison's body, and none on your car. All we found near your house were some footprints outside Ian Wright's house, and they could have been caused by anyone, even the mailman. We have nothing to go on, no forensics, no evidence. The blood we found was hers, no one else's. So we're looking into Ginger's past. I've got a detective down in Philadelphia doing some interviews, and I'm heading down there myself today." Michael paused. "You can reach me on my cell if you need me, but Steven O'Neill will be in charge here while I'm out of town. I'll be back sometime tonight."

"Can you tell us who you're interviewing?"

"Sorry, Andy, I can't. But if anything develops, I'll let you know. In the meantime, let Baker Security do their job."

"We can manage that."

"Good. We'll talk later."

"Bye," we said in unison.

"Andy!" I squealed with burning anger the moment we hung up. "So Detective Quinn was involved in the decision to bring your parents up here to get William? And to hire Baker Security? And Ian was my babysitter in the meantime?"

"Something like that," Andy retorted sheepishly. "You had been attacked, and then your father called back, so we had a conference call and made a plan."

"Who was in on the conference call?"

"Quinn, your father, a guy from the Secret Service, and me."

"Who was the guy from the Secret Service?"

"I think his name was Harris; yeah, it was Rick Harris."

"And you agreed to hire private security, hence Baker Security. Did one of them recommend them?"

"Harris did."

"Okay, then, they must be good." He seemed pleased at what sounded like my acquiescence. But I was still angry.

"They'll have someone outside Village Cooks. I would rather you not be alone inside, just as a precaution. Can you ask Sally to meet you at the store when you go in to open up?"

"I can do that, and I'm sure she will. I have to stop at the post office first to mail the postcards, but that will only take a few minutes. What about you? You'll need someone from Baker to drive you and stay with you too."

"Good point. I'll call them now and tell them we need two people." That said, we moved on.

Greg Baker sent a woman to protect me. Less conspicuous than a man, I guessed. Terry Ferrara was her name, and I liked her immediately. Soft, short black pixie hair on a small pixie body, early 30s. I was sure she was tough despite her diminutive size. She was from the Bronx, and had the accent and attitude to prove it.

"I can't cook for beans, but I love to eat," she enthused as we drove from the post office to the store after I had mailed the postcards. "I love to go to Arthur Avenue to get eggplant parm. Have you ever been there?"

"No, but I'd love to check it out. I don't know very much about Italian deli food. I know Jewish deli, however. I love turkey with Russian dressing on rye."

"Second Avenue Deli?" she asked.

"Nope, uptown, Carnegie. My family is from the West Side originally. My grandparents on both sides lived there before they had kids and moved to New Jersey."

"That's too bad. Those prewar apartments are awesome!" She chuckled.

Just two women talking about deli food and real estate. Like one wasn't in danger, and the other paid to protect her.

I got back to reality. "Are you going to come in to the store or stay outside in the car the whole time?"

"I'll be in and out, mostly out. I don't want to look suspicious by staying there the whole time. But I want you to call me if any customers you don't already know come in to the store. Ring twice then hang up. I won't know who you know, so that's the best way to do it. If that happens, I'll come in and pretend to be a customer. And keep an eye on you."

"Okay," I breathed. This was sounding pretty dramatic. And I'd have to quickly tell Sally about these arrangements.

Which I did, as soon as I got inside and found her there with our cat, Mrs. Beeton, in her arms.

"This is exciting, but not in a good way," was her concerned reaction. Then she went off to unload some boxes. She had already made the coffee and I helped myself to my second cup of the day. I reviewed the tally from yesterday, the day I missed. Sally had sold a substantial amount, to seven customers. Not many people, but a nice total. I was pleased.

"So what did I miss yesterday?" I asked.

"We had two big sales, the rest were small. The two big sales were new customers, so I got their e-mail addresses and added them to the list."

"Great!"

"One of them bought a whole set of copper pots and ordered a hanging rack. She had just remodeled her kitchen and was buying her dream pots and pans to go with it."

"Aww."

"I gave her a free set of round cake pans. Hope you don't mind. She is not a baker, but said she was interested in learning how."

"Good idea, that was very thoughtful. I'm not mad. We'll have to find her some baking lessons!"

"I'm glad you're glad. Because I have some other news." Sally sat down across from me.

"Uh-oh."

"Royal Jefferson called. He said that Elizabeth heard about Ginger, and called him."

"Oh, no. I just mailed the postcards, and I have the posters right here. Is Elizabeth Crisp pulling out of Cookbooktoberfest?"

"Not exactly. He might cancel."

"What?!"

"Well, he said he's considering it. He definitely wants to re-schedule if things aren't quieted down here soon. He said that if things are not 'safe' around here by next Monday, he'll want to discuss it with you further."

"Oh, no. Re-schedule to when? Did he give a date?"

"He was very nice about it, but he didn't say. He was indefinite. Said that we should wait until Monday and see. People will be disappointed, but hopefully they won't have shopped for ingredients or be cooking already."

"Well, I guess we should be relieved she didn't cancel altogether. Did you get the feeling that this was coming from her, or from him?"

"From him. He said he felt responsible for his client's safety, and didn't want to bring her into a risky situation. And he asked how you were and wished you all the best."

"It would have been a lot better if I'd been here. Did you tell him I was out because someone slashed my tires after the funeral?"

"Of course not, dear. I told him you were at the funeral. He called at around 2:30. You could have still been at the funeral luncheon, for all he knew."

"Right. Okay. Thanks." I gave her a squeeze. "Yes, the luncheon." I remembered. "There was more drama yesterday other than the funeral and my tires getting slashed. Did you hear about Tony Moran?"

"No, what about him?"

"He jumped out of Dennis Russo's moving car on the way from the cemetery to St. Cloud's."

"Oh my God. Is he okay?"

"Dennis has just started moving after he had stopped for a light, so he was only going about five, maybe ten miles an hour. I don't know why he didn't jump out when they were stopped at the light. I've been thinking about it. Maybe that's when he got the idea, but by the time he got the courage Dennis had started the car moving again. Still, it was pretty dramatic. Jeffrey and Miche were in the car behind him. He ran off into some bushes, and Miche was able to bring him back and calm him down. They went on to the restaurant for the luncheon, and Dennis Russo called a psychologist he knows to meet them there and talk to Tony."

"That was smart."

"Dennis is used to thinking on his feet. And dealing with crises, I'd imagine, being a school principal."

"True, but how unnerving."

"You said it. We were quite a few cars behind them but when we saw them by the side of the road, we stopped and got out and talked to them.

The situation was under control by the time we got there and they were getting ready to move on."

"Bonnie?" Sally hesitated. "I know he was her boyfriend, but do you think Tony could have killed Ginger?"

"Ian and I discussed that possibility. That maybe they had a fight and it was accidental. Or maybe he has a temper we don't know about. I really don't know, since I don't know the man."

"What does Abby think? She works with him."

"She doesn't know, she can't say for sure. She says he likes suspense movies, classics."

"This is certainly a dramatic turn of events."

"And we thought that all we had going on was Cookbooktoberfest!"

"I wish it was."

"Me too."

With that the door jingled and Sue Russo came in. The rest of our conversation would have to wait.

Sue was wearing a lovely sage hand-knitted sweater set with a cascade cardigan and gray slacks, shoes and bag. Silver earrings. A bit matchy for my taste, but she looked lovely. Then I noticed the circles under her eyes that had not been there yesterday. Her hair had been blown dry, her caramel colored highlights moved perfectly as she walked. And I got it. The old "put on a nice outfit and some lipstick to make yourself feel better" routine. I'd been there myself.

I walked over to her where she had stopped near the American cookbooks and said hello.

Then I asked her quietly, "How did it go with Tony when you got to the restaurant?"

"Dennis' friend came, you know, the psychologist Peter Kimball. We all ate, then they went into Jeffrey's office and talked for a long time. A couple of hours, I heard later. Tony's going to be staying with Miche for a few days. Dr. Kimball didn't think he should be alone."

"That's wise. Do you think she can handle it? Why isn't he staying with Jeffrey?"

"I asked Dennis that too. He said that Tony and Jeffrey have a few old issues that might come up in this heightened situation."

"That's interesting. I wonder what he meant."

"I don't know exactly. Dennis didn't say. But Jeffrey and Tony are both from the same neighborhood in Philly as Dennis."

"Hmm" was all I could think of to say.

"And Dennis' best friend was Tony's older brother."

"I knew that."

"Dennis always gets quiet when anything about Bobby Moran comes up. But, well, I don't know, this time it got me a little worried, I must confess."

"And you didn't sleep well last night, worrying about it."

"How did you know? I must look tired."

"Your outfit is too lovely for an ordinary Friday afternoon. I detected that a 'pick me up' was needed." I smiled.

"You are so right! And wise. I thought it would cheer me up, and I want to get that French cookbook everyone is talking about."

"Do you like to cook?"

"A bit. It's more that I like to read cookbooks. I don't know why I haven't been in here more often; you have a fantastic selection."

"Why, thanks," I said, handing her the book she wanted. It was *Around My French Table* by Dorie Greenspan.

"A cookbook connoisseur — my favorite kind of person!"

We laughed. I was glad that I had lightened the mood.

"I love to curl up in bed with a cup of tea and a cookbook. I love the ones that have stories about the recipes."

"Those are the best kind!" I agreed. "Have you read Pat Conroy's cookbook? It's a love letter to cookbooks, and cooking."

"No, do you have it?"

"Right here." We were still in the American section, and Pat is a well-known southern fiction author and foodie. I handed her *The Pat Conroy Cookbook: Recipes of My Life*. "It is chock full of wonderful stories, and recipes. It's one of my favorites."

"I'll take it." She walked toward the counter with the two books. "Have you ever met him?"

"Once, a long time ago. He's a great guy."

"Maybe he could be one of your Cookbooktoberfest guests one day," she suggested.

"What a great idea!" I cheered. And it was. An excellent idea for Village Cooks, and Sue was turning out to be a new cookbook-loving customer/friend. A kindred spirit. I was feeling better, and forgetting my troubles. Just a little bit. I hoped she was, too.

"I feel so much better, Bonnie. Thank you for everything," she beamed as I rang up her sale. Our new bond was confirmed.

"*Around My French Table* is a wonderful, beautiful book. I've made a few of the recipes already, and loved them. I know you'll enjoy it. And Pat Conroy's book will make you want to go to Italy."

"I thought he was a southern writer. Didn't he write *The Great Santini*? I remember the movie, with Robert Duvall," she said, her voice rising with excitement. "Oh, and *The Prince of Tides*? I loved that book, and the movie, with Nick Nolte and Barbra Streisand. I also read *Beach Music* when I was on vacation a few years ago, but I didn't know he wrote a cookbook."

"He is a novelist," I answered, "but he spent a few years in Italy enjoying the food, and in this book he writes about it."

"Kind of like a guy's *Eat, Pray, Love!*"

She left laughing, and I was now in better spirits, too. Sally had been in the back while Sue was in the store, so I went back to see what she was up to. She was on the phone when I entered the back office/storeroom.

She held up a finger to say that she'd just be a minute, so I waited.

"Whew," she said when she hung up the phone.

"Test results?" I ventured.

"Yes," she sputtered, "That was Dr. Schacht. All clear!"

I flew into her arms. We both choked up, and let ourselves hug for an extra moment before we recovered. When we separated, she continued to hold my hand, and she looked me in the eye.

"Thanks for being such a good friend," she mustered, and we hugged again. This time we let ourselves cry. Tears of joy mixed with tears of sorrow and banished fear. A good release.

A little while later Abby came in.

"My day off," she exclaimed. "And boy do I need it. Want to get some lunch at Veggie Paradise?"

"I can't." I explained about Terry Ferrara, and didn't say my other reason, that I didn't want to leave Sally alone in the store today. I wanted to be around her, I really didn't want to leave my treasured friend.

"I know what we should do. We have two extra quiches from the luncheon yesterday. Jeffrey insisted that I bring them home. I put one in the fridge and one in the freezer. Why don't I go home and get one and bring it here? We can heat slices in the microwave." She gestured at the back table that was used for packing shipments, and, sometimes, eating.

That sounded good.

"Would you mind?"

"Sure, I'll be back in a jiff."

I called Terry and offered her some. She said she'd join us, but only for a few minutes. She wanted to look like a shopper, and would need to walk out with a bag.

Thirty minutes later the four of us were gathered around the storeroom table drinking Diet Coke and eating ham and spinach quiche. Sally said that she'd wait on any customers that came in while we were back there, so we wouldn't have to put up the "Closed. Gone Home to Cook Something Delicious!" sign temporarily.

"How's Jeffrey doing?" I asked. I don't know why I thought of him instead of Miche in all of this, but I did.

"Jeffrey?" She seemed surprised too. I shrugged. "He had a few vodka tonics at the luncheon. Seemed a little nervous. Maybe he felt left out."

"Left out?"

"Well, while we were eating — a psychologist was there — did you know that?"

I nodded.

Abby continued. "It was decided that Tony would stay with Miche for a few days, and not come back to work at the restaurant until Friday, for dinner. Jeffrey looked a little put out, I noticed. Maybe he wanted Tony to stay with him. When he got up and got himself a third vodka tonic, I was surprised."

"Have you ever seen him drink like that?"

"Well, maybe, sometimes... but he always seems like he's got it all together, always perfect, and on — do you know what I mean? Except for the smoking, he always seems so smooth, put together, in control."

"He definitely gives off a suave vibe."

"Maybe it's because he's gay that he seems private, and what you see is his outer persona. Some people are like that; not everyone is comfortable being 'out'."

"Could be."

"Does he have a boyfriend that you know of?" I asked.

"I haven't heard of anyone lately."

"Lately?"

"There was a guy named Larry, but that ended around Easter. Yes, I remember — they broke up on Good Friday. On Easter Sunday we were very busy of course, and Jeffrey was a little off his game. Not his usual charming self. Pale, too. I wondered if he was drinking. I don't think the customers noticed, but I did, and I think Miche did too. I remember being glad that he said he was going to take Monday off. The restaurant is closed on Mondays, so he doesn't have to come in, but he often does."

The conversation turned to Ginger Harrison.

"I hope the killer is found by Monday," I added, after we had told her everything we could think of.

Terry raised her eyebrows.

"Because Cookbooktoberfest will be postponed otherwise."

Sally told them about her conversation with Royal Jefferson, and then explained to Terry what Cookbooktoberfest was.

"I hope they don't cancel!" Terry proclaimed and we all nodded.

Terry looked at her watch and smiled a signal to me.

"How about a cookbook and a Diet Coke in a bag for you?" I asked.

"Sure, what book, though? Do you have any paperbacks that look like they could be novels? I think I'd look a little strange with a big fat hardcover cookbook spread out on my lap all afternoon."

"Not in front of our store you wouldn't!" Sally chided.

"Nevertheless, I think I have the right book. Have you ever read *Home Cooking* by Laurie Colwin?"

"No."

"She's a New Yorker. You'll love it." I plopped the trade paperback in the shopping bag, along with a Diet Coke, and off she went.

Abby said, after the door closed, "She's nice. I like her. And I feel safe with her around."

Sally and I answered in unison, "Me too." But we didn't smile.

As the afternoon at the store wore on, I realized that I wasn't looking forward to going home. Not to another night without William there. And I didn't want to re-live the memory of yesterday. I wanted to call Andy and suggest we get a take-out picnic dinner from Veggie Paradise and have a picnic at Buttermilk Falls, maybe go for a walk. But I knew Baker Security wouldn't go for that. On Friday nights the Wilmington Library showed classic films. I went online and checked to see what they were showing. It turned out to be Suspicion with Cary Grant and Joan Fontaine. Andy would get a kick out of the irony, and whoever Baker Security sent to be with us would probably find it interesting. I called Andy.

"I don't feel like going home tonight," I started.

"Me neither," was his quick reply. "Do you want to eat out?"

"I was thinking we could have a fast Thai dinner at Thai Garden and then go to the library for their film series."

Andy hesitated. He did not love old black-and-white films the way I did. Bonnie and Clyde was about as far back as he liked to go. "What film are they showing this week?"

"Suspicion," I offered cautiously.

He didn't laugh, as I expected he would. "Haven't you seen that twenty times already?"

"Probably. But Andy, I just don't want to go home tonight. Whenever I walk in that house I miss William. And I feel like such a bad mother."

"You're not a bad mother." I could hear the disapproval in his voice. "Listen, give me a few minutes. I'll call you back."

And so he did. "Guess where we're going tonight?"

"Where?"

"To dinner with Danielle Schacht and then to a foster parents orientation meeting Bob is running at his office."

"Are we potential foster parents?" I was stymied.

"You never know, we could be, one day. We're going to support Danielle."

I was stunned. "Danielle is going to be a foster parent?"

"I guess so. All Bob said was that she was coming to the meeting. Yesterday she asked me to call her if there was anything she could do, so I thought maybe we could have dinner with her, and then go to the meeting with her. It'll keep us occupied, out of the house, and support her. Aren't the two of you becoming friends?"

"Yes, we are. And she was kind to drive me home and stay with me yesterday."

"Well, I just called her, and she was very pleased about the whole idea. It'll be interesting." He added, "We don't have to sign up or anything. It's Bob who will be running the meeting."

"Okay, sure. Where will we go to dinner? Thai Garden? Veggie Paradise? The Peacock?"

"I just put a call in to Greg Baker to clear it with him. He may have specific thoughts on where we should eat. When I hear from him, I'll call you back. We'll meet at six."

"All right." I hung up the phone and shook my head at Sally. "You'll never guess what I'm doing tonight."

When I told her she chuckled. "I wonder what William will think about that!"

"William!" I screeched. "I better call him."

He was happy to hear from me, but he was very busy with his grandparents. He told me that they did "schoolwork" in the morning, then went out to lunch and to a bookstore, and now were in the midst of a game of Monopoly. He said, "Grandma is making lemon chicken. She knows it's my favorite. I hope you don't mind."

"Of course not, honey. I use her recipe when I make it, so I am certainly not offended."

He didn't know how easy it was to roast a chicken with lemon. When he is a few years older, I'll show him how, and pass on the tradition. It is such a favorite in our house that if more than a week goes by without it, I hear wistful remarks from both William and Andy asking for it.

"When am I coming home, Mom?" His question shook me from my thoughts.

"Soon. I don't know exactly when yet. You're having a good time, right?"

"Yes."

"You'll be there tonight and tomorrow night. I don't know after that."

"Okay." He brightened when I gave him at least a partially concrete answer.

"Bye, pumpkin, be a good boy. I love you the most!"

"Bye, Mom. I love you too!"

There was a message from Andy. I called him back.

"We'll meet at Thai Garden at six. Terry Ferrara is going to stay with you, and my person, Charlie Campbell, is going to stay with me. They'll act like an interested couple at the foster parent meeting. Bob knows about it, and will play along."

"That'll be interesting, to say the least. See you then."

"Wait," I stopped him and added, "I talked to William, and he's fine."

"Great. I'm on deadline, gotta go."

I was used to that.

After a few more customers that Sally handled and about a dozen internet cookbook customers that I took care of, Sally and I said goodnight to Mrs. Beeton, who was already curled up on her carpeted perch in the darkest corner of the store, and closed the store at six. As we were locking up we saw Kay heading toward her yellow Volkswagen Beetle after closing her antique store next door.

We all hugged. Kay was like a grandmother to me. Sally frowned and said, "I told Kay the latest this morning when we opened up."

"Yes, love, I know about what happened. How terribly awful. And to have William staying with his grandparents, too! That must be so hard on you."

"Yes, but I know he's safe with them."

"That's reassuring. I have an idea. Why don't we all go to St. Cloud's for dinner tomorrow night? Ben will be in town. Why don't you check with Andy, Bonnie; and you check with Ian, Sally, and we'll firm it up in the morning?"

"Okay," we both agreed, and she popped in her yellow Beetle and was off.

"Check with Ian?" I grinned at Sally "Are you two officially an item?"

"It's starting to look that way, isn't it?" beamed Sally, before she dashed off.

I walked around the corner, where Terry had moved her car a few minutes earlier. She drove me across town to Thai Garden.

"Have you ever had to 'act' on the job before?" I asked her as we made our way there.

"Yes, and Charlie and I have been 'married' before, quite a few times in fact."

"Ah, so you're like an old married couple?" I chided.

"We sure are."

"I only met him briefly. What's he like?"

"You think I'm a loud-mouth New Yorker? I'm a little mouse compared to him."

"I can't wait."

A few minutes later we were seated, and Charlie came strolling in. We smiled up at him, and he grinned.

"Hi, Terry."

"Hi, Charlie. This is Bonnie Emerson." He shook my hand.

"We met yesterday."

"The pleasure is still mine," he said in a thick Bronx accent. A charmer and a looker. I wondered what his marital status was, since I didn't see a ring, and whether Terry was interested.

We were joined immediately by Danielle and Andy, who ran into each other outside and came in together.

Andy made the remaining introductions, and a waiter brought the menus.

Charlie was a natural, comfortable among strangers. "Decisions, decisions," he muttered, and we all chuckled.

We had just enough time for a quick appetizer, so I chose my favorite soup, Gaeng Dom Yom Gai, which is a light soup with chicken, coconut milk, and lime. I had been making it that day Zoe came to my door. Terry joined me, but the others chose various kinds of spring rolls. For our entrees, Terry chose Pad Thai, a noodle and chicken dish, while the rest of us chose either green or red curry and beef, chicken, or prawns. Charlie ordered the red curry with prawns and scallops. I asked for brown rice for the table, and was pleased when no one spoke up and asked for white, too. Since it is nutritionally empty, I disdain white rice and can't imagine why anyone would eat it when brown rice is available. I was either with a polite bunch of people, or those who agreed with me.

After we ordered and were sipping our drinks, Andy asked Charlie, "Have you and Terry been working together long?"

"About three years now, right?" He looked at Terry.

"Yes, we both started at Baker at roughly the same time, after we both got out of the service."

"The service?" Danielle asked.

The waiter brought our appetizers and we dug in. We had to be at Bob's office by 7:30.

"Charlie was in the Marines and I was in the Air Force. As it turns out, we were both in intelligence. Greg Baker had been with another firm, then went out on his own, and had contacts in intelligence. He checked us out, and offered us both jobs within a month of each other."

"How cool," I said. "Are you both from New York?"

"The Bronx," they said in unison, and we all laughed.

"Different parts, though; we didn't know each other. I'm from the Italian section and Charlie is Irish. We went to different Catholic high schools."

"High schools who played each other, so we later figured out that Terry might have seen me play football once or twice."

Terry blushed and focused on her soup. Charlie changed the subject. "What about you folks? How do you all know each other?"

"Well, we're married," Andy pointed at me jokingly, "and Danielle is a friend. And a very good doctor."

"You're a doctor?" Charlie asked.

Danielle patted invisible wrinkles in her tweed slacks. "Yes, I am." She smiled.

When she didn't say anymore, Terry jumped in. "Is there any more you can tell us about the Ginger Harrison murder? It might help us protect you."

As we were served and devoured our entrees, we filled them in. They knew that Ginger had been found dead on our property, and that my tires had been slashed at the cemetery, but that was all. They didn't know about Zoe's existence.

"Poor kid," Charlie said after Andy had described her. Terry nodded and they shared a look.

Danielle cleared her throat and surprised us with a wide smile. "I don't know if Bob told you or not, but the reason I'm going to the orientation tonight is that I'm interested in becoming Zoe's foster parent," she proclaimed.

"You're kidding!" I reached over and gave her a squeeze. "That's wonderful! Did you know, Andy?" I studied my husband.

"Not exactly, but I suspected."

I put down my fork and said, "Well I'm thrilled," then added, "I've been worrying about her." I surprised myself when I choked on my words.

Danielle took my hand. "It's okay. You are not responsible for her not having a mother. Her situation was unstable long before her mother died. Remember, she barely knew Ginger."

We ate in silence for a while, probably all thinking of Zoe. And wondering who on earth could have killed Ginger, and where that someone was.

The conference room at Bob's office held an oblong table that fit twelve. Our party was five. There were two other couples and a single woman already seated when we walked in. They had spread out, so we couldn't sit together. Our plan was to present ourselves as interested friends of Danielle's, and pretend that we didn't know Terry and Charlie. If asked, Charlie and Terry decided they would say they had fertility issues and were interested in learning about the Fost-Adopt program. They were thinking that they might foster a child first, and if all went well, adopt him or her. They wanted a baby. I wondered how much of this was true. They seemed so comfortable together, I found myself wishing their act was not a farce.

Bob brought the meeting to order with a generous "Welcome" and proceeded to hand out brochures and some application forms.

As we looked them over, he began. "No one ever said parenting is easy. Foster parenting is harder. So is adoption. But the rewards are endless. I hope that this orientation will help you make your decision whether or not this is the right path for you. I'll speak for a bit, then we'll take a ten minute break, reconvene, and then open it up to questions."

We all nodded.

He told us that there were hundreds of children of all ages needing foster parents in New Jersey "right this minute, tonight."

He explained that when children were removed from their parents' care by the state, the parents have 18 months to "get their act together." There are children that are fostered once for 18 months, and never come back in the system. They are the lucky ones whose parents get the wake-up call and succeed in putting their lives back together. On the other extreme, there are those like Zoe, who go back and forth between their parents and the foster system, because the parents are unable to care for them. He explained that drug problems are a major reason, but not the only reason. A parent's imprisonment, illness, or mental illness could have caused the child to be placed "in the system." Many of them are abused or neglected. They may have a complicated history, having been passed around to relatives or through other foster parents.

"What they need," he told us, "is an environment with rules and predictability. They need love and affection, school, food, and a roof over their head, but they mainly need stability."

He went on. "These children come to us with inevitable scars. They have been through emotional roller coasters and, because their brains are not fully developed, they don't have the intellectual ability to fully process their situations. Some of them act out, some don't. Most need counseling, some don't. They all need to know that there will be someone there putting out their cereal bowl for them in the morning, and making sure there is cereal and milk in the house. Someone who will be there for them after school to help with their homework, and to put dinner on the table. To make sure they have clean clothes and a warm bed."

My heart was breaking. These were all things that William took for granted, and that I did too growing up. But right now our home wasn't a safe place, and William couldn't be there.

"If you think you can provide that, for two days or for 18 months, then we will be happy to have your participation in our program." Bob smiled warmly. "But there are requirements you must meet. You must be over 18. I think everyone here has already met that qualification." We laughed.

"You can be single or married, divorced, widowed or in a civil union. We accept foster parents of every race, religion and sexual orientation." He paused and looked around, then continued. "You must show financial stability, provide references, be fingerprinted and shown not to have a criminal record in the state or federal jurisdiction, and you must endure several home consultations. Yes, we come to your house, uninvited and unannounced." Someone chuckled nervously. He went on.

"You also have to go through a 30-hour pre-service training program. At the training program we cover everything from discipline to attachment issues these children often have."

He looked at us sternly. "If I haven't scared you off, come back in ten minutes and I'll answer any questions you may have."

I took a deep breath and looked at Andy. He was grinning fondly at Danielle, who looked as poised and determined as I had ever seen her. At that moment I felt great admiration for my new friend.

"What do you think?" I said to no one in particular.

"Let's go outside for a few minutes," Andy answered, and the three of us went outside. We took turns using the rest room, then gathered in the hall. Terry and Charlie were still in the conference room, but facing the open door so they could see us. They were talking to another couple who looked similar to them in age. I wondered if they were having the opportunity to use their infertility story. In a few minutes Charlie came out, nodded hello to us, and used the rest room. He returned, and Terry did the same. I noticed they were taking turns so that one of them was always keeping an eye on us.

When we were back inside Danielle asked the first question. "What about health care? Are the children included in our health insurance plans, or does the program provide coverage?" *Good question*, I thought.

"We provide Medicaid coverage for them. And because they are in the system we find that some children get more attention and better care than they might otherwise, because they are fully examined and tested." He went on. "There are children with health problems and special needs who are waiting for parents."

Terry raised her hand. "How long does the process take, from application to fostering a child?"

"Didn't I mention that?" Bob laughed. "I must be slipping in my old age. It takes about five months."

The woman in the couple Terry and Charlie were talking to raised her hand. "Are there ever cases when there is more than one child in a family that goes into foster care?"

"We have many cases where there are sibling groups that need a home. We try not to break up sibling groups, but not all foster parents are willing or able to take more than one child. We are especially looking for foster parents who can."

Andy spoke up. "What is the maximum number of children that can be fostered in one home?"

"Four," Bob answered.

Andy nodded, and asked another question. "Is there financial compensation?"

"Yes. We call that 'board rates' and you would get approximately $700 per month for each child, more if the child has additional emotional or physical needs."

People around the table were taking notes. These were good questions. I wondered if Bob had purposely left this factual information to the questions period, and his introduction served as just that, an introduction.

"What about Fost-Adopt?" Charlie asked. "How does that work?"

"The goal of each situation is to have the child returned to his or her parent. When that happens, we call it a success. But there are some children who, for a variety of reasons, cannot return to their parent or parents, or a relative, and those children are eligible for what we call the 'Fost-Adopt' program. We place about 1,000 children a year in permanent homes through this program. Many are older, or have special needs, but there are some younger ones available as well."

Danielle shifted a little in her seat. I knew she was thinking of Zoe, and that this was what she hoped to do.

"Any more questions?" Bob asked. No one spoke up. "Well, if you have any more, please feel free to call me or e-mail me."

After a chorus of "thank yous" we all got up to leave.

As we filed out Danielle stopped and spoke to Bob for a minute. Andy and I nodded goodbye to him, then waited in the hallway. Andy had already filled him in on our need for security. The others, including Terry and Charlie, filed out, but Terry and Charlie lingered in the hallway. Pretending we were strangers, Charlie said to Andy and me, "Very interesting, don't you think?"

"Yes, indeed," answered Andy.

"Do you think you'll go for it?" Charlie asked.

"We'll have to discuss it more."

Charlie laughed heartily. "Aha, us too. Me and the wife."

Then Danielle came out and we all took the elevator to the lobby, and filed out to our cars.

Chapter 7

Banana Nut Bread

Makes 1 large loaf.

This bread — really almost a coffeecake — is good sliced thin and toasted. We use it to make one of my favorite sandwiches too. Just spread some whipped cream cheese on one slice, top with another, and nectar and ambrosia couldn't taste any better.

1. Preheat oven to moderate (350° F.).
2. Cream together until light: ½ cup butter and 1 cup sugar.
3. Beat in 2 eggs.
4. Sift together: 2 cups all-purpose flour, 1 teaspoon baking soda, and ½ teaspoon salt. Stir into butter-sugar mixture, blending well.
5. Stir in 1 cup mashed ripe bananas and ½ cup chopped walnuts.
6. Spoon batter into a well buttered 2-pound bread tin (9-1/2 x 5-1/2 x 2-3/4) and bake in the moderate oven for 1 hour, or until loaf tests done.
7. Cool for 5 minutes, then turn out on rack to cool completely.

Vincent Price, *A Treasury of Great Recipes* (1965)

Saturday at Village Cooks was very busy, as usual. I grabbed a moment to send out the email blast to our customer list. The postcards would be arriving. People would only have a week to plan, but this was the best I could do under the circumstances. I knew my customers would understand. About a dozen copies of *Holiday Delights* had sold in the last two weeks, and Sally and I had casually suggested to customers that Cookbooktoberfest might feature Elizabeth Crisp. By the time they received the postcards or e-mails that stated the name of the cookbook and the author, they would probably not be surprised.

"I have to run out and put up posters," I called to Sally during a moment that was somewhat quiet — only four customers in the store. "I'll be right back."

I took my tape and made the rounds of shops on the "strip," as I thought of the part of Willow Lane that housed shops and restaurants.

When I got back twenty-five minutes later, Mrs. Beeton greeted me with a "meow" and followed me around as I helped customers. Some were doing early Christmas shopping, and several bought gifts that they wanted shipped. Terry was in and out all day, discreetly checking out all of the customers and making sure I was not in danger. I didn't even look at the time until Andy called, when I noticed that it was almost 4. Since William was with Andy's parents and I was at the store, he decided to put some time in on a big investigative story that he had been working on for a few weeks.

He said, "The medical examiner's report is in. There were no drugs in Ginger's system. She died from a blunt trauma to the head. There were no other marks or bruises on her body. Cause of death uncertain."

"Uncertain? What does that mean?" I asked.

"She could have been walking along in the woods and tripped and fell, and hit her head on a rock. Which would make it accidental. Or it could have been murder. Ginger could have been hit by someone who left the scene and took the murder weapon with them."

"There was a lot of blood. Did that tell them anything?"

"Heads always bleed a lot."

"Really?" I didn't know that.

"It's a fact. Ask Danielle next time you see her."

"Hmm." This was a lot to mull over. "I had hoped for something…"

"Definitive?"

"Yes."

"Well, there is no physical evidence of a crime on the scene, and now no certain cause of death."

"Does that mean the police won't look for the killer?"

"Well," Andy hesitated, "Maybe Michael learned something when he went to Philly. Without evidence, they'll look to her known associates, the closest people to her, and their only hope is a confession. They have to find out something about someone in her past that is strong enough to bring that person in for questioning, some kind of motive. From someone they've already checked out and they know had the means and also the opportunity."

He paused again. I heard his phone buzz. "Listen, I have to go meet this guy for an interview. I'll meet you at the restaurant tonight."

"You're not coming home first?"

"I'll be lucky to finish the interview and meet you there by 6:30. I'm lucky he agreed to see me, and he probably only did so because it's Saturday and I'm meeting him away from his office."

"Where are you meeting him? Or is that a secret?"

Andy chuckled. "I'm meeting him at a diner twenty minutes away, that's all I can say. Don't worry, Charlie is following me. Believe me, he's not letting me out of his sight. That guy never stops."

I didn't laugh.

"Like I said, I'll be there by 6:30. That's the time, right?"

"Yes, I saw Kay this morning and confirmed it. Ben will be joining us." Kay's son Ben lives in New York, and often visits on weekends. He keeps a horse at Morris Farms.

I sighed. "Goodbye. Love you."

"You too." He signed off.

As it turned out, Ben and Kay and Ian and Sally were all at St. Cloud's when I arrived. Andy was not. The four were seated at a round table for six near the floor-to-ceiling clad windows in the back of the restaurant, with a beautiful view of the autumn leaves in the woods outside. October is spectacular in northwestern New Jersey. Most people think they need to go to New England for autumn leaves, and ours are just another of the unsung aspects of the "Garden State" that have not made it into popular culture, which prefers television shows like The Sopranos and Jersey Shore as New Jersey symbols. Miche was in the front of the restaurant talking to a waitress, and she smiled and greeted me.

"Hi, Bonnie, it's lovely to see you." I wore my black shirtdress from work, but I had switched the matching tie belt for a woven gold belt and added a white silk scarf tucked in around my neck.

"How are you, Miche? How is Tony doing?" I asked. "I heard he's staying with you."

She pulled me aside. "He's not doing well. The police went through his apartment and found a gun. They're examining it now. I don't know if it's legal or not, I can't get Tony to tell me. They have his cell phone too. We've been fighting about it all day." Her eyes were wide with tension and fear. "I'm afraid they'll take him in, and I just don't think he'll be able to handle it." She fought back tears. I stroked her shoulder to comfort her.

"Where is he now?" I asked quietly.

"He's in the kitchen, working. I don't know how he can do it, but he's back there chopping away. I don't think the chef knows what's going on."

"Why not?"

"Chef Lemoine is sometimes, not always, in a world of his own. He gets so involved in what he's making that there could be a tornado outside and he wouldn't notice. He's one of those driven artists. Have you ever met him?"

"No."

"He's a genius in the kitchen, but a little hard to talk to. He's very quiet and shy."

"But is he a nice person?"

"Absolutely." Miche replied. "And he's so tall, he looks down at everyone. He's a lamb deep down, but comes off a little scary. "

"Is that why you don't call him by his first name?"

"Ha!" she laughed. "I can't imagine calling him George."

"But he's well known, he has managed to be successful here. St. Cloud's is highly Zagats rated, thanks to him." I quoted what Jeffrey had once proudly told me.

"Yes, he has, and it's been wonderful. Jeffrey really is the 'face' of the restaurant, anyway. So we let Chef Lemoine be, and let him have whatever he wants. And he doesn't want much conversation in the kitchen."

"But they have to talk about the food, right?"

"Not as much as you'd think. Once the menu is worked out each day at their meeting, each person back there knows what they have to do, and they just go about their business. One thing I can say for Chef Lemoine, he has an extremely well-organized and calm kitchen. No yelling or chaos back there. In fact, they play classical satellite radio from Chef Lemoine's laptop. The orders come in, the assistant, Barb, reads them aloud, and Chef Lemoine, Tony and the others nod, and they all go about doing what they need to. Chef has already organized and taught each one their duties for each recipe. The only person he ever really chatted with that I can remember is — " she paused — "was — Ginger Harrison. She used to come in to visit Tony, and we were surprised that Chef let her. He was actually very nice to her."

"Fascinating. Have I met Barb?"

"I guess not." She glanced out the window. "Listen, you better go to your friends. I see Andy outside on his way in. Ah, here he is."

The front door opened and Andy rushed in.

"Sorry I'm late," he said, and gave me a kiss. "Did you just get here?" He smiled and said hi to Miche while he waited for my answer.

"Yes, just a moment ago. The others are seated already." I nodded to the right to indicate to him that Terry and Charlie were in the restaurant already, having dinner at a table in the back but facing the door so they could see everyone who came in and out of the dining room. Their drinks were just being delivered.

Andy took my arm and smiled at me. We joined our group. "Hi everyone, sorry we're late," Andy said as we were seated.

I loved seeing the blooming relationship between Sally and Ian. The chemistry between them electrified the table. Sally looked lovely in drop pearl earrings and a hand-knitted rose boatneck sweater that showed a little bit of her shoulders.

"Not at all, not at all. Ben has been telling us about the case he just finished," Ian said.

Ben ran his hand through his thick black hair. Longish for an attorney, I found myself thinking. "Enough of that for now," Ben jumped in. "Let's order."

To a few chuckles we all perused our menus.

"What is cervelle de canut?" Kay asked the waiter, who told us his name was David.

"It is an herb cheese and vinegar spread served on warm croûtes. The spread consists of shallots, garlic, and herbs."

"Sounds delicious," piped in Sally. "What does 'cervelle de canut' mean in English?"

David, a handsome red-haired twenty-something who, I later learned, was working his way through graduate school at Rutgers, laughed. "It's known as silk weaver's brain. You can understand why we prefer the French name."

The table reacted in the expected oos and aahs. "Hardly anyone ever asks what it means." David smiled at Sally. "It's named after silk workers in Lyon who developed the spread in the mid-1800's."

"Why don't we try that, and the tomato tatin?" Andy asked, and everyone nodded.

"We need one more appetizer to share. The basil palmiers are very good here," added Kay. Unlike regular plain palmiers, I knew that the basil palmiers that St. Cloud's served had a pesto-like filling of fresh basil and garlic. They were one of Andy's and my favorites.

"It's settled, then," said Ben, and the waiter nodded and went off to get our appetizers.

We continued to read over the menus. Andy and Ben chose the pan-seared duck breasts with apples, Sally the chicken basquaise, Ian the short ribs, and Kay and I both decided on beef bourguignon. We skipped soup and salad in favor of the appetizers, and I knew I, for one, wanted to save room for dessert, since they were all made by Abby.

After the wine order was made, we relaxed into conversation.

"Mom told me that William is with your folks." Ben directed his words to Andy, by way of showing us that he knew about what had transpired in Wilmington this week, even though he had been in New York.

"Yes, he is, but he's having a good time. I think it's harder on us than it is on him." Andy brushed my hand with his.

Ian cleared his throat. "Have there been any developments, Andy?"

"Well, the latest is that the medical examiner determined the cause of death to be blunt trauma to the head."

There was a collective sigh at the table. Kay put her hands together in a prayer-like pose, and put her head down. Her bracelets jangled a bit as she did so. She was wearing a matching pumpkin-colored knit dress and jacket with chocolate brown piping, and a triple-stranded necklace of multi-colored beads in golds, browns, and oranges. Her hair was pinned up in her usual loose French twist.

"Meaning it could be an accident?" Ian asked. "Or murder?"

Andy repeated what he told me earlier. "Blunt trauma to the head. No evidence on the scene. She could have been out for a walk in the woods and tripped and fell and hit her head. Or someone could have hurt her."

Ben asked, "No evidence at all?"

"There was blood around her head, but she didn't hit it on a rock."

"What a mysterious young woman Ginger was," Kay put in. "We don't know how she died, and she doesn't seem to have any family."

"Except for Zoe," I said.

Our dinners arrived and we continued to discuss the death of Ginger Harrison and its effect on us.

"Where did she live?" Ben asked.

"Hmm," I pondered. "They found Zoe at Mayfield Manor, so we assume she had a room there."

I looked at Andy. "Did you hear anything about the police searching her room and finding anything?"

"No, but that's a good question. I'll ask Michael Quinn the next time I speak to him."

"Do the police know the time of death?" Ben continued.

"As a matter of fact, I forgot to tell you," Andy said as an aside to me, then turned toward Ben. "They are certain it was within an hour of when Bonnie found the body."

"Dear Lord!" I cried. "That close!"

Sally grasped my hand.

I choked. "I could have seen the killer. Maybe that's why my tires were slashed. Maybe the killer thinks I saw him, or her."

"Or maybe they were nearby and saw me from a distance," I added, shuddering.

"Now Bonnie, calm down this minute," Kay ordered in no uncertain terms. Sally was still holding my hand. What caring, comforting friends I have, I thought. I'm lucky. Terrified, but lucky.

Andy was eating. He probably couldn't think of anything to say. So were Ian and Ben, all busy with their knives and forks.

I smiled. "I'm okay. Sorry I got carried away." I took a bite of my beef. Now was definitely not the time to tell them about the gun being found in Tony's apartment. "Someone change the subject, please."

"Sally is going to teach me to cook," declared Ian. "My first lesson is tomorrow."

"Really, how wonderful!" Kay exclaimed.

Sally took her hand away from mine.

"I'm going to start with baking. We're going to make banana nut bread."

Andy looked up. "Umm, one of my favorites. With cream cheese."

"Not just with cream cheese," Sally added, "cream cheese smothered all over it."

They all laughed.

Sally went on. "You won't believe what cookbook I got the recipe from." She eyed Ian flirtatiously, then winked at me.

Ian leaned back in his chair and rubbed his stomach. "No clue."

"Vincent Price's cookbook. It's called *A Treasury of Great Recipes*."

Ben chuckled. "Vincent Price the actor? From those horror flicks? He wrote a cookbook?"

Kay answered. "As a matter of fact, darling, I used that cookbook when you were growing up. Remember that rich chocolate ice cream I used to make in the freezer?"

"That was Vincent Price's recipe?"

"Not exactly," Kay went on. "He and his wife Mary traveled the world going to what were then the best restaurants. He convinced the chefs to give him his favorite recipes, and he included them with facsimiles of the menus in this extraordinary cookbook."

"The great part about it," Sally joined in, excitedly, "is that Vincent and Mary went home and prepared the recipes themselves. It is not just a collection of recipes from landmark restaurants all over the world. Anyone could have done that. This is a collection of those recipes gathered on wonderful occasions and then later cooked at home, with Vincent's anecdotes and stories included with each one. On the title page it says 'Famous specialties of the world's foremost restaurants adapted for the home kitchen.'"

Ian laughed. "How did you remember that?"

"Because I've looked at that page hundreds of times!" We all laughed at Sally's answer.

"It's one of Bonnie's favorite cookbooks, isn't it?" Andy proudly added.

I nodded. "Yes, a treasure. Out of print now, I'm afraid."

Sally added, "But we keep on the lookout for them and acquire them whenever we can, and keep a stash of them in the storeroom. We have five of them in back right now, in varying conditions."

"Really?" Ben asked, sounding truly surprised.

"Yes, indeed; every few months a customer will call, write, or come in and ask for it," answered Sally.

"When it first came out, people went to those restaurants and collected the menus too, and placed them in the cookbooks. Some of the used ones we acquire have the old menus in them, right next to the facsimile ones Price has included."

"Wow. I never knew." Ben again. "Did you do that, Mom?"

"When we were first married, when things were good, your father took me to Luchow's in New York, and I saved that menu in the cookbook. And that time we went to Paris we went to Lasserre, of course, and I saved that menu too."

A collective sigh followed, as we all knew that Kay had left her abusive husband in Japan when she was pregnant with Ben, and Ben never knew his father.

Ian broke the silence. "My expectations for tomorrow's banana nut bread are exceedingly high, after all of this discussion."

Sally's eyes lingered on his with the greatest affection.

Although the dinner was superb and the conversation blessedly distracting, by the time it was time to order dessert, I felt like crying. I had participated in the conversation and even enjoyed myself, but it was an effort. I was tired of feeling like my life was in danger. I felt like I couldn't get away from this nightmare that caused me to have my son go stay with his grandparents and Andy and me constantly kept under surveillance. Even though Charlie and Terry were right there in the corner of the room, I was still anxious. I excused myself and went to the ladies' room.

As I rounded the corner, I ran into Tony. He must have been in the men's room, and was on his way back to the kitchen.

"Hi," I said.

"Hi," he replied, without much interest. I couldn't let him go. I had to say something. I hadn't spoken to him at the funeral. Although I was there with him at the cemetery, and by the side of the road after he had jumped out of the car, I couldn't remember if we'd ever been officially introduced.

"I don't know if we've ever been introduced," I said quickly.

"What?" he asked, distractedly.

"I'm Bonnie Emerson."

"I know, I've seen you. You're the one who found her."

"That's right, I did. I'm so sorry."

He finally looked at me.

"It's good that she died on your property," he muttered.

"What?"

"She loved nature. The woods. She loved trees. She loved animals — she wanted to get a cat. She always wanted to learn how to ride, so I got a friend to give her riding lessons at Morris Farms."

"Oh..." I started.

"It's good that she died in the woods."

And then he was gone, into the kitchen.

Whew, that was intense, I thought. I found the woman he loved dead, so it stands to reason that at some time we would have had to talk. We had a connection, and it had to be verbalized. I was glad that it had. I actually felt a little better, and went back to the table.

In honor of the season, we all ordered apple tarts for dessert. To our surprise, Jeffrey was with David when he brought them to our table. I hadn't seen him all night. I hadn't seen him do his usual chatty rounds around the restaurant, greeting everyone and asking how their meals were. But here he was, in a gold merino wool turtleneck sweater that emphasized his fair hair and skin and made him look like the California golden boy that he was, kissing both my cheeks, and laughing.

He fell into me a little bit, then leaned on me. He touched my shoulder and whispered, "I'm glad to see you out and about."

And as suddenly as he appeared, he was gone. My second quick but profound interaction of the night.

Andy's eyes widened. "That was strange."

"He usually chats up the table, doesn't he?" Ian asked. "And goes around?"

"Yes, he does. But tonight he was only interested in Bonnie," answered Kay.

I told them, "I smelled alcohol on his breath. That's probably why he didn't make the rounds like he usually does."

"Hmm. Where did he go?" Sally asked.

"He's gone back into the kitchen." Ben could see the kitchen door from his seat. "You know, I've never been introduced, but I recognize him from somewhere. Maybe a bar in New York?"

At that moment my cell phone rang. As I reached in my bag for it I looked across the room and saw that Charlie was talking on his cell phone too, and Terry was listening intently to his end of the conversation.

It was my father.

"Hi, Dad." Everyone at the table was quiet. The former president was on the phone.

"I know it's last minute, but I'm calling with an invitation for tomorrow. Would you like to go to a Phillies playoff game? It's the National League Championship Series. They're playing the Cardinals."

"Uh, I don't know."

"Carol and Paul can bring William. You and Andy can meet them there. Your mother has the details all worked out."

"Hold on a minute." I quickly told Andy about it. He agreed. Sally nodded — it was her Sunday to run the store.

"Thanks, Dad. We'd love to."

"Great, honey. We want to see you, and this is a way we can. We have a box, so don't worry about a thing. Your security people have already been informed, and will get you to the ballpark in time. Talk to them."

"Okay, Dad, I will. Miss you. See you tomorrow."

Our phone conversations are always brief.

"Love to Mom," I added, signing off.

"I guess we're going to a baseball game tomorrow!" Andy was excited.

"And we'll get to see William," I added, my heart a little less broken now.

Chapter 8

Sunday was bright, beautiful and not too crisp, a perfect day for baseball. I had mailed the postcards, sent the email blast, hung posters in store and restaurant windows around town, and put up the large poster. The poster read "Make a dish from Elizabeth Crisp's HOLIDAY DELIGHTS and bring it to Cookbooktoberfest October 16 at 1 p.m. Elizabeth Crisp will be here for the contest to judge the best execution of one of her recipes. Come and vote for a friend! Or just come for the food!" In smaller print, it said, "Win a gift certificate to Village Cooks. First prize $500. Second prize $250. Third prize $100."

I could relax, and enjoy the day. I'd get to see William, and Carol and Paul. And my parents.

I got up early and turned on the oven. Baking always relaxed me. I loved the precision of measuring out the ingredients, and was fascinated by the chemistry that magically turned them into something entirely different than their components. When you cooked a steak and onions on the side, you had steak and onions. But when you mixed sugar and flour and chocolate and butter, there were endless possibilities. Cake, cookies, brownies, fudge. While the oven was preheating I made scrambled eggs and rye toast for Andy and me. Then I baked more of the chocolate chip cookies from the extra dough I had frozen from the batch I had made a few weeks before, this time to bring to William. His favorite. Andy loves what I think of as "super" chocolate chocolate chips — chocolate cookies with huge chocolate chips, but William likes what he calls the "original kind." Think Toll House. I prefer Hillary Clinton's version, with oatmeal mixed in. I like oatmeal mixed in a lot of things. Especially meatloaf, as a replacement for breadcrumbs.

119

While they cooled I took a shower and put on my green zip-up cable sweater over a gold flowered long-sleeved blouse, and jeans. I love it when everything works out like that. I call it multi-tasking heaven. Pure efficiency mixed with love.

At ten Charlie drove the two-hour ride to Philadelphia, with Terry in front riding shotgun, and Andy and me in back. We chattered a bit about the teams, and then Andy snuggled up to me and fell asleep. He had stayed up late watching a Yankees game. While he napped I stared out the window and pondered. I finally decided the time was right to tell them all about Tony's gun. I didn't want to lose the chance while we were all four together in private. I knew Andy would be mad that I hadn't told him last night. I wasn't usually a procrastinator; in fact, I'm the opposite. But since the day I found Ginger Harrison on the edge of the woods near our house, I have found my behavior surprising. I broke one of my top five life rules: never wake up someone who is sleeping and doesn't absolutely have to get up.

"We had such a nice time at the restaurant, and I didn't want to talk about it during dinner," I explained to a cranky Andy, after I recounted what Miche had told me about the police finding a gun in Tony's apartment, and about their taking Tony's cell phone.

"And then Dad called, and invited us to the game, and you were so excited, I didn't want to break the mood," I went on. "By the time we got home you rushed to put on the Yankees-Red Sox game. And I was afraid if I talked about it I'd get all worked up and wouldn't sleep."

I added, "Being at the house is a bit unnerving for me."

Terry broke in, softly but firmly. "We could put you two in a safe house if you'd feel more comfortable." She looked over at Charlie. Charlie nodded.

"A safe house!" Andy's voice rose, unusual for him. "I'm a reporter, I can't go to a safe house. I can't hide out."

I raised my eyebrows. "I guess we've nixed that idea."

What a relief to finally arrive at Citizens Bank Park. Terry and Charlie led us up to the Hall of Fame Club on the second level, where two Secret

Service people greeted us. Charlie shook their hands, and we were let in. Then came the best part.

"William!" Andy and I cried in unison and threw open our arms. I tried not to cry as we all hugged, and grinned weakly at all four grandparents standing right there watching us. They were all smiling. Mom wore a rust-colored silk shirt I had seen before, with a brown tweed pantsuit I hadn't. Her lovely short blond hair framed her face. Carol was all in oatmeal, a pretty knit pant set with a cowl collar that contrasted with her curly red hair that fell in waves around her shoulders.

"Mom, the car we drove here in had a TV in it!"

"It did? Wow, that's amazing."

"Not a DVD player like we have in our car, Mom, it was a real TV. With channels."

Paul came over. "We watched CNN."

I smiled. "Ah, that explains it."

Andy and Dad had moved away, and were talking. Or should I say "conferring." Andy was talking, Dad listening. Probably telling him about the gun. Which Dad probably already knew about. He was nodding and replying.

We were on the second level, near the press seats. With Terry, Charlie, the Secret Service people and the seven of us in our family, we were a pretty large group. We filled the box. A private set of rest rooms and a concession stand were adjacent to the box. William asked, "Can I have a cheese-steak, Mom? It's lunch time."

"So it is." I nodded to Mom and Carol and we all went over to the concession stand. William approached the stand first, and spoke to the guy who worked there. He was a skinny tall guy in his fifties, with longish thin hair cut in a choppy shag. He looked like a weathered Rod Stewart.

"We have hot dogs all the time at home during the summer. My Grandpa said you have cheese-steak sandwiches here. Can I have one of those, and a bottle of water, please?" William asked eagerly.

"Sure can," the concessioner said. "Where's home, champ?"

"Wilmington, New Jersey. You probably never heard of it."

"As a matter of fact I have." He looked at me, nodded and smiled. "An old buddy of mine is a school principal there."

William was excited. "Do you know Mr. Russo?"

"Yes, I do. Dennis Russo. We go way back." He grinned and leaned forward. I thought he seemed like a nice man. But you couldn't be too careful, so I was keeping an eye on things.

"How far?" William asked. The innocent inquisitiveness of youth. Mom and Carol were listening closely.

"To when we were younger than you, about kindergarten," he said. "We went all through school together, graduated high school together too. Dennis, and me, and another buddy, Bobby. Dennis went off to college, and Bobby joined the service."

"What did you do?" Again, youthful curiosity.

"Me? I stuck around here in Philly. A little of this, a little of that. But now I've got it made." He handed William his sandwich and bottle of water. "I get to go to all the Phillies games."

"You're lucky." William said, and he took the gooey cheese-steak sandwich from the man. "Thanks."

"Not a problem. You come back if you want anything else."

"I will."

The opening music signaled that the game was about to start, so the rest of us didn't get anything. I smiled and said "We'll be back" to the guy, and we joined the others getting settled in their seats.

"I was lucky to get my food first," William preened.

"Yes, you were. Now let me hold it while you go sit next to Dad."

"Where are you sitting?"

"Next to you, and Terry."

"Who's Terry?"

"A nice lady who works for Grandpa." It was a stretch, but you could say that, sort of. "She's really cool, you'll like her. She's from the Bronx."

"Awesome," said William. As he sat down, I handed him back his food, and we joined in the opening festivities.

"Give me a bite," Andy whispered to William.

"Say 'please.'"

"Please."

William passed it over. Andy closed his eyes in an act of blissful joy as he chewed, and William giggled. Andy winked at me. Things were looking up.

The stadium was sold out, but with mostly Phillies fans, according to the sea of red and white shirts in the crowd. St. Louis was pretty far away to draw fans, but I noticed a handful of white shirts with the two famous red cardinals on them mixed in with the striped white and red Phillies shirts. Both teams wore red baseball caps, and so did their fans, with either the entwined "STL" or the single "P" distinguishing them.

By the end of the third inning the Phillies were losing 3-2. But Ryan Howard had hit a home run to close the inning, and the crowd went wild with glee and anticipation. Although William had gotten a cheese-steak sandwich, I hadn't eaten lunch, and I was hungry. It seemed like a good time to get some food.

I reached over William and poked Andy's shoulder. "Do you want anything? I'm going to get something to eat."

"Sure. Other than a bite of William's cheese steak, I haven't had anything since that huge breakfast you made." I had made pancakes and sausage and cooked apples. He leaned over and kissed my cheek. "I'll have a hot dog and some of those fries with chili and cheese on them. And a beer. Anything more for you, fella?" he asked William.

"Nachos?" He looked at me.

"Sure, I can carry all of that."

"Do you need help?" Andy started to stand up.

"No, they'll give me a box to put it all in. I'll be fine."

As I stood up Mom saw me and stood too. We walked to the ladies room together.

"I've been so worried about you," she started, when we were alone.

"I'm fine, Mom. But it's hard having William at Paul and Carol's. That's the worst part of all of this."

She squeezed my arm, then laced hers through mine. "I hate that this all happened while we were in Japan. And your father didn't even tell me until we were back in the country. I was so mad at him. Coming here today — this was the only way we could see you."

"I know. I missed you so much, Mom. I'm glad you're here now."
"This will be over soon," she said, patting my arm. "Your father said they have a good lead on the killer. When he's arrested William can go home. And we'll be able to come and visit."

"Allowed" to come and visit is what she was thinking, but didn't say, I knew. Within all of the glamour of world travel and expensive private boxes at ball games, life could still be restricted for a First Family, even after the term in office was over.

"Really? They have someone?"

"Your father said they're very close. A matter of days. Now let's go get some grub," she added in her most refined voice. I laughed.

The Rod Stewart look-alike was still behind the counter.

"How ya doing?" he asked.

"Fine, thanks. But we have a pretty big order. Do you have boxes?"

"Sure do," he answered me. "Or I can get someone to come over and help. We have 'waiter service' up here, too, if you want it. Although it wasn't ordered for this game, I can get it for you. No problem."

"I think I can manage for William, Andy, and me. What about you, Mom?"

"Your father wants a cheese-steak sandwich and a beer, whatever's on tap. I'll have a crab cake sandwich and a bottle of water. Will all of that fit in one box?"

"Sure will."

My turn. "I'll have the crab cake and water too, and an order of nachos, and a hot dog, and fries with everything on them, and a beer."

"You mean the fries with chili, cheese, and jalapenos?"

"Sounds like a heart attack, but that's what the man wants."

Rod Stewart was startled. "The President?"

"No, my son-in-law. He's a lot younger, don't worry," she said.

Mom laughed. He smiled.

"It's an honor to serve you, ma'am. I got to meet the President earlier, and we took a picture using my cell phone. Very cool." We could tell he was trying to be professional and control his excitement.

He added, politely, "It's going to take few minutes to grill the crab cakes. Everything else is ready, but that takes some time."

"That's fine." Mom smiled.

"Do the crab cakes come pre-made, or do you make them yourself?" I asked.

"They come pre-made, and we heat them. But they're from a terrific place in Baltimore. We get a shipment every morning."

"I guess you don't have time to make them yourself."

"Yeah, I'm pretty much a short-order cook here. But at home I make some mean ribs. About a dozen different kinds. Chili, too."

"Ah, the manly diet." Mom laughed.

"You should write a cookbook with that name," I added.

Rod Stewart chuckled. "You'd be surprised how many cookbooks I have at home. Maybe thirty, forty. I love to try new recipes."

"I have a cookbook and cookware supply store. You should stop by if you're ever in Wilmington."

"Really? That's cool."

"It's called Village Cooks and it's right on the main road, Willow Lane. We sell cookbooks, pots and pans, knives, cooking gadgets, that kind of stuff."

"Are you married?" Mom put in.

"Mother," I glared at her.

"That's okay," Rod Stewart answered. "I'm divorced, no kids. Dating a little, but no one serious."

He put the crab cakes on the grill and addressed me as he was assembling the other pieces of our order.

"So, you know Dennis Russo. I haven't talked to him in a while. Do you know Sue, too?"

"Yes, I do."

"What a girl. Love her. Great couple. She's the best. She kept Dennis going when Bobby died. We lost him in the Gulf War."

"I heard," I said.

"We used to call ourselves the three musketeers." He choked a little, and recovered quickly.

"What is your name? So I can tell him I saw you."

"Pete Cannavale. Call me Pete. 'Bobby, Dennis and Pete.'" He sighed.

"We did it all. Together. From kindergarten. Played kickball in the streets, listened to music in our rooms at each other's houses, stood up for each other in school. And with the nuns. It was great."

"Did you know Jeffrey Sloane too? I believe he was from Dennis' old neighborhood."

He gripped the spatula. "Jeffrey Sloane? You know him too? Does he live up there in New Jersey?"

"Yes, he does."

"Holy cow. I always wondered where he'd end up."

"He owns a restaurant in Wilmington."

"He *owns* a restaurant?"

"You're surprised?"

"No disrespect, but I thought he'd be dead by now. I'm surprised Dennis didn't tell me. But like I said, we haven't really spoken in a couple of years. How long has he been there?"

"Let's see. St. Cloud opened about three years ago."

"St. Cloud?" He snickered. "St. Cloud?"

"What's wrong with that?" I said, and Mom and I looked at each other.

"Again, no disrespect, ladies, but the Jeffrey Sloane I knew was always in the clouds, if you know what I mean. As in high in the clouds. We used to joke about it. And he helped others get there, too, if you know what I mean." He laughed and looked embarrassed. But he went on.

"And he made a lot of money off them. Him, and Bobby's little brother, Tony. That dude. He was an evil piece of work when he was high. Which he always was. It was his idea to sell drugs. Before that Jeffrey just liked to get high, you know. And party with the ladies. He was a man of action, never stayed with one girl too long. Always a charmer. I heard Jeffrey ran off to Florida after that girl died. I don't know what happened to Tony. He's probably dead too."

"What girl?"

"Some girl at Drexel. Drexel University."

He spelled it out, knowing we weren't locals. We nodded.

"I forget her name. She was really quiet and shy. A chemistry genius, something like that, everyone said. There weren't that many accomplished female chemistry physics students around back then, so it was a big deal when she died. From some bad stuff that Jeffrey gave her."

"He gave her drugs?"

"Her and half this side of Philly." He paused and considered. "No, that's not right. By then he was specializing in the college part of town, University City. Drexel and Penn. Dennis had gone off to Rutgers and barely ever came home. He met Sue there. I didn't know Jeffrey too well myself, I mainly knew him through Dennis and Bobby, and since Bobby was away too…" He trailed off. Flipped the crab cakes.

"She was a friend of Jeffrey's, sort of. Well, they were partying together. Who knows, maybe she was using her physics to help him whip up chemicals. It turned out the chick was allergic to the stuff he gave her. He flipped out. How could he have known? No one else got sick, or died, off it. But he was so freaked out he dyed his yellow lab black and headed off to Florida. That's what I heard."

He packed up the crab cakes and then the rest of the food.

"He dyed his dog black?"

"Yup, and the funny thing about it was the dog's name. Sunshine. I remember after he left we all were wondering if he was going to change the dog's name, since he wasn't yellow anymore."

"Wow" was all I could muster. Mom wasn't saying anything. But she didn't know Jeffrey or Tony; to her this was just interesting chat. I couldn't wait to tell Andy, and get home and tell Abby.

Mom smiled her First Lady smile at Pete, and thanked him. I did too. He bent his head down, and signaled that although he was connected to us, he was in fact at work. And his job was to serve us food. So we left with it.

"What took so long?" Andy asked as I got back to the seats and passed out the food to them. William immediately pulled a huge piece of cheese off the top of the nachos, put his head back, and dropped it in his mouth.

"I'll tell you later." I nodded at William, and Andy knew I couldn't talk about it in front of him.

During the seventh inning stretch Dad went down to the stands to meet and greet people. A secure section had been set up, and we went with him so William could be part of the fun. One little boy asked

William, "Why aren't you getting President Billings' autograph too?" and William answered, "Because I already have hundreds of them!" The little boy beamed and slapped him five. The boy's mother snapped a picture.

When we went back up and reached the lounge area, Dad stopped me. "We'll be right with you," he said to the others.

He playfully tousled my hair and said, "Come on, peach, I want to talk to you." "Peach" was his pet name for me. "Let's sit down over here."

We sat down at a table and chairs out of anyone's hearing distance. Pete Cannavale was watching us, but trying not to look like it. He busied himself wiping the counter.

"How are you doing?" he asked.

"Hanging in there." I shook my head. "The hardest part is being away from William. I feel like such a bad mother, putting my child's life in danger. All of our lives." I looked around. Other than the two Secret Service agents over on the other side of the room, Pete was the only person in the lounge, and now he had his back to us.

"You're not a bad mother." He reached across the table and took my hand. "A mother protects her cubs. That's what you're doing. You're a terrific mother. You learned from the best. Elaine."

His big blue eyes — those eyes that had seen so much, fought in Vietnam, loved and married Mom, served in the Senate, protected the American people for eight years — were rimmed with tears. His big paw patted my hand. "Don't worry. It's going to be over soon."

"I hope so."

"There's some news. I don't know what it means yet, and the police are following up on it."

"What is it?"

"It could mean nothing. When they searched Ginger's room at Mayfield Manor they found a letter. A note."

"Really?"

"They identified the paper. The top was torn off, but the part of the heading with a school address was partially visible. They were able to match it to Wilmington Middle School stationary."

He went on. "The note said, 'Stop what you're doing. Now. Please. Dennis.' It was hand-written, and they've been able to match the handwriting to confirm that Dennis Russo wrote it."

I was shocked. What did Dennis have to do with Ginger? "Oh my God," was all I could say. Dennis? What was going on?

"Are they going to arrest him?" I asked.

"Not yet. Detective Quinn will be bringing him in for questioning, probably tonight or tomorrow. They're checking his financials first. Looking for motive."

I remembered that Michael had made a trip to Dennis and Tony's neighborhood in Philadelphia to do some research that might lead to a motive.

"Did he find out anything when he went to Dennis' old neighborhood? When was that, Thursday?"

"He told me that Dennis' uncle, Joe Russo, died a few months ago, and Dennis is handling the sale of his house. Apparently he was a widower without kids."

"Boy, Dennis sure has a lot going on," I noted. "With school, Tony, his uncle's house... I don't know him very well, but he has seemed anxious lately." I started to add that Sue seemed surprisingly calm in the midst of all of this, then remembered our conversation about "putting on a happy face" at Village Cooks when she came in the other day. She was better at covering her troubles than Dennis was.

"Detective Quinn is very good. And he's got a lot of help on this one, believe me. Behind the scenes."

He brushed back a tuft of silky white hair, an unconscious gesture I had seen many times. It meant he was ready to move on, get to the next thing. A busy man with a lot on his mind, even now that he was out of office. Sure enough, he let go of my hand. He stood up and said, once again, "Don't worry."

I instinctively stood up and he drew me into his arms. While we hugged I quietly said "I won't, Dad, I won't." But I knew I was lying. He did too.

The Phillies won 5 to 3. Close game. While the crowd was cheering wildly, we were shepherded down an elevator to our waiting cars. I kissed Mom and Dad goodbye in the elevator.

"I'll call you tomorrow," I told Mom, "as soon as we hear anything I will call you." But I knew that if there were any official news, Dad would hear first. Michael Quinn had come to Philadelphia to research Ginger's past, and we hadn't heard anything about her background. I wondered if Dad had. But it wasn't the right time to ask.

It was torture saying goodbye to William before he got in the car with Carol and Paul. "It should only be a few more days," I promised. Andy pulled me away before William could see that I was crying. "Bye, sweetheart! I love you!" I choked out.

On the way home I told Andy, Terry, and Charlie about Dennis' note. Then I told them what I had learned from Pete. It's a good thing it was a long ride.

Charlie said, "The plot thickens." A regular Sherlock Holmes, from the Bronx. He had a way with words.

But Andy was silent. He looked like he was brooding. I nudged him. "Andy, do you know something you're not telling us?"

"Dennis applied for a license to open a school called Moran Academy."

"I know," I said. "Remember I told you about that the other day? It's going to be a school for dyslexic kids. I think it's a great idea."

"Tony Moran is dyslexic," Andy said.

Terry turned around from the front seat. "So?"

"I don't know; I'm trying to figure it out." I paused and considered. "Ginger was Tony's boyfriend, Tony is Dennis' childhood best friend's younger brother that he obviously feels responsible for, Tony is dyslexic, and Dennis is starting a school for dyslexic kids. I'm just wondering how and if that has anything to do with Ginger's death. And why would Dennis start a school, when he already has a job as principal of Willow Middle School? And why would he send a note like that to Ginger?"

"Excellent questions, all," said Charlie from the driver's seat. Sherlock, again.

We drove in silence for a while, as we all pondered the puzzle pieces Andy had just described. About ten minutes from Wilmington, my cell phone rang.

"Hi, Abby," I chimed. I was glad to hear from her. We had just gotten off the highway, and were on local roads.

"Tony Moran overdosed on Xanax." She got right to the point. "I'm at Miche's apartment, waiting for the ambulance."

"Oh my God. We're a few minutes away. We'll be there soon. Is Miche there?"

"She's on the phone. She has been trying to get hold of Jeffrey. It's the dinner rush. Someone has to be out front. But if she doesn't reach him and tell him that she won't be there, the waiters will be on their own."

"Oh, no. How awful. Is Tony alive?"

"They're working on him now."

"Miche must be so upset. You, too."

"Don't worry, I'm not alone. Bob's here. We were together when she called him."

"Good." I breathed. "We'll get there as fast as we can."

I hung up and relayed the news to Andy, Terry, and Charlie. Terry called their boss, Greg Baker, and told him what was happening. Charlie sped up a bit and got us there in six minutes.

The ambulance was still outside when we pulled up in front of the big yellow house. Miche's apartment, on the first floor of a subdivided Victorian, was on a quiet street on the other side of town from the hospital. She had told me that a young couple with a baby lived on the second floor, and a single grad student who was rarely around lived on the third floor. Apparently he spent most of his time at his girlfriend's place.

As we jumped out of the car, we saw Tony being carried down the steps and loaded into the ambulance. We got there in time to see him lying there, his wild black hair more disheveled than usual, his eyes closed as if he were asleep. An IV was attached to his arm, as was a blood pressure machine.

Miche came out right behind him, along with another woman who was holding a baby. The other woman was very pretty, and looked to be in her mid-twenties. She wore jeans, a t-shirt and a gray hoodie, her chestnut hair in a ponytail. Young Mommy clothes.

Andy and Charlie went over to talk to the ambulance workers. Terry stayed with me.

"Hi honey," I cried as I grabbed her and threw my arms around Miche. She was sobbing. "Don't worry, he'll be okay. He'll be fine." I went on, trying to comfort her.

Andy came over and interrupted us. "They're leaving now. We'll take you to the hospital, Miche."

The woman with the baby burst into tears. "It's all my fault," she cried.

I started to ask "Why" but was interrupted by Miche.

"Guys, this is Nicole Rue, my upstairs neighbor," she said. "Her baby is Maxim. They're from Quebec too."

Terry took charge. "Let's all sit down on the steps and calm down for a minute. It will take them a while to get him into the hospital and situated. Let's just take a moment."

We all obeyed. I sat on the top step with my arm around Miche, who was sputtering as she tried to slow her tears. She held Nicole's hand.

Terry took the baby, who was asleep, thank goodness. Andy sat on the bottom step and Charlie stood, pacing back and forth in front of us.

"Why do you think it's your fault?" Andy gently asked Nicole.

She started to answer, but Miche wouldn't let her. "It's not her fault, it's mine."

"What do you mean?" I turned to Miche. "What happened?"

"I took him to the psychologist, you know, Dr. Kimball. They had a special 9 o'clock appointment. Afterward I was going to take him with me to church, because Dr. Kimball said he shouldn't be alone. Especially today, a week from the day Ginger died. That's why they had the special appointment." Miche fished in her pocket for a tissue and wiped her nose.

"But he was so shaken when he came out of his appointment that I knew I couldn't have him sitting in church. I was afraid he'd walk out. Or cry, and embarrass himself. He was such a mess. I was supposed to do a reading from the Old Testament, so I had to be there. It was too late to cancel, so I called Dennis and asked if I could bring him over to his house, and then drive Tony to the restaurant later because he had to be at work at two. Dennis and Sue's house is on the way to my church. Dennis said that was fine, that he was home and could do it."

She sniffed and went on. "So I brought him over. What a relief. Frankly, I was so glad to have some freedom that after church I went and got a pedicure. It was a spontaneous decision — I needed to relax. It's been pretty stressful having to watch him all the time. He used to be so strong, but now, now he seems so ... weak. At night sometimes I check on him to make sure he hasn't left the apartment and run off to hurt himself." Miche sniffed again, and looked down at her feet.

Andy and I exchanged looks. I was thinking that if Tony were this fragile, he should be in the hospital. What if he went back on drugs? I wondered if Dr. Kimball really knew the extent of Tony's depression over Ginger's death.

"Not that he wasn't sweet and agreeable. He went along with everything I said; he didn't interrupt my routine at all. We went to work together last night. He was no trouble at all. But still, I have been anxiously waiting for the police and Dr. Kimball to say Tony could go back to his apartment. I think the responsibility is a little much for me."

We all nodded sympathetically to Miche's plight.

Nicole broke in. "But he didn't stay at Dennis'. Dennis brought him over here, to get his medicine. He had forgotten to take it. When they got here they ran into me in the hallway. David had gone to work and Maxim was up from his nap. I needed to go to the drugstore, so I offered to take Tony to St. Cloud's, because it was on my way. The drugstore is just a few blocks past the restaurant, and I would be passing it." Sadness passed over her face.

"So Dennis left," she continued, "and Tony was helping me get the baby in the car when his cell phone rang. He was making funny animal sounds to the baby, he was having a good time. He seemed fine, he was cheerful." Nicole started crying again.

"When he got off the phone he told me that that was his boss on the phone, that he didn't need to go to work, they were giving him the night off since Sunday was a slow night." She broke off.

She said quickly, "I didn't know anything about his mental state, that he shouldn't be alone."

She paused, took a breath, then said, "I thought he was Miche's new boyfriend, that that was the reason he moved in the other day. I was happy for her. I see the way she looks at Maxim…"

Her eyes met Miche's, who nodded sadly, and looked away.

She continued, "So I went off to the drugstore with Maxim, and Tony went back in the apartment. He said Maxim was a cute baby and I was lucky to have a son. I figured maybe he and Miche were going to settle down together. He was very pleasant, a nice guy. What did I know?" She burst into sobs.

"That must have been when he took the pills. It was about a quarter to two, right?" Miche asked.

Nicole nodded. "Yes, about that," she nodded slowly, calming down.

Miche took over. "And I got home around 4:30, with my pretty pink toes and some groceries. I was in such a good mood — and then I found him on the futon in my second bedroom, where he's been staying. The door was open. I was surprised, because he usually keeps the door closed. I couldn't believe it when I saw him lying there. I couldn't imagine what had happened — I left him with Dennis just this morning. It was only a few hours ago!"

Miche studied her hands, then shuddered and said quietly, "He had white froth coming out of his mouth."

"Oh God," said Terry.

"So I freaked out and tried to shake him awake." She grabbed Nicole's hand and squeezed it. "And I couldn't get him to wake up. I just couldn't."

She let go of Nicole's hand, and was crying again.

"I thought he was dead. I called 911. Then I called Jeffrey, and when he wasn't at the restaurant and didn't answer his cell, I called Abby."

"We came right over," Bob said. "I took Tony's pulse and saw that he was alive."

Miche choked out the words, "I was so relieved."

"I know, honey, I know." I held her.

"And then I called you, and then the ambulance came, and then you arrived." Abby spoke with an air of finality. "And here we are."

Andy stood up and stepped off the steps and stood next to Charlie Campbell. He looked down at Miche and Nicole. "It's not your fault, Miche, or yours, Nicole. Tony is responsible for what he did. Not either of you."

"Let's get to the hospital, guys." Charlie reached for Miche and took her hand to help her up.

She turned to Nicole, and said, "You don't have to come. Don't bring the baby to the hospital. Stay here. Will David be home soon?" David owned Cheese, Please, a few shops down from Village Cooks.

"Any minute."

As she said it, a blue Honda Civic came around the corner and pulled in the driveway. A red-haired man with black-framed glasses wearing a yellow t-shirt with "Cheese, Please" printed in large black letters on it in jumped out of the car and ran to his wife. "This is David," she sobbed as they hugged. I knew him, and nodded a greeting.

The others muttered "Hi'" to him and "Goodbye" to both of them and went off to the hospital.

A couple of blocks from the hospital, Abby called my cell phone.

"Just wanted to let you know that Bob called Dennis and told him about Tony's overdose. We forgot to tell you at the house. But he wanted you to know, in case you were planning on calling him, you don't need to do it."

"Okay."

Sure enough, Dennis and Sue were already there when we got to the emergency room waiting area, and rushed over to us.

"They just brought him in. We can't see him yet." The words burst out in blasts from Dennis. His eyes were frantic; he looked a wreck.

Sue nodded her hello and said, "We can't see him yet. They told us to wait here. Someone will come out and tell us what's what."

"Soon, I hope," said Miche, as she took Sue's arm. "Let's go sit down."

We all followed. But only Abby, Miche, Sue, and I sat down. Dennis was pacing, and Andy and Bob stood near him. Terry and Charlie were seated on the other side of the room, acting as if they didn't know us and just happened to come in to the waiting room at the same time. Terry was already flipping through a magazine, but her head was cocked toward Charlie as she listened to something he was saying that I couldn't hear.

The waiting room wasn't too crowded. There were only a handful of other people there, I was relieved to see. That meant that Tony would get a lot of attention, I hoped.

"Not too crowded. That's good for Tony," I said. No one answered. Andy just looked at me.

There were beads of sweat on Dennis' hairline. "I brought him home to get his medicine. He needed to take it before he went to work. He forgot to bring it with him earlier. I watched him take it. He only took one." He looked pleadingly toward Miche.

"I know, I know, Dennis."

"Did he seem upset about anything?" Bob asked.

"No, he was fine. Annoyed with himself that he hadn't brought the pill with him earlier when he went to the doctor. He just forgot. Other than that, he was getting ready for work mode. All business. Getting things done. You know what I mean." He looked at all of us for confirmation. Sue gave him a weak smile and lowered her red-rimmed eyes.

Michael Quinn arrived a few minutes later. He nodded at the group of us, but spoke to Miche.

"Ms. Lombardi, would it be possible for us to search Tony's bedroom? We have already searched his apartment, as you know. It would be a great help to us if you would give us your permission."

Miche nodded, then looked over at Andy for confirmation, who nodded back. "Sure, I don't see why not. The pill bottle is still there, on the end table."

Michael replied, "Thank you very much," and was gone.

"What do you think they'll find?" I asked no one in particular.

Andy answered. "Maybe he left a note. If he killed Ginger, it might be a confession. Remember, he's a key person in a murder investigation. The police always look at the significant other as the 'bad guy.' Sometimes they feel they know right away that the person is guilty. Then they go off and do background work to find evidence, opportunity, and motive. Once they have a solid case, they bring the person in."

Everyone was listening attentively. Andy continued. "I don't know whether or not Tony has an alibi for the time of Ginger's death, but a suicide attempt, if that's what this was, sure makes him look guilty. Especially on the one week anniversary of her death."

"Do you think he could have taken a bunch of pills to get high, because of his grief, and not to kill himself?" Sue asked.

"That's a good possibility, given his history," Andy replied.

"Not uncommon," added Charlie.

"I hate waiting like this. Where are those doctors?" I asked.

"I'll go see if I can find out anything." Dennis seemed glad to have a job to do.

Terry rifled her bag and brought out some mints. "Who wants a mint?"

We all partook.

"I used to chew gum. But my mother said I looked like a cow. Not an attractive image for prospective boyfriends, so I quit." She chuckled. The mood lightened a bit, just for a moment, as we all had something to do. After we were back in our seats sucking on our mints, the tension returned. And silence.

Eventually Dennis came back. "He's still alive. They've pumped his stomach. That's all they would tell me." He shook his head and slumped into the seat next to Sue, who covered his hand with hers.

An interminable twenty minutes later, a pale, dark-haired woman in a ponytail and wearing a white coat came out and approached us. Her name tag read "Lauren Ruskin, M.D."

"I'm Doctor Ruskin," she said with brisk authority and a slightly friendly tone. "Are you folks here for Tony Moran?"

"Yes," we said in unison.

"Who is immediate family?"

"He's been staying with me," Miche whimpered.

"None of us are relatives, but we are friends, and we all brought him in," I said, secretly hoping that she would recognize me as Bill Billings' daughter and that her recognition would give me some authority, so that she would tell us — or me — what was going on.

"Okay, then I guess I can speak to all of you. Well, there's good news and bad. The good news is that we pumped his stomach and gave him charcoal to absorb the Xanax he took. He was having trouble breathing, and we had to perform a tracheostomy."

"Oh no," cried Miche.

Dr. Ruskin continued. "It was successful. But we don't know exactly how long it was between when he took the pills and he came here. There may be some organ or brain damage. We're monitoring him, and doing everything we can."

"Is he awake?" asked Dennis.

"I'm afraid he's in what I can describe as a mild coma."

"Jesus Christ!" Dennis slammed his hand on his thigh.

"Dennis, take it easy," Sue pleaded. She looked up at Dr. Ruskin. "Is there anything we can do? Should we stay and wait?" It was clear to me that Sue wanted to get Dennis out of there. I felt the same way.

Dr. Ruskin got it. "Since he's non-responsive, there's nothing you can do but wait. We'll call if there's any change. I think you should all go home for tonight."

Andy stood up, taking the lead. "Thank you, Doctor, we'll do that."

"All right, all right," Dennis muttered and stood up to go. "We'll be back in the morning."

As we gathered up our stuff, Miche said, "I'll call you if I hear anything during the night."

"Will you be all right alone? Should I stay over?" Abby asked her.

Miche started to answer, then shook her head. The tears came. Abby put her arms around her and walked her out. I was glad she would be bringing her home, and hoped she'd spend the night at Miche's place.

The rest of our downtrodden, troubled group filed out after them. I don't think we even said "Goodbye" to each other as we went to our separate cars in the small emergency room parking lot. It had been a week since I found Ginger's body, and now her boyfriend Tony was close to death too.

Chapter 9

Riviera Fish Soup

The first time Michael and I went to Cannes, the playground of the stars, it was out of season, our hotel was out of fashion, and we were almost out of money. The conditions sound a lot less than ideal, but the reality was great. With the summer crowds gone, we had the beaches to ourselves; our hotel was adorable, and the hotelier even cuter (he must have liked us too; since he sent us home with a bottle of wine from his cellar); and our frugality turned up a find: an affordable restaurant (that we returned to three nights in a row) with a view of the beach and a fish soup that I dreamed about for years.

I'm guessing that it was made from the tiny little creatures that I'd see in the market every morning. Tucked into the corner of the fishmonger's display would be an assortment of very small fish and a large metal scoop. The fish were labeled something like "fish for soup," and you bought whatever came up in the scoop, no picking out the pink ones from the gray ones or the skinny ones from the chubs. Of course, these little rockfish were part of what made the soup a regional treasure, but there was more. There was the texture: thin but with enough fish bits that you felt you were eating the soup as much as sipping it; the mysterious base flavors: saffron and pastis (a licorice-flavored liquor); and the ritual that went with enjoying it: floating a raft of grilled bread, rubbed with garlic and doused with olive oil, in the soup; topping it with rouille, a peppery rust-colored mayonnaise (rouille means rust; you can use aïoli if you prefer); and figuring out how to get all three elements into every spoonful.

To make the soup in the United States, I had to give up on the idea of small fish by the scoop, but I discovered that I could get a lot of flavor from fish that were local to my fishmonger. Red snapper, a fish with Mediterranean relatives, is great for this soup, as are other lean white-fleshed fish like flounder and sole. More important are the saffron and pastis and a food mill.

Here's the recipe that will get you the texture, the flavor and the ritual — I leave it to you to add the beach view.

1 whole red snapper (about 2 pounds), cleaned and scaled (head on, if
   possible)
3-4 tablespoons extra-virgin olive oil
2 medium onions, chopped

2 carrots (1 if it's very thick), trimmed, peeled, and chopped
4 garlic cloves, split, germ removed, and smashed
1 small fennel bulb, trimmed, tough core removed, and chopped
1 28-ounce can plum tomatoes
¼ cup tomato paste
3 pinches of saffron threads
2-4 tablespoons pastis (I use Pernod or Ricard)
1 wide strip orange zest, any white pith removed
A bouquet garni: 2 parsley sprigs, 2 thyme sprigs, and 1 bay leaf, tied
    together or wrapped in cheesecloth
Salt and freshly ground pepper
Piment d'Espelette or cayenne

For the accompaniments:
4 slices country bread
1 garlic clove, split and germ removed
Extra-virgin olive oil
Rouille or Aïoli

If your fishmonger is your friend (or if he's not busy), perhaps he'll chop up the snapper for you. If not, grab a heavy chef's knife or a Chinese cleaver and go to work, removing the head (save it) and then cutting the body of the fish into small pieces. The smaller the better here — 2 inches on a side is ideal but difficult, so just do the best you can.

Place a large Dutch oven or stockpot over medium-low heat and put in 3 tablespoons oil. When the oil is warm, toss in the onions, carrots, garlic, and fennel and stir everything around so that it's glistening with oil, then cover the pot and cook slowly, stirring around once or twice, for 10 minutes, to soften but not color the vegetables.

Add the fish chunks and head to the pot and stir well; if the mix looks a little dry, add another tablespoon of oil. Cover and cook for 5 minutes.

While the fish is cooking, drain the liquid from the tomatoes into a large measuring cup. Keep the tomatoes in the can and, using a pair of scissors (easier) or a long knife, cut the tomatoes into chunks (don't worry about getting everything even).

Turn the tomatoes into the pot, add the tomato paste and saffron, stir to incorporate, and cook for a minute or two. Add enough water to the tomato juice to make 6 cups of liquid and pour it into the pot, along with 1 tablespoon of the pastis. Toss in the zest and bouquet garni, season with salt, pepper, and piment d'Espelette or cayenne, and bring to a boil. Lower the heat so that the soup simmers gently but steadily and cook, uncovered, for 40 minutes.

If using a food mill, fit it with the medium disk and place the mill over a bowl. Ladle the soup (liquid and solids) into the food mill in small batches (discard the head and the bouquet garni when you come to them) and puree, scraping the solids that accumulate on the underside of the disk into the bowl and discarding the solids that build up in the mill; pout the soup into a clean pot. If using a food processor or blender, puree the soup in batches, discarding the head and bouquet garni, and then, if you'd like, press the soup through a strainer into a clean pot.

To make the accompaniments:
Preheat the boiler. Give the slices of bread a rubdown on both sides with the cut sides of the garlic. Brush or drizzle a little olive oil over the bread and put the bread on a baking sheet. Run the bread under the broiler until it's lightly browned on one side, then flip the slices over and brown the other side. Put the warm bread on a plate and the rouille or aioli in a bowl.

Meanwhile, reheat the soup over medium heat and taste it. Add more salt and pepper if needed (you'll probably need more salt) and 1 more tablespoon of pastis. For some, that will be just enough; for others, another tablespoon or even 2 should be right. (I usually add at least 3 tablespoons.)

Serve the soup with the toasts and sauce.

Dorie Greenspan, *Around My French Table* (2010)

The phone rang, waking me up. I looked at the clock. "Ten o'clock!" I said out loud. Monday, I thought, then relaxed. The store was closed, William was with his grandparents, and I didn't have to be anywhere. It had been a rough night. Andy slept well, but I tossed and turned for hours. I think I finally fell asleep around five. I guess Andy had decided against waking me up when he got up for work, since he knew Village Cooks was closed and I didn't have to be anywhere in particular.

It was Kay Lannigan. "I'm glad you're home, dear. How are you?" I sat up and gave her a brief description of the last twenty-four hours, then got out of bed and slipped on a robe and slippers. I brought the cordless phone with me to the kitchen, where I poured myself a glass of water from the pitcher in the refrigerator, and popped in a quarter lemon from the covered glass bowl I kept there. A diet aid, I've been told. It's easy to do, and every little bit helps. My tale was over by the time I plopped myself down in one of the Ethan Allen reproduction Windsor chairs at our round kitchen table. Sure enough, there was a note from Andy: "Went to work. Hope you got some sleep. A."

Kay was suitably stunned by my news. Then she got to the reason for her call. I knew that Lannigan Antiques was closed on Monday, like Village Cooks was.

"I'm sorry to bother you on your day off, but she's going to be leaving town next Saturday and I know you won't have a day off before then."

"Who's leaving? What are you talking about?" I noticed that the sun was shining, and the colors of the trees in our backyard had gotten more golden since yesterday morning, the last time I had sat at the table eating pancakes with Andy before we went to the baseball game, which now seemed like a month ago.

"I'm sorry, let me start at the beginning," she fussed. "A young woman from Australia came into the shop yesterday afternoon. Her mother, Mary Pettit, passed away recently, and she came over to take care of things. Her mother lived in Wilmington Commons." The townhouse community where Abby lived.

"Do you know the name?" Kay asked.

"Sorry, I didn't know her."

"Well, her daughter's name is Tracy Brown, and when she was going through her mother's things she found hundreds of cookbooks."

"Hundreds of cookbooks?" I parroted.

"Yes, she doesn't know how many, exactly. She said there is one bookcase full of them, plus about a dozen boxes filled with them, in the garage."

"She kept them in the garage?" I didn't like the sound of that. Not much of a caretaker of her books, I thought, envisioning damp, musty book covers stuck together.

"They were double-boxed, she said, and her mother kept a dehumidifier going in the garage."

"Really?" I can't say I was impressed, but I was pleased.

"I know you don't deal in rare or out-of-print cookbooks, but I was wondering if you would go out there and take a look at them and advise her on what to do with them. I'd go, but I know china, not cookbooks. I told her I'd ask you."

I pondered for a moment. I didn't have any plans for the day other than finding out about Tony's condition and calling William. Unless Tony awoke, there didn't seem much reason to go to the hospital.

We had two shelves in the back of the store for "Gently Used Cookbooks" that were fairly successful. Some were out-of-print, like *A Treasury of Great Recipes*. I had been considering enlarging the section to a full-fledged "Rare, Used and Out-of-Print" section (with a snappier name), but had never done anything about it. Maybe it was time. If I could buy these books in a lot...

"Sure, tell her I can be there at one."

"You can?" Kay said in a lilt. "That's wonderful. She said she'll be there all day today. I'll call her. She's a very nice person, you'll like her. And I hope you'll find the books interesting."

"Thank you. It'll be a good distraction for me. William's not here, and it will give me something to do. Lord knows I don't feel like grocery shopping. I don't want to go and sit around the hospital and feel useless. And I'm sure Terry won't mind the drive over there." Terry's car was in the driveway, so I knew she was out there, watching over me.

I fed William's rabbits, Edison and Einstein, and leisurely took a shower and got dressed. I was about to call Terry and tell her about going over to Tracy Brown's, that is, Mary Pettit's townhouse, when I remembered that I hadn't eaten. So I sat down and ate a blueberry yogurt as I read the newspaper Andy always left on the couch in the living room. Just as I was reading an article about a new exhibit of manuscripts related to food that had just opened at the Morgan Library in New York, the phone rang again. This time it was Andy.

"No change," he said before I could utter a word. "I just talked to Michael Quinn. But there is other news."

"What?"

"They found Dennis Russo's fingerprints on the pill bottle, and in various other places in Tony's room in Miche's apartment, and in the bathroom."

"What on earth does that mean?" I didn't understand the implication, and Andy sounded serious.

"That he handled the pill bottle." He paused. "Bonnie, they didn't find a suicide note. And Dennis' fingerprints were all over the pill bottle, along with Tony's."

"And?" I had a feeling I should be sitting down, and was glad I was already doing so. I uncurled my legs and sat up straight on the couch.

"The implication is that Dennis could have had something to do with Tony's overdose."

"No!" I exclaimed.

"Add that to the note found in Ginger's room, and you have solid evidence. Michael's going to be questioning him today."

"You're kidding!" I shouted. This couldn't be.

I lowered my voice. "Questioning Dennis? As a suspect in Tony's overdose?" I couldn't believe it. "Do you think this has something to do with Ginger Harrison? Why would Dennis kill Ginger and try to kill Tony?"

"Calm down, honey. We don't know the answers to any of that. We'll have to wait and see. I know it's a terrible thought, but remember the closer the police get to finding the killer, the sooner we'll know that we are safe and we can bring William home and go back to our lives."

William had been at his grandparents' since Thursday night. Although Carol and Paul had been sent a week's worth of schoolwork for him, I hated that he had missed his school and his routine, and of course being home with us. I felt responsible. Bob, Abby, Miche and I had informally agreed that night at the Peacock Inn to try and find out who the killer was, but we hadn't gotten very far, and we never made a real plan. We hadn't really done anything. Events had gotten in the way. Events like having my tires slashed and Tony's OD. I needed to get back "on the case," as they say. I had an idea, and maybe Andy could help.

"Andy," I said in a calm, even tone, trying to impress him with it, "can you check your newspaper's archive and see if there is an obituary for Bobby Moran?"

"Sure, I can do that. Where are you going with this, hon?"

"I don't know. But he was Tony's brother and Dennis' best friend, along with that guy I told you about who was behind the food counter at the Phillies game. I can't help thinking that their link is the key to all of this, something that happened back in Philly."

"What was his name again?"

"Pete Cannavale."

I could tell he was writing it down.

"I'll check him out, too. You never know."

"You're the best."

"Gotta go."

"Love you."

"Me too."

Now it was 12:15. I called Terry. "Can you come in the house?"

"Sure, be right there."

A moment later she was ringing the bell. Today she wore a chocolate brown pantsuit and a robin's egg blue silk blouse that made a striking combination.

"You look pretty!" I couldn't help but blurt as I opened the door.

"Thanks. Date tonight." She grinned and stepped inside.

"With?" I grinned back.

"Yes, yes, it's Charlie Campbell. We've been dating for a few weeks now. But we haven't told Greg, so please don't say anything. We're trying to find out what Baker Security's policy is on inter-office dating."

"That's great, Terry. Andy and I were talking about you two, hoping you were a couple. You're great together!"

"Thanks. Anyway, what's up?" The front door of our house opens directly into the living room. She walked over toward the sitting area, and I followed, sat down on the couch, and motioned for her to do the same. She did.

"Is it Tony Moran?" I saw the alarm in her eyes.

"No, no. Andy called and said there's no change. I called you because I have to go over to Wilmington Commons. I need to be there at one. There's a woman there cleaning out her late mother's townhouse, and she found a lot of old cookbooks. She checked with Kay Lannigan, the antiques dealer, who recommended me."

"But you're not an antiquarian book dealer. Are you?"

"No, I'm not, but I know cookbooks. She said these didn't go back any earlier than the thirties. I have nothing else to do today except worry, so I agreed to take a look. Would you like to have a quick grilled cheese sandwich with me and then go over there?"

"It's my job, so, sure."

And so we did.

Wilmington Commons is on the north side of town, set into a lovely wooded hillside. There are about a hundred townhouses that snake around the winding streets in the gated community. Built in the nineties, the brick exteriors resemble colonial townhouses, with black or red doors, shutters, and brass knockers. Each one has a small deck in back. There's a pool and a tennis court for residents, as well as a playground which declares it a family rather than an over-55 community, like so many townhouse communities. About a third of the residents have school-age children.

The streets are all named after United States presidents. When I teased Abby about living on the corner of Lincoln Lane and Washington Street, she said, "Be glad I don't live on 'Billings Road.' Besides, it's better than having fake British names, like 'Oxfordshire Square' and 'Stoneham Court.'" She had a point. After all, this is America. And Washington's Army spent the frigid, snowy winter of 1779–1780 in nearby Morristown. We often brought out-of-town visitors to the Ford Mansion, Washington's headquarters, and to Fort Nonsense. Sometimes we also brought them to Morristown National Park, where the soldiers lived in wooden huts on the hillside, and near Tempe Wick's cottage with its lovely herb garden.

Mary Pettit had lived on Truman Road, in one of the middle townhouses on the lower side of the hill. I banged the knocker. A woman with a short reddish bob and purple-framed glasses opened the door. Her feet were bare and she wore jeans. But she wore a sweater that was like none I'd ever seen. Cowl-necked, the cowl section was made of purple wool with pink ribbons knitted into it. The left arm and half of the front, in a diagonal, was made of lavender boucle, and the other side, and the right arm, of yarn made of varying shades of rose darkening to purple. It was startling, eye-catching, strange and spectacular.

I think I did a double-take as I took it all in, because the woman laughed and said in an Australian lilt, "Hi, I'm Tracy Brown, and yes, I knit."

She must have noticed our stares.

"You must be Bonnie Emerson."

She reached out and shook my hand. I laughed and introduced Terry. We decided beforehand that we would say that Terry was my friend, and that we had just had lunch and she was merely along for the ride, out of curiosity to see the cookbooks. I wonder what Tracy Brown would have thought if she had known that Terry was my "protection."

She led us into a living room with traditional furniture and a multi-colored oriental rug. The fireplace mantle was painted Wedgewood blue, and an oil painting depicting a waterfall that looked like it could have come from the Hudson River School hung over it.

"Come on into the dining room, that's where the cookbooks are," she instructed. We followed her into a small separate dining room, large enough for a table for six and a sideboard. On the side wall near the entrance to the kitchen stood a seven-foot tall bookcase filled with cookbooks. The back wall contained sliding glass doors and a small patio facing onto a meadow. Not an end unit, but it had a nice view.

"Did Kay tell you there are more in the garage?"

"Yes, but let me take a look at these first."

Terry studied them politely for a moment, then pulled out a dining room chair.

"May I?" she asked.

"Yes, of course," said Tracy, and sat down opposite her.

I remained standing, transfixed by the array before me. I took a deep breath. My first thought was, "Even if they're not worth anything, I've got to have them."

They were all in what rare book dealers would categorize as "very good" to "fine" condition. The top four shelves were international cooking. The two middle oversized shelves were a mix of oversized, illustrated cookbooks, and the bottom three shelves held American cookbooks. That much I could see at a glance. Among the American cookbooks there was a whole shelf of New York cookbooks, including

Molly O'Neill's *New York Cookbook*, a signed first edition in hardcover, published in 1992, and charmers such as *The Madison Avenue Cookbook: For People Who Can't Cook and Don't Want Other People to Know It*, by Murray Tinkelman, published in 1962. There was a cookbook with recipes and reminiscences of one of the most famous New York restaurants, and a favorite of my parents, *Luchow's German Cookbook: The Story and the Favorite Dishes of America's Most Famous German Restaurant*, by Jan Mitchell, published after the restaurant moved from its famous Fourteenth Street location to the theatre district and then closed a few years later. My parents went to the new location, but said it just wasn't the same. The original restaurant, at 110 E. Fourteenth Street, had been there for 100 years and had hosted the likes of Teddy Roosevelt when he was the New York Police Commissioner, Enrico Caruso and Diamond Jim Brady. It was next to the Palladium Theatre. I'd heard they were both torn down and replaced by NYU dorms. Kay had just been talking about Luchow's at dinner Saturday night.

Looking at Mary Pettit's collection reminded me that many cookbooks are not just about food, but are also about places, and tradition, and memories. I knew I was going to enjoy looking through these. But it could take all day. And I didn't want to keep Terry here long, since it was supposed to look like she was my friend, tagging along. Tracy wouldn't expect us to stay long.

"Did she have a list of her cookbooks, by any chance?" I asked Tracy.

"I haven't found one, but the boxes in the garage are numbered, so there may be a key list somewhere. I just haven't found it yet. I'm still going through her papers. It's very hard — "

"I'm sure it is," said Terry. "When I lost my Mom it took me weeks to get it together to even begin to look at her things. I don't know how you are doing it, and all by yourself."

"She moved here when my Dad died six years ago to be near my brother and his family. He has four boys. I live in London now, but I travel a lot for my business. My daughter Tina is in college in New York, and I come here two or three times a year to see all of them."

"Are you originally from Australia?" I asked.

"Yes, born and bred in Perth. But when Mom sold the house there, that was the end of our ties to Oz. It's a small family, and what's left is in the U.S. now."

"So you're staying with your brother? Does he live in Wilmington?"

"No, I'm staying here. He lives in Wilmington, but he also travels a lot. He's a corporate accountant and he works in either New York or Singapore. He was here for the funeral of course, two weeks ago, but then he left for Singapore, and his wife Peggy has her hands full with the kids, so I'm doing this myself. I go over there for dinner most nights."

"What do you do?" Terry asked. It was hard not to ask questions of this interesting woman.

"I am a knitwear designer. I have a studio with four employees, plus a shop, Heath Wear, in Hampstead Heath, which is in north London. I travel to buy yarn in China, South America. Most people think of Scotland and New Zealand, but Argentina, Turkey, and China are major suppliers these days. Last summer Mom and Tina flew over and met me in Turkey, and we traveled all over, and went on to Greece and a few of the Greek islands." She was starting to lose her composure.

I grabbed a thick blue Greek cookbook off the shelf, *Vefa's Kitchen*, by Vefa Alexiadou. "Did she buy this on that trip?"

"Yes, she did. Vefa is a famous chef and cookbook author who is on television in Greece. That book is supposed to be the first authoritative and all-encompassing Greek cookbook in English ever published. She has stores all over Greece; they're called 'Vefa's House.' We met her in a tiny restaurant in Santorini, and of course we had no idea who she was, we were typical tourists — but we started talking while we were waiting for our tables, and she and Mom hit it off. The next day they cooked a dinner for all of us in the hotel kitchen. Mom and Vefa. It was brilliant."

I looked inside. It was inscribed, "For my dear friend Mary. I loved cooking with you. Always, Vefa."

"Would you like to have some lemonade?" she asked. "I found some Crystal Light and mixed some up."

"Sure."

I sat down at the head of the table while Tracy went to the kitchen, got the glasses out and poured.

After she brought the glasses to the table, she sat down opposite Terry. "So what do you think?" she asked me. "Are these the sort of books you would be interested in buying?"

"Are there any that you want to keep for yourself?" I asked gently. I couldn't believe she'd want to part with some of these gems.

"I think I'll keep *Vefa's Kitchen* as a keepsake. But that's probably it. I don't cook very much since I travel a lot, although I do like to bake bread when I have a chance. Mom gave me some baking cookbooks over the years, which I treasure."

"Cool. Which ones? Do you remember?"

She giggled. "When I was in high school she bought me The *Tassajara Bread Book*, you know, the one written by a Zen monk?"

"Of course I do. That was one of my earliest cookbooks!" We both laughed.

"I have quite a few, in fact. She often gave me baking books as gifts. Let's see. She loved Dorie Greenspan, and gave me that book where she baked with Julia Child. But the ones I use the most are Dorie Greenspan's *Baking: From My Home to Yours*, and my other favorite, *Baking Illustrated*, by America's Test Kitchen."

"I love Dorie Greenspan too, and we carry all of her books. Her latest is *Around My French Table*. It's a spectacular book," I said. It was hard to hide my enthusiasm, I was getting excited. Terry just grinned.

Then I noticed something out of the corner of my eye. Two men walking in the meadow outside. One was carrying a clipboard. They were walking toward us. They looked familiar. As they got closer, I saw that the men were Dennis Russo and Pete Cannavale. Pete Cannavale? Dennis Russo? Together? Pete had said that he hadn't seen him in a while. What did he say? Years? Months? I couldn't remember. And why were they walking around outside Wilmington Commons? Last night at the hospital Dennis had seemed so upset about Tony. What was he doing here, now, calmly walking around with a clipboard, and Pete Cannavale? I opened my mouth to say something, but as I did Pete and Dennis turned toward us. Terry met my eyes. She had seen them too. She stood up and asked to use the bathroom, but lingered in the doorway watching before she left. Watching out the window. During that moment they walked away, out of our view.

When Terry came back she said, "I left my cell phone in the car. I'll be right back, I want to go get it."

"Sure," said Tracy. "Shall we go take a look in the garage? There are about 12 boxes down there."

"Let's wait for Terry," I answered. "She'll be back in a minute."

"Okay."

And she was. She nodded at me, and I assumed that meant that everything was okay out there. "We're ready to check out the books in the garage. Wanna come?"

"Of course," Terry said, and Tracy led us through the kitchen and through the door to the garage. Tracy turned on the light and we all entered the garage. A collection of twelve numbered boxes, four piles of three boxes each, was neatly stacked on one side, on wood slats. Further down were more wood slats, but they held plastic storage containers, also numbered. About twenty of them. And a large rectangular box that said "Christmas tree" on it. Sure enough, there was a dehumidifier going. Other than that, the garage was empty.

"I took her car out so we'd have room to walk around."

"Very neat," murmured Terry.

"These are the cookbook boxes," Tracy said, and opened a top box in the far-left pile. I looked inside. And was very pleased with what I saw.

All of the cookbooks in this box were about meat. I gathered that she had them organized by subject. That would make my decision easier. And I was pretty sure that if every box was similar to this, I'd buy them all. There was everything from the British favorite from about fifteen years ago, *The River Cottage Meat Book* to *Falling Off the Bone*, Jean Anderson's recent book that I carried in Village Cooks. The subject was ripe for whimsical titles, and Mary had quite a few, including *The Meat Club Cookbook: For Gals Who Love Their Meat!*, *Meat: A Love Story*, and the Time-Life book *Monday Is Meat Loaf and Burgers and Pork Chops and Steaks and More*. She also had the classic Lobel Brothers' *Meat* and *The Complete Round-the-World Meat Cookbook*.

I moved over a few rows and opened another box. It contained all of the Ina Garten Barefoot Contessa cookbooks and all of Elizabeth Crisp's books. I turned to Tracy.

"How about a thousand dollars for the lot?"

She stood there with her arms folded, and shrugged. "Perfect. When can you pick them up?"

"Well, I can probably fit about six or eight boxes in the car now. I'll come back for the rest tomorrow. Is that okay?"

"Sounds good."

"I'll write the check now." We went back upstairs where I had left my purse. From Terry's expression I knew we had to get going. She was uncomfortable, I could see, and wanted to get us away from there. *Where had Dennis and Pete gone*, I wondered.

After I wrote the check and handed it to her, Tracy said, "I'll box up the rest tonight and have them ready for you tomorrow. What time will you be over?" She nodded toward the pile of flat new boxes stacked against the wall.

"How about nine?" That would give me time to make two trips if necessary and open Village Cooks at eleven.

"Brilliant," she said, her smile wide.

"Well, it's been very nice meeting you," Terry reached out and shook Tracy's hand. "Let's go down and load what we can from the boxes in the garage."

We were able to fit six boxes in the back and three in the back seat. We drove over to the store. Thankfully there was a spot right in front. I unlocked the door, and we each carried a box in. Then Terry started taking them out of the car and piling them up on the sidewalk near the door. "Do you have a hand truck?" she asked.

"Oh, that's right. I do!" I raced in back to get it. By the time I got back she had the seven remaining boxes neatly stacked in two piles, and the trunk door was back in place, the car doors closed and, I assumed, locked.

I held the hand truck while Terry leaned over to move the boxes on to the hand truck. She lifted the first box and set it on the metal base. It made a loud "thump" as it landed on the metal. Terry started to raise her body to reach for the second box but was stopped short by the sound of two shots and the sudden crashing of glass falling onto us as the left store window near us broke into pieces. Terry grabbed me and pulled me down. We crouched, Terry covering my body with hers. I think I screamed. Or maybe I cursed. I don't know. I do know that my senses sharpened and my body was filled with more adrenalin than I've ever felt in my life. Hyper-alert, I had a crazy sensation of well-being. How could I feel this way, I thought, when I am terrified? I could be shot at any moment. It all happened in a flash. I tried to get up, but Terry blocked me. "Don't move! Quiet!" she hissed.

A moment passed. We didn't hear any more shots. Kay came running out of the door of Lannigan Antiques. "I called the police," she hollered. "Come on, scoot on over here."

Terry nodded and pulled the two of us, still crouching, over to Kay's doorway.

We got inside and Kay gave us a huge hug. "Thank God you're all right!" she cried. Terry reached behind her and slammed the store door closed. "Kay, please lock the door."

"Of course," said Kay, letting go of us. She did so.

We looked around. The store was empty. "Do you have a back room?" Terry asked quickly.

"Yes, that way." Kay pointed.

"Okay, Kay, you go first. Then Bonnie. Now!"

We obeyed her orders and ran to the back room. She followed a second later. Then we heard police sirens.

Next to her desk, Kay had a work table. There were two folding chairs folded next to it. Kay opened them and motioned for us to sit down. I did, Terry didn't. She paced. Kay sat down at her desk, and turned to me.

"Lean over, let me get the glass out of your hair."

I obeyed. She collected a few pieces and put them in a pile on the table. Terry's hair was full of glass too, but she apparently hadn't noticed. She continued to pace, a stern look on her face.

I had all of my fingers and toes intact, I reminded myself. Terry is fine, Kay is fine. A window is broken, but we are fine, and that's all that matters. *I should calm down*, I thought, willing it so. An officer I didn't recognize knocked on the door. Terry went out and spoke to him. A few minutes later, they both came back.

"This is Steven O'Neill," she pronounced. I had heard about him, but hadn't met Michael Quinn's number two man until now.

Kay stood up. "How do you do? I'm Kay Lannigan." She shook his hand.

I didn't stand. I murmured, "I'm Bonnie Emerson" and put out my hand as well. He shook it, and nodded. "Ladies." He was on the short side, with medium brown hair, not too short, and a round, impish face and laughing blue eyes that belied his serious demeanor.

His eyes met mine. "Are you all right? Do you need an ambulance?"

"I don't think so. Kay's been collecting glass from my hair. Terry needs to get the glass out of her hair, too. That's about it. I guess we were lucky he missed."

Terry nodded. "Do you have a rest room, Kay? I'll go in there and shake out my hair."

"Yes, dear, it's over there," Kay said and pointed to a door at the other end of the rectangular back room that ran the width of the store. "Do you need help?"

Terry turned and walked away. She spoke over her shoulder. "I'll be fine."

"What's with her?" I said, and was surprised to hear that I'd said it out loud, and not just thought it. I guess I was a little shell-shocked.

Officer O'Neill answered, "She's upset with herself."

"Why? It wasn't her fault. I think she saved my life."

"Whether it was her fault or not, I can't say just yet, but I know she's beating herself up about it."

"Oh, dear," clucked Kay, and reached out and held my hands in hers.

After a moment of silence I let Kay's hand go. O'Neill cleared his throat. Terry was not back yet. The door opened, and Andy rushed in, and ran, as fast as a grown man could through aisles of tables filled with china, to the back room. I stood up and hugged him.

"Oh, Andy," I whimpered.

"Bonnie, Bonnie, are you okay?"

"I'm fine. Just shaken up."

He looked around, nodded at Kay and Steven O'Neill. "Where's Terry?"

"In the bathroom. She's cleaning herself up," answered Kay.

The bells chimed again and two more officers, a man and a woman, came in. Charlie Campbell was with them.

"Bonnie, are you all right? Where's Terry?" he barked.

"Right here," she called as she came walking toward us. Charlie rushed up toward her, got close, then paused. He didn't touch her, but spoke softly to her, "Are you okay?"

"I guess so," she half whispered.

Together they walked back over to us.

Charlie took charge. "We should get you home," he said to me. Then, to O'Neill; "I need to get them off the premises. Can you interview them at the Emersons' house?"

"Of course, not a problem. I'll drive them over now," answered Officer O'Neill briskly. He added, "Mrs. Lannigan, would you mind closing up the shop and coming with us?"

"Actually, the store is not open on Mondays. I was here doing some paperwork when I heard the noise, called the police, and ran out and found the girls." We were grown women — me over 40, and Terry, over 30 — but, I guess to her, we were girls.

"Let's go, then," Charlie said.

Chapter 10

> "I don't feel very much like Pooh today," said Pooh. "There there," said Piglet. "I'll bring you tea and honey until you do."
>
> A.A. Milne, *Winnie-the-Pooh*

O'Neill drove the police cruiser that took Kay and me to our house. Andy drove his own car, followed by Charlie and Terry in Greg's car. As we pulled up, Greg Baker arrived, with another man.

We went inside and sat down in the living room. Greg and the man stood, and Greg introduced him. "This is Bill Fritz. He works for Baker Security and is going to take over for Terry and work with Charlie." Bill Fritz was taller than Greg, lanky, with dark hair cropped close and bushy black eyebrows rimming intelligent blue eyes.

"For the rest of today and tonight," he added. I was relieved. I liked Terry, and wanted to keep her around. I also didn't want her to get in trouble.

He went on. "We haven't determined yet whether or not you folks can stay here or whether we need to take you to a safe house."

"A safe house!?" gasped Kay.

"You'll have to stay with them for the immediate future, ma'am, since you were a witness. We need to make sure you're all in a safe place. And we need to interview you both," he nodded at Kay and me, "and Terry."

"Who will interview us?"

"We're waiting for Detective Quinn to get here. He's talking to the Secret Service, so it might be a while."

"The Secret Service?" Kay's shriek was softer this time. "I thought they only protect sitting presidents."

"They protect ex-presidents and their spouses for life," Andy answered, "and their children up to age 16."

156

He chuckled. "Bonnie is obviously older than that. But given the circumstances, an Executive Order was issued to protect Bonnie and her family."

"It was?" I asked. This was news to me. Frankly, I was accustomed to Secret Service protection from my youth and hadn't really thought about it. "I thought this was an extension of Dad's protection," I said.

"It is, because Ginger Harrison's body was found on your property, but it required an Order. Not a problem. Your Dad called the White House, and it happened immediately."

"That's cool," I said quickly.

They all looked at me strangely. I laughed.

Then Andy laughed too, and said, "An extra layer of protection can't hurt. They have the resources to supplement the behind-the-scenes work that the police force is doing, and they have authorized Baker Security to be our on-site protection."

"You may think that Terry, and Charlie, and Bill here are the extent of our protective services," added Greg, pulling up a chair. Since he had done so, Bill sat down, too. "But they're not. There are always at least two, sometimes more, 'invisible' agents backing them up. Today, Bonnie, when you went to Wilmington Commons with Terry, Charlie and Bill were right there. You just didn't see them."

"Really?" I was stunned. "And when we went to the Phillies game?"

"We had four people that day, plus a few Philadelphia undercover police officers, and the usual four Secret Service special agents that travel with your parents at all times."

"Impressive," said Andy. "I had no idea, but I'm glad your services are so extensive."

"What about when we went to Bob Lee's adoption meeting?" I asked, remembering that room with about a dozen people in it.

"You had Terry and Charlie in the room with you as you know, and we had two people outside and one in the building, checking the hallways."

"Wow. And when we went to eat?"

"At restaurants we have people seated at other tables posing as customers, and people outside in cars watching all entrances and exits."

"That's very thorough," Kay chimed in. "Very James Bond."

I giggled. So did she. We were starting to relax. That is, Kay and I were. The rest of the people in the room were holding themselves stiffly, betraying their tension. This was serious business, I reminded myself. Suddenly I remembered something. "Mrs. Beeton!" I cried.

"Who's that?" asked Greg.

"My cat. She lives at the store. And now with the window broken, she'll be so scared!"

"I'll take care of it," Steven O'Neill said, and walked out of the room, pressing numbers on his phone.

He came back a moment later. "They already found her, safe and sound, in the back, under a table. An officer lured her out, and now Animal Protection has her. They're bringing her right over."

"Thank God she wasn't shot," I cried, and moved closer to Andy on the couch, entwining my arm in his.

The next thing I knew, I was in tears. The thought of sweet Mrs. Beeton, all alone, with the sound of the shots, and all of that glass and commotion, and then the police there… and me, forgetting all about her, when she could have been hit, and I didn't go to help her… I finally broke. Andy held me while I sobbed.

"You were in shock, dear," offered Kay. "Don't feel guilty. You had just been shot at. And then there was all of that glass." She tsked.

"I know, I know. But I still feel awful. I feel responsible." That word reminded me of how badly I felt about finding Ginger Harrison and how that led to my tires being slashed, William having to go and stay with Paul and Carol, Tony's overdose, and now this. Too much to bear. I was trying to pull myself together to say something to that effect when the doorbell rang and Michael Quinn opened the door and walked in.

After saying "Hello" to all of us (he didn't need to be introduced to Bill Fritz, so he apparently already knew him), he looked over at the wooden bench by the window, and then at me, and said, "May I?"

"Of course," I answered, and he brought it over, next to the big wooden coffee table, opposite Kay, Andy, and me on the couch.

He sat down. "I have some news."

"Did you find the person who shot at us?" I asked, excitedly.

"Not yet, but we will, don't worry. We found casings across the street, in the alley between A House in Provence and the empty store. We're checking out the empty storefront now."

"Dear Lord," uttered Kay.

He leaned forward toward those of us on the couch, and looked me in the eye squarely. Uh-oh. The room was silent.

"It's Tony Moran. He didn't make it."

"Oh, no." I don't know who said it, or how many said it. It sounded like a cacophony of voices to me. Suddenly my forehead was sweaty, and everything began to whirl.

I fainted. Sitting on the couch. Yes, it is possible to faint from a seated position. I knew that. I once knew a woman who fainted in her car a few times. She had to give up highway driving alone. Now I'd proven that it's possible to faint while seated on a couch, with one's husband's arms surrounding one.

When I woke up Andy and Kay were looking down on me. Sally and Ian were there, too. The room seemed filled with people.

"When did you arrive?" I croaked to Sally and Ian.

"We got here a moment ago, just in time to see you collapse."

There was a wet dish towel on my forehead.

"Kay got you a wet towel. Don't worry, you're all right, you just fainted," cooed Andy.

I sat myself up the best I could and looked at the others in the room.

"Tony," I remembered.

They all nodded, sadly. No one spoke.

Kay handed me a glass of water. I drank some and felt better. Strike that, I didn't feel "better"— but I no longer saw stars, and the room was right in front of me where it belonged, instead of swimming around me.

Michael Quinn was speaking. "You know we've been in touch with the Secret Service. Rick Harris, the lead special agent in charge of President Billings, is on his way here. He'll be here with a few other special agents within the hour. Once they assess the safety of this house, Rick Harris, Greg Baker, and I will meet and decide about sending you and Andy to a safe house."

Andy asked, "Do you have an opinion on that yet, yourself?"

"I think we can keep you safe here. But whoever shot at Bonnie and Terry Ferrara probably knows where this house is. It's been on the TV news, you may recall."

He paused.

I groaned.

He went on. "I've got my people working on a few leads, and maybe we can wrap this up soon."

A thought jumped into my head, and before I could stop it I burst out, "Wait a minute. Tony couldn't have killed Ginger, because he couldn't have shot at us. He was in the hospital dying when we were shot."

Duh. Everyone stared at me. I guess I deserved some leeway for being slow on the uptake, having just been shot at, fainted, and all.

Michael said, "The killer is not necessarily the person who shot at you. They could be two different people, or not. We don't know yet."

He went on. "From the shell casings we know what kind of gun was used in today's attack. We found a gun in Tony Moran's room, and confiscated it. It was a .22, and it was stolen three years ago. Obviously he didn't do today's shooting. It's a different gun altogether."

"What kind of weapon was used today?" Ian asked.

"A Ruger."

Before I could ask "What's a 'Ruger'?" the phone rang. Sally was closest, and answered it "Emerson residence."

A moment later she said, "Certainly, President Billings, here she is."

It was my father. I brought the cordless phone into the kitchen and sat down at the table. "Hi Dad," I tried to chirp cheerfully.

"How are you? Your mother is very upset," he quipped. I knew he meant "your mother and I are very upset" but wouldn't admit to his part.

"I'm fine. Really, I wasn't hurt. Just shaken up. And Michael Quinn just came over and told us about Tony Moran."

"Terrible, isn't it? Drugs…" and he muttered something I didn't quite catch, but could imagine, as I knew the war on drugs had been a major focus of his presidency, and his work since he left office.

"Now Peach, I want you to think back to when you arrived at the store. When you pulled up, did you notice any strange cars around, anything out of the ordinary?"

"Let's see," I pondered, glad he was asking me questions and not telling me that he had decided we had to go to a safe house, no ifs, ands, or buts.

I started. "I was surprised and pleased that there was a spot in front of the store. Well, no, wait, that's not right — there wasn't a spot at first. As we pulled up, a car pulled out."

"Do you remember what it looked like?"

"Hmm." I thought for a minute. "It was a Ford! I saw the Ford label on the back! An SUV, maybe an Escape. It was dark blue, I think."

"Thank you. That was great. Now I'm going to put your mother on. She's right here."

"Bonnie, are you all right?" came my mother's worried voice.

"Hi, Mom, I love you," I answered, and started to cry. She did too. After a moment I said, "I'm all right, really. I wasn't hurt." But we both knew I could have been killed. And they had already lost one daughter.

Our conversation went on like that for a while — me trying not to whimper, and her, anxiously mothering and cooing. If someone had shot at William I would have been hysterical. She was a mountain of calm in comparison. What a lady.

As we were saying our goodbyes Andy and Michael appeared in the kitchen doorway.

"We've got a full house in there. Dennis and Sue just arrived," said Andy.

"So I'm going to interview you right here, if that's all right." Michael pulled out a digital recorder and placed it on the table.

"Do you carry that around with you?" Andy asked.

"In the trunk. You never know," chuckled Michael.

He nodded at Andy, turned on the machine, and we began the interview. There wasn't much to tell because Michael already knew my new exciting bit of information — the dark blue Ford SUV. While I had been talking to my mother, my father had obviously called him.

What else was there to say? We reached Village Cook's block on Willow Lane, a dark blue Ford SUV parked right in front of the store pulled out, we pulled in, got out, opened the trunk, and each carried a box in, and then Terry piled up the rest by the door to carry in while I went inside and got the hand truck. I held the hand truck while Terry put the first box on it. Then the world exploded.

But we survived. With a little bit of glass in our hair, but none the worse for wear.

Andy nodded and smiled. I guess I had done all right.

"So what do you think?" I asked Michael, when I had finished. "This has been a crazy week, and I'd like to know what you think is going on."

Michael studied me for a long moment, as if he were deciding whether or not to speak his mind. Finally he did.

"I cannot rule out Tony Moran's involvement in Ginger Harrison's death. He was her boyfriend, so there was a connection. He had a job that he apparently handled quite well for the last year or so, until Ginger's death. He had an apartment. He didn't have a record. But he was an unstable ex-drug addict who kept a stolen gun in his apartment. And when someone dies, nine times out of ten the spouse is responsible. We always look at the spouse first — husband, wife, boyfriend, girlfriend — whoever."

He shook his head sadly and lowered his voice and met my eyes. "He was not a good guy, Bonnie. I'm not saying he was a bad guy, I'm saying he was troubled. Very troubled."

I nodded sadly in agreement.

Michael went on, "He could have killed her, or been with her when she died. It could have been an accident. Maybe they were hiking and had an argument and he pushed her. Maybe she fell. Maybe she was alone taking an early morning walk in the woods on a nice fall morning and tripped and fell and hit her head. It could have been as simple as that, that she was out taking a walk and fell. These are all valid possibilities."

"But it was raining. She wouldn't have been taking a walk in the rain," Andy put in.

"You said that you didn't notice if she'd been there that morning when you left for the birthday party at 11:30. It was sunny early that morning, and bright. It had been clear the day and night before. The clouds didn't kick in until 10:50 a.m. I checked."

He stopped and I saw the pain in his soft brown eyes. I had seen that same expression in my father's eyes. Frustration and sadness, the weight of the world on his shoulders, the knowledge of secrets he could never reveal. An unsolved case just had to gnaw at him.

Andy asked, "But don't the two attacks on Bonnie suggest that someone might think that she knows something, since she found the body?"

"Yes. Which leads us to think that the killer might think or know that Ginger had something on her person that Bonnie could have found, and the killer could think that Bonnie has it. Or…"

I interrupted him. "Why would I keep whatever it was? And why would I touch a dead body?"

"Perhaps Ginger was alive when the killer left, and the killer suspects that she could have said something to you, the 'last words of her dying breath.' The killer doesn't know the timeline or where you were exactly between when he or she left Ginger and when you found her. He doesn't know your movements that day."

I asked, "Do you mean the killer could suspect that Ginger told Bonnie the name of the killer?"

"It's a possibility."

I took in air. "And he could be after me to keep me from talking?"

"Happens all the time."

"All the time?" I squealed. "Good Lord."

He didn't say anything.

Andy came into the room, saw that the recorder was turned off, and looked at Michael questioningly. When he nodded, Andy sat down and joined us.

"What about Dennis?" I asked quietly, since he was in the living room. "What about the note from him that was found in Ginger's room?"

"That's certainly something we are looking at, but it's not entirely incriminating. It doesn't threaten her life. We don't know what he meant by 'Stop what you're doing. Now. Please.' Maybe she was taking drugs again, and he was pleading with her to stop. Maybe they were having an affair. I don't know the nature of their relationship. He seems to have taken on a 'big brother' role with Tony — maybe Ginger was giving drugs to Tony, and he wanted her to stop. That had been their background, you know. Tony and Ginger met in rehab in Trenton."

"I think I knew that," I said. "But I wonder what Tony was doing with prescription drugs if he's supposed to be clean."

Andy asked, "And what about Dennis' fingerprints on the pill bottle Tony overdosed with?"

"Do you have something against Dennis?" I heard myself snap at him.

"No, I'm just trying to work it out in my head. There's the note and the fingerprints. And, I don't know, hon, it just seems like he has secrets."

"We all have secrets," I admonished.

"You know what I mean. There's something a little dark or fishy there, and I always sense that Sue's protecting him, trying to make sure it doesn't come out."

"Really? I like Sue," I said.

Michael broke in. "I think Andy's trying to rationally take those two pieces of evidence and combine them with his perceptions of Dennis, and see how it adds up."

"That's right, I am."

"We do that all the time," Michael said. "But we are trained to know that evidence can be evaluated many different ways, like I just explained about the possible interpretations of Dennis' note to Ginger. These things take on power as they add up, but they are not enough. We need motive. Right now we don't have a motive for Dennis to murder Ginger, or, for that matter, Tony. We need to be absolutely sure we have a solid case before we make an arrest."

"Does that mean that Dennis is a suspect in both of their deaths?" I asked.

"He's a person of interest. He has been questioned already, and he will be questioned further. That's all I can say right now," answered Michael.

We returned to the living room. Abby and Bob had arrived. When she saw me Abby rushed over to me and gave me a hug. I could see Sue warily watching us from across the room, and tried to smile at her.

"Are you okay?" Abby cried.

"A little shaken up, a little confused, but I'll be all right."

"Jeffrey called me and told me about Tony. I was over at Bob's office. We came right over, and when we got here we heard that you were shot at?"

"I was, but I'm okay. Some glass in my hair from the broken store window. Guess whoever did it was a lousy shot."

She didn't chuckle, as I hoped she would.

"Bonnie, I'm so glad that you're all right," she whispered. She was still holding me.

I pulled away. I saw she was wearing her clogs with autumn leaves hand-painted on them. The last time I had seen her she had been wearing blue ones with angel fishes. I wanted to say "Aww, you're wearing your fall clogs. I love them!" but I knew I didn't dare. It was not the right time to discuss shoes.

So I tried to reassure her instead. "Don't worry. I've got excellent protection. Terry Ferrara, the woman from Baker Security, pushed me down and covered me, she protected me. She probably saved both of our lives. And now the Secret Service is on their way over. They'll be here soon to do an 'assessment.'"

"Assessment?"

"We may have to go to a safe house. They're going to check things out. Then there will be a meeting. Then we'll be told our fate." I enunciated the word "fate" slowly. I don't know why.

I went on. "I'm a little scared. It seems like such a drastic measure."

"Bonnie, they've already sent William away. Your tires were slashed and you were shot at. This is serious. You should be more than a 'little' scared. I'm terrified." She reached over and gave me another squeeze, then let go.

"Let's go sit down," she said. "There are a lot of people here."

"I know," I muttered.

The spot where Andy and I had sat on the couch was still open. Abby and I took it. Kay was still on the end, and Ian was near her, in one of the wing chairs. Dennis and Sue were sitting on the love seat. Sue nodded to me. I smiled back, weakly. Dennis was talking to Andy, who was in the other wing chair. Bob was over by the wall of windows looking out back to the woods, talking in a group with Charlie, Terry, Greg and Bill. When Michael Quinn walked in, the room became silent.

Except for stupid me.

I giggled. First a little, then a lot. Not too much. Not like a crazy wild woman. But enough to be inappropriate. Andy's expression mixed anger, embarrassment, and surprise.

"It's as if he's Hercule Poirot, and he has gathered all of the suspects in the drawing room," I finally got out.

Abby laughed, and so did Kay, heartily.

I could tell that Michael fought a chuckle as he said quickly, "Afraid not. But I wanted to let you know that the Secret Service people are here, and they'll be milling around. I'll introduce you when they're ready to come in. In the meantime, your cat is here. They just pulled up. O'Neill went outside to get her."

"Thanks," I said.

Steven O'Neill came in the front door a moment later carrying a cage with poor Mrs. Beeton.

Sally and I sprung up. "We'll put her in the bathroom. She's never been here before, so that will be a safe place to let her out," I said as I reached her. Mrs. Beeton glared at me. Then she hissed.

Yikes. I cringed. "Oh, Mrs. Beeton, I am so sorry," I cooed.

I took the cage. Sally went ahead into the kitchen and was opening cabinets. "What are you looking for?" I asked.

"Tuna. Do you have any?"

"Yes, here." I reached with my other hand.

She took the can out of the cabinet. Then I reached in the drawer and pulled out the can opener, and handed it to her. Mrs. Beeton was crying.

"I'll bring her into the bathroom," I said.

"I'll be in in a minute with tuna and some water."

"Right."

I brought the cage into the half bath that opened from the kitchen. I closed the toilet seat, and rested the cage on top. Sally came in and placed a bowl of water and a bowl containing some tuna on the floor under the pedestal sink.

"I'll be right back," she said. And she was, carrying the day's newspaper.

"Let's tear it up," she said, "for litter."

"Okay." So we did, and placed it on the other side of the toilet, as far away from the food as possible. Mrs. Beeton was quiet.

"Now what?" I said. "Should we take her out?"

"Never reach in and take a cat out of a cage," Sally admonished. "Especially an angry cat. No matter how much the cat loves you, at that moment, they hate you."

"So what should we do?"

"Open the cage and leave the room. Close the door. She'll jump out when she's ready. She'll be fine. She knows us, and knows this is a better situation than the one at the store presently."

So I opened the cage door and left it ajar. I peered in. Mrs. Beeton hissed at me again. "I love you, Mrs. Beeton. Please don't be mad," I said in my most loving soft voice. "Come down and have some tuna."

"Time for a treat," cooed Sally in her singsong British accent, in a tone that Mrs. Beeton had heard before. Hopefully that would comfort her, and she would smell the tuna and get the idea that she was now safe and well cared for. She didn't come out, so we left the cage open for her to go out when she was ready, and we left her there.

We went back into the living room. Terry, Charlie, Greg, and Bill were gone. Probably outside with the Secret Service people. Michael Quinn and Steven O'Neill were gone, too.

Kay and I went back to our spots on the couch. The assembled group looked up at us.

"How did it go?" Andy asked.

"Fine, except for a few hisses," I answered.

"She'll be fine, she just needs a little time," said Sally.

I changed the subject. "So, Abby, you said Jeffrey called you and told you about Tony's death?"

"He was at the restaurant. He told me that he and Miche were at the hospital when Tony died."

"When did he die?" Ian asked. "What time?"

"About one o'clock this afternoon. They were visiting," Abby said, weakly.

Dennis looked like he would choke. Sue eyed him.

"Are they coming over here?" I asked. I almost added "too" but I stopped myself.

"I don't think so. That is, it didn't come up. I didn't tell him about the, uh, incident at your store. Jeffrey said that Miche dropped him off earlier and that he was having a cocktail. He said he thought Miche was coming back later, but he didn't know for sure, and that he might go out."

"A cocktail, this early?" asked Kay.

"You don't know Jeffrey," Abby answered. "He said that he and Miche were standing there in Tony's hospital room not knowing how long they should stay, because Tony was asleep. Then suddenly there were lots of beeps and bells and nurses rushed in, doctors too, I guess. Apparently they worked on him, but it was too late. Since they weren't family, a nurse told them to go home."

"Wow," said Andy, staring.

"How sad," added Ian.

Abby continued. "So Miche brought Jeffrey back to the restaurant — apparently they had met there and she had driven them over to the hospital — and dropped him off there. It couldn't have been earlier than two, right? I got the feeling that Jeffrey had been drinking since he got back. He talked like he does when he's in that manic kind of high he gets when he's drunk but still functioning, in fact he was breathing very excitedly. Rushed."

"Hmm," said Sally. "I guess seeing one's old friend die is a good reason to get sloshed early in the day."

"In Jeffrey's world, it is," agreed Abby, sadly.

Kay said, "I wonder why Miche left him alone." She looked at Abby. "Does she know he drinks?"

"I'm sure she does."

"Hmm," said Sally again, then, "I wonder what they'll do with Tony."

Dennis spoke up. "There won't be a funeral. He didn't want one. When Ginger died he told me that. He said he wanted to leave his body to science…" he snorted, choking up. "He said they could probably learn a lot from his f#$%ed-up brain. Excuse me, ladies."

We nodded in understanding.

He went on, "Believe it or not, he had it marked on his driver's license that he wanted to be an organ donor. When Dr. Ruskin called to tell us that he was… gone, I reminded her of that, and of his wishes. She said she'd take care of it right away."

"They interviewed Dennis twice, already, once at home last night and once at the police station this morning," said Sue.

"Really?" I sounded more surprised than I was.

Dennis shifted uncomfortably in his seat, then said, "Yes, the first time was right after the overdose. They came over last night right after we got home from the hospital. We were exhausted."

"And very upset," Sue put in.

Dennis continued. "Michael Quinn and another guy, O'Neill, came over, rang the bell, and said they had some questions for us." He spluttered and coughed, and stopped to compose himself. Then he went on.

"They found a note I wrote to Ginger a long time ago, when I went to visit them once. They were both passed out when I got there, so I left them a note. I was trying to get Ginger and Tony to stop doing drugs. She had a kid, for Chrissakes!"

His eyes bulged.

"That's not all. They found my fingerprints on Tony's pill bottle. I think they thought that I tried to kill Tony!" he burst out.

Sue reached over and entwined her arm in his, bringing him closer to her.

"He dropped the pills, and I helped him pick them up. I would never hurt him. For God's sake, he was like a little brother to me. Bobby's little brother… all these years…" he broke off, into tears. He didn't try to hold back this time.

"I don't know if they believed him," said Sue. "They asked a lot of questions about the school, too."

"The school?" asked Ian.

She looked at Dennis, who nodded through his blubbering. Then she said, "Moran Academy. Bobby left some money to start a school, but it wasn't really enough, so Dennis invested it. It's been almost twenty years now, and it's done really well, despite the recent problems in the stock market. With the real estate market down Dennis was able to buy some property over by Wilmington Commons, and has applied for the licenses and variances he needs."

"Why did Bobby leave money for a school?" I asked.

"Because," Sue choked, and struggled to continue, "Tony was dyslexic. Poor Tony…" She stopped again, then said, "Bobby knew what a hard time he had in school learning to read. It really messed him up. He finally got help in high school. Bobby was impressed with the programs that helped Tony, and told us that since he wasn't married and didn't have kids that he wanted his life insurance and savings to go for a school for dyslexic children. He wanted it to be named Moran Academy, and he wanted it to start with kindergarten, so that kids wouldn't have to suffer waiting for help in high school — if then — the way Tony did. He wanted it to go from K through 8, maybe someday go all the way through high school. Before he left he put it in his will. He knew he might never come back from the Gulf, and set this all up before he left, just in case…"

Now she was crying too. Softly.

Everyone was quiet. After a few minutes Dennis pulled himself together and continued, "He knew I had an education degree, and was going for my Master's. He made me promise to start the school if anything happened to him over there. There weren't a lot of casualties in that war, and it was so short, I didn't think anything would happen to him. He had no idea how much a school would cost, or what was involved, and I went along with him just to shut him up. He just wanted to help other people if anything happened to him. I never thought I'd actually be doing this, twenty years later. But Tony seemed to be getting it together, and I thought it would motivate him to stay straight, and then the Donovan land went on sale, so it seemed like a good time. I never thought they'd both be dead… and Tony's girlfriend, too."

He was interrupted by Abby and Sally bringing in two trays, one with coffee, milk, and sugar, the other filled with mugs, followed by Kay, who had put some cookies out on a couple of plates. They set it all down on the coffee table.

Ian took a mug, and added milk and one sugar. Then he reached for a cookie, dunked it, took a big bite, and gave me an embarrassed Cheshire grin.

Dennis stared at the wall of windows that faced our backyard. He said, "They asked me where I was last weekend, and last Sunday, the day you found Ginger. I was in Philly, I told them…." He broke off, and noticed the coffee mugs, sugar, creamer and plates of cookies in front of him. He started to reach for a mug, but changed his mind. His eyes filled.

"I feel so… responsible!" he exclaimed.

Sue stood. "It's been a terrible day," she said. "I think we need to go home."

They said their goodbyes. I got up and walked them to the door. I kissed them both on the cheek, and whispered to Sue, "I'll call you tomorrow." She looked surprised but said "Okay." I don't know why I said it, or what I planned on calling for. But they were both so upset I couldn't just let it go at that.

A few minutes later Michael Quinn, Greg Baker, and a somber group of six or eight other people walked in. They were all in suits. *Must be the Secret Service*, I thought.

They approached us en masse. Michael, Greg, and two other men stood in front of the group.

Michael addressed us. "Good afternoon, everyone." He looked around. We nodded.

"All of you in this room are closely connected to Bonnie," he paused and nodded at me, "or the late Tony Moran. And you all know that shots were fired at Village Cooks, Bonnie's store, while Bonnie and Terry Ferrara, of Baker Security, were unloading boxes of books in front of the store at about 3 p.m. this afternoon. President Billings has been informed of these developments. Additional Secret Service assistance has been authorized under the circumstances."

Michael motioned to a trim, early-forties Pierce Brosnan look-alike to his right and said, "Folks, this is Special Agent Rick Harris, and he's in charge." Then he waved another man forward. Taller, a few years younger, equally handsome, but with thick black hair, premature salt and pepper at the temples creeping upward. "This is Louie Nicholas, second in command." We all nodded at them, and there were a few quiet "hellos" uttered.

Michael's arm swept over the rest of the group who were gathered behind them, and started with the three women on the left. "This is Ruth Cohen, Rachel Johnson, and Michal Ann Wilson." We nodded again. "And Adam Swift, David Jorgensen, and Ron Miller." More nods and quiet greetings all around.

"The reason we have brought this group to you is that you will be seeing these agents in your immediate surroundings for the foreseeable future. We have decided that the Emerson family will return to their normal activities."

I gasped.

"Yes, Bonnie, William will come home. Your family will not have to go to a safe house."

"Why?" asked Andy.

"Whether or not Tony Moran killed Ginger Harrison, there is still someone out there who is trying to endanger Bonnie. Today's action was evidence of that. We want the shooter, who may or may not be the killer, to believe that we think that Tony Moran killed Ginger Harrison, and that his death has ended our concern. We want him to think that we've called off the security detail, and see that we are allowing William to come home. We will be providing extremely close security that he cannot see. We want him to think that the Emerson family is operating as if it is all over. It is our hope, our expectation, that he will reveal himself. We think he will do so quickly. It's a calculated risk."

He turned to face me. "Bonnie, we want you to have Cookbooktoberfest on Saturday, as planned. We can have a private discussion about the author and her publicist and how to communicate with them about it, if need be."

"Really? We don't have to cancel?"

"There will be agents among the guests. We want all of you" — he gestured toward the group of us seated in the living room — "to remember the faces of all of us standing before you. You already know some of the folks at Baker Security." He nodded at Greg. "You also already know the people in our police force."

Michael took a deep breath, and continued in a louder, firm voice. "If you are around anyone in the Emerson family — Bonnie, Andy, or William — and see anything amiss, notice anyone suspicious, see a suspicious package, receive a phone call, overhear a conversation, or just have an odd sensation that something is off, look around. One of us is sure to be nearby."

He looked around at the group surrounding him. Then he went on. "But we don't want you to walk up to one of us and say so. We want you to use a code word. And the code word is 'red.' If you're in Village Cooks and something fishy happens and you see Rachel," he paused and nodded at her, "in the corner scanning an Italian cookbook, go over to her and say something like 'Have you seen a red pen? I dropped one here somewhere…'"

A few people chuckled. He continued. "Then, follow the agent's lead. Depending on the situation, they'll know what to say, and what they say will clue you in to what to do to get to a private location where you can tell the agent what you observed. If you are in a situation where you are able to call and report whatever it is, call me or call the police department. Not 911, call the regular number, and say you have a 'red report.' They'll connect you to someone knowledgeable who will handle it."

"Excuse me," said Kay. "What kinds of things do you think could happen? What should we look out for?"

"Be alert and follow your gut. That's the best I can tell you. It's possible that nothing will happen, that you won't see or hear anything strange. All of this is predicated on the chance that something could happen, so that you will know who we are and that we are there to protect you. We want to be prepared. Chances are good that nothing will happen, that in our close observation of the Emerson family we will find the attacker on our own, without any of you noticing anything." He smiled confidently and nodded, his remarks completed.

This meant that our family was being used as bait, I thought. I wasn't reassured at all. But I had to save face, I had to say something public to this group to show support for the plan. I had learned from my parents how to put on a public face and hide my true emotions. So I gave it a shot.

"Thank you," I broke in. "All of you. I — we — really appreciate everything you are doing for our family."

Abby reached over and squeezed my hand. I must have been believable.

Michael began walking around the room handing out business cards. "I'm handing out my card to each of you. Feel free to call as needed. My cell phone is always on."

While Michael made his way around the room, Greg spoke. "Terry Ferrara is going to be visibly off the case, because of her involvement today. She may have been spotted. Bill and Charlie will be visible, and we'll have some other people working behind the scenes, including Terry, that you won't see."

Then Special Agent Harris spoke. "Just remember, folks, if you are in sight of anyone in the Emerson family, one of us is nearby. At all times. Twenty-four seven."

Michael finished giving out his cards, and was back standing next to Rick Harris.

"Any questions?"

He looked around the room. No one spoke.

"All right then. Thank you very much," he said, and turned. The others followed him into the kitchen.

"I guess I'll call my parents and tell them the good news," said Andy.

Ian shrugged. "I hope this works," he sighed.

So did I. But I had my doubts.

Chapter 11

Childhood smells of perfume and brownies.

David Leavitt

After the crowd of security folk dispersed, and Andy had gone upstairs to call his parents, Abby said, "Anyone for more coffee?" There were quite a few takers among our bittersweet group.

"I'll help," offered Sally.

"Me too," said Kay. And off they went.

Ian pushed back in his chair, and after a deep sigh said, "This is an interesting turn of events. I'm not sure they made the right decision."

"What do you mean?" I asked. I had my doubts too.

"I'm not convinced that 'flushing out the bad guy' is the best tactic. I hope they continue to pursue other methods with equal gusto."

"I'm sure they are. And they'd have to keep close watch on us if we were in a safe house anyway. This way, they'll watch us, but we get to go on with our lives. I'm glad for that."

"I'm still concerned about your safety. Your whole family's safety." Ian's expression was somber. He clearly disagreed with the plan.

Andy came back into the room. "My parents and William are on their way. They'll be here within the hour," he said, excitedly.

Ten minutes later we had ordered pizza for dinner, and were awaiting its arrival as well as that of Paul and Carol, and most importantly, William. Sally, Ian, Abby, and Bob were still at our house, as were Greg Baker and Louie Nicholas and a few of their assorted security folks, private and federal, now working together. Andy had ordered five pies and six bottles of ginger ale. I remembered that I had brownies in the freezer, and went into the kitchen to get them out to defrost. As I put them on the counter, Sally came into the kitchen.

"Can I help?" she offered.

"I know this is not exactly a party, but I thought I'd get some brownies out of the freezer. They'll be a little cold, but in half an hour or so they should be soft enough to eat after the pizza."

"Good idea," she said, "Where are your cooling racks? If you put them on there the air underneath will help them defrost."

"Never thought of that," I said, and went to the lower cupboard where I kept them, and drew out two of the larger ones. "What a great idea."

Sally helped me open them up and lay the plastic bags of brownies out on them.

"It's the same principal as cooling, in reverse." She smiled. "Are you sure you're okay?"

"That coffee helped, and..." Before I could go on to say that William's pending arrival and the news that we could go back to life as normal had cheered me up and distracted me from the shooting, the front door burst open and I heard William's excited voice proclaim, "Mom, Dad, I'm home!"

I rushed into the living room and swooped him up in my arms. Andy quickly joined in. I found myself crying.

"What's wrong, Mom? Are you okay?"

"I'm wonderful," I stammered, "I'm so happy you're home."

"You're crying because you're happy?"

Carol came over and patted our backs. "Sometimes people cry when they're happy, honey. It's a form of release."

"Exactly," I agreed, and noticed that Andy was sniffling the tiniest bit, too. I looked over at Paul, who stood about two feet away. Like his son, he was fighting back tears.

"I know that," William said. After a moment that I wish had been longer, he stepped away and added, "Who's all here?"

"Bob and Abby, Sally and Ian, and some other folks from the security company," I answered evenly, eyeing Carol. How much had they told William? She nodded reassuringly. Then William said, "Mere and Pop told me there would be security people here. Just like Grandpa has." He lowered his voice. "Do you think they have guns?"

"Yes, I'm sure they do," answered Andy matter-of-factly, "and they are well trained. We'll introduce you."

"How long will they be around?"

"Maybe a week or two, I don't think they'll be here longer than that." Andy turned, and his expression said "Help!"

I said, "Someone was fooling around and shot the window of the store. The security people are going to keep an eye on us just to make sure nobody bothers us again, and the police are getting closer to catching them. It should be over soon."

"What about the guy who killed that lady you found outside? Did they catch him?"

"They think so," I said, stretching the truth. I hated doing so, but the situation was too complicated to explain to him.

The doorbell buzzed behind us, startling us. It was Bill Fritz from Baker Security, standing next to a teenage boy carrying a stack of five pizzas. Bill was holding the bag that I presumed held the soda.

Paul took the pizza boxes and carried them to the dining room table, while Andy paid for them. I went to the kitchen to get glasses. Bill nodded and said, "Be right back." Then he and the delivery boy left. He walked him back to his car.

"Never mind, Bonnie, they sent paper cups. And paper plates too!" called Carol.

"Okay!" I went into the living room and told the group that the pizza was here. One by one, Baker Security, Wilmington Police, and Secret Service people came in to line up and get their slices and ginger ale and take them into the dining room. Bill said, "We don't usually get fed on the job. This is a treat. Thanks."

"It's been a hard day on all of us, and it's our pleasure," replied Andy.

"There's dessert, too," I added, and Bill brightened.

After we ate I said I'd be right back and got up and started toward the kitchen.

"I'll help," offered Carol, and before I could reply, she was following me in.

"I defrosted these brownies," I said. "We just need to get them onto serving plates." I reached up into the cabinet and brought out two white platters. I set them on the table and we each took them one by one off the cooling racks and placed them on the platters.

"I wanted to talk to you," Carol started. "It's about William."

I turned quickly and faced her. "What?"

"The first few days he slept well, and acted like he always does when he visits us overnight. But the last few days I think he got homesick, and didn't sleep very well. Last night he got up and made himself a dish of ice cream in the middle of the night."

I stopped moving the brownies onto the plate. "Oh, no, I'm so sorry. I feel like the worst mother in the world."

"Oh, Bonnie, stop that. You're a great mother. I think William missed you and Andy, and being home. After a few days the novelty of being with us wore off. And I had to do some everyday things — like laundry, and grocery shopping — that I don't usually do on his shorter visits."

"Do you think he'll be all right?"

"I think he'll be fine. But he might sleep late tomorrow, glad to be home in his own bed."

"But he has school tomorrow."

"I'd let him sleep till he wakes up, take him to school late if you have to. Take it easy on him tomorrow." She finished moving the brownies off her tray. "There, we're all done," she said.

I hadn't noticed that I'd finished too. "That's a good idea," I said. "I'll do that."

We each carried a platter into the living room.

"Who wants homemade brownies?" I trilled cheerfully.

Later, after everyone (that is, everyone except the security people and Bill Fritz, who was planning to stay in the living room all night) had left, and William had allowed Andy and me to come into his room and kiss him goodnight after I lightly tucked him in, Andy and I took our showers and settled down for bed.

After Andy turned out the light, lay back, and put his arm around me, he said, "What a day. I'm glad that's over."

I snuggled into his shoulder.

"Do you think it's worth the risk, Andy?"

"There are a lot of people making sure that we'll be safe, and they have your father to answer to."

There certainly were a lot of people involved, now. The following morning I was already feeling like the walls had ears. Everywhere I went, even when accompanied by agents or security people I knew, I felt like there were more watching. And they were.

William slept an extra half hour, and I took him to school myself. The Secret Service had arranged for a "teacher-in-training" in William's homeroom who would stay with the class as they went through their day to various subjects in other classrooms. This "teacher" was one of the younger of the Secret Service agents we had met, Rachel Johnson. By the time William got there it was the middle of first period, Social Studies, and Rachel was already in class. Ruth Cohen was going to be one of the lunch ladies who served the children.

It was hardest on Andy. He didn't like the idea of having someone trail him through his day at all. And he thought he didn't need the assistance. Nevertheless, David Jorgenson was to accompany him on his assignments. He was the youngest of the agents, and with his round face and soft wispy blond hair, looked even younger. Andy was to tell people that David was an intern. Andy was used to working alone, and although I suspected he would like the company at first, I knew how focused he got when he was writing a story, and expected that someone near him — "breathing down my neck," I could hear him say — would cramp his style.

When I arrived at the store at 10:45 the guys from Wilmington Windows had just finishing installing the replacement window, and were cleaning it. I thanked them, while Michal Ann Wilson watched from the car. She had followed me to the store, and was sitting in her car, unobtrusively reading a newspaper. Mrs. Beeton would be glad she could go home soon. I'd see if the agents would allow me to go home and get her later in the day. I knew she hated being cooped up in the bathroom, but thought she was probably asleep right now.

Cheered by the newly replaced window, I rushed inside to the back office and called Royal Jefferson. I told him that the man presumed to be the killer had died of an overdose, as Michael Quinn and Rick Harris had instructed me to say. It was the truth, but not the whole truth.

"Well, that's pretty fine news, darlin'. For you, not for the dead guy. Poor soul."

"I know, it's very sad."

"Who was he?"

"Ginger Harrison's boyfriend."

"The boyfriend? You're kidding. Guess he couldn't take the guilt."

I didn't have to say we weren't sure whether or not he was the killer, did I? I chose not to. "Yeah, well…" I commiserated, then said cheerfully, "So that means we're all set for next Saturday, right?" I held my breath.

"As a matter of fact," he paused — for effect, I knew — "I never told Elizabeth about the problem. But I had to protect her just in case."

"Royal!"

"I know, I know. You can sock me in the arm when you see me!" He teased.

"You can bet on it," I teased back.

"Elizabeth's excited. This is going to be different from all of the other book signings she's ever done. There's going to be a photographer there, right? I told her there would be."

"Yes, Andy's friend Kathy Post is a photographer for the News-Journal. We always hire her to take pictures at Cookbooktoberfest. She does a wonderful job. She took the pictures that are on the Village Cooks website."

"Oh, good. I'll tell Elizabeth that."

"Great. What train will you be on?"

"The one that arrives at 12:30. Will you be there to pick us up?"

"I'm afraid I have to be at the shop. But my friend Abby Alexander will pick you up. She's a pastry chef at St. Cloud. And she can't wait to meet both of you."

"You mean Elizabeth. You don't mean me."

"You, too. I've told her all about what a charming big old Southern teddy bear you are."

"Aww."

"She loves New Orleans, and will want to talk restaurants with you. She hasn't been there since Katrina, so she'll want to know the latest."

"All right, all right. I'll wear my Southern gentleman white suit and hat, and bring my gold-tipped cane."

"You will?"

"Just wait and see."

"Okay. Listen, even though the event starts at one there will probably be some people on line in front of the store when you get here. Would you like Abby to bring you somewhere to freshen up first? My house is on the way between the train station and Village Cooks; you could stop there."

"Let's see what Elizabeth says."

"Good plan. I'll tell Abby, just in case. She has a key."

"All right, then, sweet girl, we'll see you on Saturday."

"See you then," I signed off. I didn't tell him that they were going to have a police escort. An unmarked police escort, that is.

The important thing was: they were coming. It was on! I took a breath and enjoyed the moment. Then I called Abby and told her the good news.

There were several emails about Cookbooktoberfest, including one from the local newspaper I had sent a press release to, stating that they were sending a reporter. And New Jersey Country Magazine was sending a feature writer and a photographer. Grand! It was nearly noon when I was finally able to leave the back office and go out to help Sally in front. Because of the "situation," Rick Harris had asked her to extend her hours this week, to come in at 11 and stay until 6. She cheerfully agreed, and said she always enjoyed the frisson of excitement leading up to Cookbooktoberfest, and this would give her more time to talk to customers about it. What an angel she was.

The police must have brought the boxes of cookbooks inside. They were stacked neatly in the back room. I'd have to call Tracy about the remainder, I reminded myself. Then I noticed that Michal Ann was looking at cookie sheets, comparing dark to light ones. I'd have to explain the difference to her.

But first I checked on the register area, where I found Sally talking to a man I recognized. Pete Cannavale! What was he doing at Village Cooks? For that matter, what was he doing in Wilmington? With the excitement of having the window shot out, I had forgotten about seeing him with Dennis Russo in the Donovan meadow behind Wilmington Commons yesterday. It seemed like a century ago.

"Pete," I said and could not keep the surprise out of my voice, "What are you doing here?"

"Mrs. Emerson, hello, hello," he crowed. "How are you?"

"Fine, fine. But I'm surprised to see you. I thought you had never been to Wilmington."

"I hadn't. I saw you on Sunday at the game, and then Sunday night I got a call from Dennis Russo out of the blue. I'm telling you, I was surprised at the coincidence."

He paused and looked at his feet for a moment. Then he looked me in the eye and said quietly, "He called to tell me about Tony's overdose. So I drove right up. We stayed up late talking about old times, and of course about Tony. He let me crash in their guest room but I didn't get a wink of sleep, strange place and all. I think he got a couple of hours sleep, and then, before visiting hours at the hospital, he took me out to show me where the school Bobby wanted is going to be. It was intense. Then we stopped at a florist. Dennis wanted to pick up flowers to bring to Tony. While we were there buying them Dennis got the call that Tony had passed. Jesus H. Christ. First Bobby, now Tony."

I eyed him warily. "But Dennis and Sue came over to my house yesterday afternoon."

"By that time I couldn't keep my eyes open, and Dennis brought me back to the house. Tony was dead, there was nothing I could do, and I really needed to sleep. I can't take the all-nighters the way I used to. I guess Dennis and Sue went to your place while I crashed. When I woke up, they were home, but they said they'd been out at a friend's and had just gotten back. I didn't know it was you."

All right, then.

"What are you doing here now, in my store?"

"Sue is such a sweet lady. She's a living doll. She cooked chicken parmesan last night, after all that upsetment. She said it calmed her to cook. We should have just ordered a pizza, but she wanted to do it. I offered to help, but she wouldn't let me. Chicken parm is one of my specialties." He paused and scratched his head. "Anyway I thought I'd get her a little something as a thank you, you know, and I saw these shops when I drove into town. When I saw the sign that said 'Village Cooks' I remembered you, and that you had invited me to stop in. I knew that she liked to cook, so I came in to get her something. Maybe something for myself, too."

"That's very sweet," I said. "What have you picked out?"

"Well, I happened upon the new Bobby Flay cookbook. For me."

He grinned.

"And a set of mixing bowls for Sue," said Sally. "The Pyrex ones with different colored lids."

"They'll be handy, right? Even if she already has some?" asked Pete.

"You can never have too many. They're indispensable," I said. "She'll love them, and she'll use them whenever she has leftovers or has to bring a dish in a bowl — like potato salad or cole slaw — to someone's house. It's very thoughtful of you."

"Thanks." He almost blushed.

"I'm going to go wrap them up. I'll be right back," said Sally, and she disappeared in the back.

Now, I wondered, was this a "red" moment? Should I say something for Michal Ann to hear? It was kind of suspicious that Pete Cannavale was here. On the other hand, he had a plausible explanation. And he seemed harmless enough. But what did I know? I decided to hedge my bets, and use the word "pink" so that Michal Ann could hear it.

"We have some pretty wrapping paper," I said, "It's not pink," I said loudly, "but it is feminine. Blue and white. It's what's called a toile pattern, a country scene."

He looked at me a little strangely, and said, "Okay, I'm sure she'll like it."

Michal Ann got the message, and came over. Smart cookie. She examined the measuring cups that were displayed near the counter.

"Where are you going after you leave here?" I asked Pete, so that she could hear.

"Back to Dennis and Sue's. Dennis took the day off. Even though Tony didn't want a funeral, Dennis wants to have a memorial service in a few weeks. I think he's making calls."

Then Sally came out from the back room, package in tow.

"Very nice!" said Pete. "Looks gorgeous. Thanks."

"I'm sure she'll like it."

"Thanks, ladies. It was good to see you, Mrs. Emerson. Take care. I guess I'll see you at Tony's memorial service, whenever that is. I'll come back from Philly for it."

He gestured a wave then picked up the package and walked toward the door.

Michal Ann rushed over and held the door open for him.

"Thanks, ma'am," he said, then called to us, "Bye, ladies."

Michal Ann ran her hand through her short thick black hair. Tall and athletic, she looked like a runner. She had amazing posture. "What is this about 'pink'?" she asked me. "Were you trying to tell me something?" She laughed warily. "Did you forget the color? Should I go after him?"

I chuckled. "I said 'pink' because I'm suspicious of him, but not completely sure I should be. Think of it as 'code light red.'"

"Why are you suspicious of that guy? Do you know him?"

"His name is Pete Cannavale and he's an old friend of Dennis Russo and Tony Moran."

"Yeah, I heard him telling you that Dennis Russo called him."

"I don't know, I just think you should keep an eye on him, and check him out. His story is probably true, but there may be another piece in the puzzle. I thought you guys should know about him."

"Thanks for that. I'll call it in now." She made a call, and then Ruth Cohen appeared within three minutes.

"I'm taking over for Michal Ann for a little while," she said. And Michal Ann went out to, I guessed, call it in, and have Pete Cannavale checked out.

Ruth looked around at the pots and pans, the rows of baking supplies, the knife display, and the blenders, mixers, food processors, ice cream makers, and other kitchen machines with excitement in her eyes. "I love to cook," said Ruth. "I'm only here for a few minutes while Michal Ann is out because I have to get back to the school for the lunch rush. I'm a lunch lady!" She laughed. "But I'm glad I'm here. As a matter of fact," her gray eyes crinkled, "I need to buy some new cookie pans."

"Michal Ann was looking at them before. Come on over, I'll show you what we have."

I showed her the cookie pans that we carried.

"Do you have any nonstick?" she asked.

"No, we don't. Most nonstick pans are dark, and they tend to overbrown the cookies."

"Ah, that's why that always happened." She smiled and nodded, her blond ponytail bobbing.

"We prefer shiny light brown baking sheets. The cookies brown more evenly on them. And it's always a good idea to use parchment paper. Makes the cookies the same color, and it's easier to slide them off."

"No digging with the spatula, right? No broken cookies?"

"Not with parchment paper. And if you really want to get them off easily," I reached for another pan, "try this. One end is rimless, so you can slide the parchment paper with the cookies right onto your cooling rack."

"That's fantastic. Is it expensive?"

"$9.95."

"I'll take two," she said.

"Great."

We walked over to the counter, and I started to ring up her purchase. I lowered my voice, even though there was no one else in the store. "Are you supposed to be doing this while you're on duty?"

"Not a problem. Don't worry about it. I'm a legitimate shopper, right? And I'm using my own money." She gave me her credit card.

"Okay, then," I said.

Michal Ann came back inside. The four of us were alone in the store, but she came close, and she too lowered her voice. "Pete Cannavale's got a record," she said brusquely. "Armed robbery."

"Cheese and crackers!" burst Sally.

"He was in prison for 11 years."

"Oh my God, where?" I wondered.

"Pennsylvania. He was involved in a jewelry store robbery in Wayne, a town west of Philadelphia. It happened a long time ago, in '96."

"So what happens now?" Sally asked.

"We've got people keeping an eye on him. And we're checking him out further."

The doorbell tinkled and a customer came in. Ruth left with her purchase, and Michal Ann stayed and browsed the international cookbook section.

The customer wanted cake pans in standard sizes, so it was easy for me to help her despite being distracted by the shocking news of Pete Cannavale's history. As I had explained to Ruth that dark cookie pans can brown or over-brown cookies, the same thing happens with cake pans. The darker the pan the darker the crust. Some people, believe it or not, like a dark crunchy cake crust. I'm not one of them. Neither was this customer. She had seen the Cake Boss on television, and wanted to get started baking. I sold her *The Cake Bible* by Rose Levy Berenbaum, a classic, and *The Cake Mix Doctor*, a book the purist in me didn't approve of, but the business owner in me loved, because it sold well. I had tried one of its hybrid cupcake recipes, and it worked well, so I could sell it without concern.

When the customer left I said, "Sally, I have to go in the back and do some things for Cookbooktoberfest."

"No problem. I'm fine out here." She was filling in holes in the displays of spatulas and wooden spoons from our stock in the back.

"Can I help?" asked Ruth. "I have an hour before I have to get back to the school."

"Sure. I'm packing nutmeg graters with a half-dozen nutmegs in gift bags for all of the participants. And one for Elizabeth."

"What a nice idea," she said enthusiastically, and followed me into the back room.

I opened a cabinet and brought out the supplies. A box of nutmeg graters, two bags of nutmegs, tissue paper, blue and white toile gift bags that matched our signature gift wrap but sported "Village Cooks" labels, and yellow ribbons.

I laid out the materials and we set to work. "It's a thrill for them to meet the author and participate in the contest, but I always like to surprise them with a gift," I chatted. "Actually, it's not exactly a surprise. The repeat participants know there will be a 'goody bag.' When they ask me what it's going to contain, I never tell. It's always an autumn cooking theme gift. The nutmegs are for baking apple pies."

"Or pumpkin," Ruth added with a grin. "What was last year's gift?"

"Silicon pot holders. I think they're the greatest. You can scrub them yourself or throw them in the dishwasher."

"I use them too," said Ruth.

"Do you cook a lot?"

"When I can, mostly on weekends. Sundays. This summer I tried to make perfect brownies, and tried four of five recipes before I came up with one I liked."

"Where did you get it?"

"The Barefoot Contessa."

"Aha, I should have known. Everyone loves her recipes; they don't have too many ingredients."

"True."

"She has a brownie mix you can buy, too."

"I've seen it in the grocery store. But I wanted to try making them from scratch first."

"Good for you."

After we had finished packing the goody bags, Ruth said, "Will that be enough?"

"I think so. We have twelve people signed up so far, but more always come through in the last few days. I think some people test the recipes and wait until they feel confident to register. And *Holiday Delights* has some complex, special holiday recipes. I want to make sure we have plenty."

"Do you think we could go back to my house and get Mrs. Beeton?" I asked.

Ruth looked at her watch. "I still have time. Sure, let's go check with Michal Ann."

We asked Michal Ann, who said she'd take me. Ruth would stay at the store with Sally.

When we got to the house, I was surprised that poor Mrs. Beeton jumped into the carrier.

"Sweet girl, you'll be home soon," I promised.

A few minutes later, back at Village Cooks, Mrs. Beeton leaped with fervor out of the carrier, and started racing around the store. Looking for new scents, I figured. Maybe a tiny spider in a corner somewhere. There were no customers in the store.

"How did it go?" Sally asked.

"No problem, I said, "She was happy to come, to get out of that bathroom."

"Uneventful," Michal Ann told Ruth.

"Who followed?" Ruth asked.

"Ron Miller. He'll be in soon."

Ruth went back to the school. The rest of the day was "uneventful," as Michal Ann had said. Michal Ann brought me home and dropped me off in time for William's arrival from school.

"How did it go today?" I asked him after he plopped his book bag down in the corner and came to the table for his afternoon popcorn and cider snack.

"That assistant teacher that they sent — Miss Johnson — she was great. The kids had no idea she was really Secret Service. She's really good at math, Mom. One time, she went to the board and taught us an algebra game!"

"Wow, cool."

"It was, Mom."

"So, you think this will work out having her there?"

"For a while," he said.

I hoped it wouldn't be too long.

After dinner William asked if he could have some time to play an Xbox game with two of his friends talking on the internet. While at Carol and Paul's he had begun doing so; they had played together at 7 p.m. every night for half an hour.

We don't play "against" each other, Mom, he had said, "we play 'with' each other."

"All right, all right," I agreed.

That gave Andy and me half an hour of blessed privacy to talk. I made tea, and we settled in the living room on opposite ends of the couch and compared notes. I told him about Pete Cannavale's visit.

"Did you ever get a chance to search your newspaper archive for Bobby Moran's obit?" I asked.

"I did it today." He handed me a printout. It read:

"Robert Moran (4/15/68–2/26/1991). Sgt. Robert Moran of Philadelphia died from wounds received while conducting a reconnaissance of the Iraqi border in Operation Desert Storm. He attended Temple University. He graduated from Franklin High School in 1986. He was a pitcher on the high school baseball team all four years. He served honorably for his country. He is survived by his brother, Anthony Moran of Philadelphia."

I shook my head. "That doesn't tell us much."

"It tells us they were each other's only family. I looked up their parents, too. Their father, Patrick Moran, died in September of 1979. Their mother, Florence, died in January of 1987. So six months after Bobby graduated from high school his mother died. Could explain why he didn't finish college, and signed up for the service." He paused. "It also may explain Tony's descent into drug use."

I thought for a moment.

"Hey, wait a minute. That means that Tony must have been eight when his mother died. Did he live with his brother, then?"

"I wondered that too, so I called Bob Lee and he checked it out. Tony lived with his brother from September 1987 to June of 1990. That must have been when Bobby enlisted. Tony would have been eleven or twelve."

"Where did he go then? Would Bobby have enlisted and let his brother go to a foster home?"

"This is where it gets interesting. Tony moved in with Dennis Russo's uncle Christopher. The one who just died, remember I told you?"

"Yes, I do. Go on."

"Christopher Russo was his foster parent."

"Okay, let me get this straight. It's June 1990. Tony is eleven or twelve, just ending, say, sixth grade. He has been living with his older brother, who quit college after one semester when their mother died, for two-and-a-half years. Who knows what happened during that time. Bobby must have had a job. Then he decided to enlist in the Army, and made arrangements for Christopher Russo, Dennis' uncle, to take custody of Tony to raise him as his foster son."

"That's what it looks like. It gets better."

"Really?"

"When Michael Quinn went to Philadelphia last week he learned that Christopher Russo had recently died and Dennis was handling the sale of his house."

"You told me that already."

"I didn't tell you that Dennis is the executor of his estate, and that Christopher left his estate jointly to Tony and Dennis. An equal split. And it was sizeable, four million. The guy had been a jeweler. Never married, no kids. Russo Jewelers, around the corner from his house, was, apparently, his whole life. He liquidated the business last year. Michael suspects he did so when he found out he was terminally ill. Cancer."

"Wow."

"There's more. Guess who lived next door to Christopher Russo?"

"Pete Cannavale?"

"No, he lived three doors down from Russo Jewelers. Good guess, though. Anthony and Dana Sloane, Jeffrey's parents, still live there. They're retired now. Michael interviewed them. Anthony 'likes' the horses, and Dana is a great Italian cook. She came over from Italy in 1962. Anthony is originally from Virginia. He told Michael he came to Philadelphia for a job in printing, and met Dana at an American Bandstand taping."

"Dick Clark's American Bandstand!"

"Yes, indeed. May 30, 1963. Leslie Gore sang 'It's My Party' on the show that day. They told Michael all about it."

"That's pretty cool. Now I know where Jeffrey got his love of music."

"How do you know about Jeffrey's love of music?"

"When we went to the Peacock Inn he and I sang karaoke together. He was having a ball dancing and singing."

"Oh, that's right, I remember you telling me about that."

"Did the parents tell Michael anything else interesting?"

"They said that Christopher was very religious, went to mass every Sunday. And that he always wanted children, but never met the right girl. And that taking care of Tony was too much for Bobby. He was just a kid himself, really. So they worked it out. Dana said she used to cook for Christopher and Tony sometimes; especially when Tony first moved in, she would send over food."

"Sounds like a nice lady."

"Michael said she was."

We sipped our tea in silence for a while, both of us lost in imagining a time long past in Philadelphia, and two lost brothers and the kind people who helped them.

Chapter 12

Cook-books have always intrigued and seduced me. When I was still a dilettante in the kitchen they held my attention, even the dull ones, from cover to cover, the way crime and murder stories did Gertrude Stein.

Alice B. Toklas, *The Alice B. Toklas Cook Book* (1954)

By noon on Friday, twelve more copies of the book had sold, and seventeen people had signed up to make recipes from *Holiday Delights*. Twelve women and five men. The deadline to sign up was 6 p.m. Friday, the night before the event. I had learned to allow last-minute sign-ups the hard way. The first year I held Cookbooktoberfest I closed registration on Thursday at 6 p.m., knowing that on Friday I'd be getting ready. Separately, three women came in Friday afternoon and implored me to let them be included. I had made extra gift bags (that year the gift was a piecrust shield — my inaugural cookbook had been *The All American Dessert Book* by Nancy Baggett), so I let them register. So this year I was expecting, or at least prepared for, a few more.

I had the store floors professionally cleaned on Thursday night. We had swept the floors after the window was broken, of course, but I was glad to have them cleaned to make sure every particle of glass would be gone. Today the store was open, but customers could see we were busy setting up.

When I designed the store, I had a vision of events like this, so I had six waist-high white rolling bookcases built. They "lived" in the front of the store and were constantly moved around to suit specific seasonal store displays. The tops of the bookcases always featured something new, and that something was always a combination of cookbooks, pots and pans, table linens, cooking tools, etc. Sally and I loved setting up the displays.

For Cookbooktoberfest, Sally and I moved the rolling bookshelves into back-to-back pairs, set up the three "tables" and covered them with yellow toile tablecloths. We set them up in a "T" formation, with two pairs side-by-side, and one pair down the center. I set up a table for the author and piles of the chosen cookbook against the far left wall, and put a small table with paper cups of apple cider next to the author table. October was a little late for sunflowers, but Sebastian Blooms always managed to find a large bouquet for me, which I put in a large blue ceramic vase and placed on the left side of the drink table, so that the flowers were between the author and the cider. All of this was visible from the large front window. The brand new bright and shiny front window.

Mrs. Beeton scampered around our feet and wrapped herself around our legs. With the furniture-moving excitement, she was a little jealous. I picked her up and cuddled her in my arms.

"In less than 24 hours we're going to have quite a crowd here," I told her, "so you better give yourself a good bath beforehand so you look pretty."

"I'll brush her before I leave tonight," Sally offered.

"Hear that, Mrs. Beeton? Sally is going to make sure you look especially gorgeous for the big day tomorrow," I crooned. She blinked at me and squirmed out of my arms.

The doorbell tinkled and Tracy Brown came in, carrying a box.

"Look at all of this! It's brilliant!" she cried.

"Yes, we're almost all set up," I said.

Ruth, who was seated in the big blue armchair in the corner reading *The Oxford Companion to Wine*, caught my eye, and I nodded to signal that I believed Tracy was "okay."

After I introduced Tracy to Sally, Tracy said, "I'm leaving tomorrow, and I wasn't sure whether or not I'd have time to pop by before I head to the airport. I was so upset after you called and told me what happened at the store, so you couldn't get back to pick up the rest of the books. So I thought I'd bring them over myself." She smiled. "I also wanted to say goodbye and thank you for making a good home for all of my mother's beloved cookbooks."

"You're very welcome." I was touched by her sincerity. "But I'm afraid I haven't unboxed the others yet, they're still in the back room."

"Busy with your event, I guess," Tracy said. I detected a hint of disappointment in her voice. She had probably hoped to see her mother's books on display before she left.

"That, and life in general," I said. If she only knew.

"I'll be working on them next week, and plan to do a special Thanksgiving display focusing on beloved used cookbooks as representative of tradition and remembrance."

Tracy said, "Oh, that sounds lovely. I better get the rest of the boxes. It's getting dark out there. Looks like rain."

Sally and I had been so busy that we hadn't noticed the weather.

Sally asked, "What's the forecast for tomorrow?"

I had been watching the weather reports closely. "We're due for rain tonight, but it's supposed to pass over and be clear and lovely tomorrow. I, for one, am confident we will have a magnificent sunny autumn day for Cookbooktoberfest. And for your flight," I added.

"So am I," Sally chimed, her British accent a bit more noticeable in Tracy's presence.

Seeing her books had brought home for me the connection between loved ones that used, treasured cookbooks represent. I couldn't wait to unbox them when things quieted down. After Cookbooktoberfest, after Michael Quinn and Greg Baker and Rick Harris and all of their people found and arrested Ginger's, and maybe Tony's, killer. Tracy's cookbooks could lead to the development of another branch of the business. I knew that people bought and sold used cookbooks online, and that it was a thriving business. I could do that too, but also offer them in the store, where customers could browse and see them. Maybe I'd learn about rare antiquarian cookbooks, too. Who knew?

"Sounds lovely," Tracy said. "Will you email me a picture?"

"Sure, I'd be happy to. I have your email address."

"Thanks," Tracy said, and gave me a peck on each cheek, the European way. "Stay in touch!" And she flew out the door.

"That was quick," uttered Sally.

"She's heading back to London where she runs a knitwear company. She's a knitwear designer. I think she has a show to prepare for."

"How interesting."

"I guess with all of the excitement of the shooting, and now Cookbooktoberfest, I never got a chance to tell you about the cookbooks I bought from her."

"No, you didn't. I wondered what those extra boxes were."

I grinned. "Time for a break?"

She smiled. "Past time."

Since there was no one other than Ruth in the shop, we headed to the back for a cup of coffee and some chocolate-dipped biscotti Sally had brought in.

I told her all about Mary Pettit and her interesting daughter, Tracy Brown.

"Hampstead Heath, why, that's a lovely area to have a shop. Must be high-end."

"I'd imagine."

"Next time I go over I'll look her up."

"That would be nice…. Are you planning a trip soon?"

"Ian and I are chatting about it, but haven't made specific plans yet. We're thinking we'd like to go over and show each other our old haunts."

"London is lovely in November, as I recall," I told her.

"Who knows, maybe we'll have an American Thanksgiving in Hampstead Heath," she said, dreamily. "Or Christmas."

The promised storm materialized later that afternoon. Still, Sally had one call-in and two in-person additional registrations after Ruth took me home. That made 20 in all. Plentiful. I had made 25 gift bags, more than enough. I was feeling pleased and optimistic when Ruth drove me home. The rain fell in torrents, but she drove slowly. I watched the wipers fight the sheets of rain, and prayed it would end before tomorrow.

William was happy that it was Friday. Not only did it herald the weekend, but it meant no homework. I usually let him have free time to do what he wanted on Friday afternoons if he didn't have anything scheduled. Which he didn't, today. So I stuffed a chicken with a couple of lemons and quickly cut up some potatoes and carrots, nestled them around the chicken and popped it in the oven. David Jorgensen was in the kitchen working on his laptop, his gun on the table beside him. I got in and out of there fast.

Then William and I cuddled up to watch a movie together. William couldn't get enough of "Star Wars." The whole series had recently come out on Blu-Ray, and his grandmother bought it for him for Christmas. We had seen it, as we had seen all of them, as a family together, but he still enjoyed watching them over and over. When he wasn't watching Dr. Who.

The dark ambience of the movie matched the chilly darkness outside. The wind rapped at the windows. After about an hour I took a break to go into the kitchen to check the chicken and turn the vegetables, and William came with me. He invited David to watch the movie with us, but David said he hadn't seen any of them, and if he were to do so, he'd start with the first. Good idea, we agreed. But William was incredulous. "You haven't seen any of them?" he cried.

"Not a one," said David, shaking his head while trying to not look impatient as he rubbed his hand through his unkept hair.

"If you ever want to have a Star Wars marathon to catch up, let me know," said William, eagerly.

David cocked his right index finger like he was pointing a gun. "Will do," he said.

Once we were back in the living room curled back up on the couch, sharing our favorite big old quilt, the phone rang. I looked at William.

"It's all right, Mom, answer it. I know tomorrow is Cookbooktoberfest. And we did see this in the theatre. We own the DVD. I'll keep watching, go ahead."

Impressed with my son's maturity, I answered the phone. It was Abby.

"Hi, Abs."

She said, "I just called to check in on you, see how you're doing. Tomorrow's the big day."

"It sure is. And when it's over, we have a riding date. Monday morning, okay?"

"That'll be great. We also have book group next Wednesday. Did you finish the book?"

We were reading *The Dante Club*. I had finished it three weeks ago and it was now a distant memory. Our group met once a month, and sometimes I read the book right away and nearly forgot it by the time of the next meeting. I had lobbied for bi-monthly meetings but the members of the book group wouldn't hear of it. Many of them had other evening commitments and were on town committees or attended church or temple meetings. Our group, the "Wilmington Irregulars," read mysteries. *The Dante Club* is what I'd call a literary mystery. It's about some Harvard professors who translate Dante's Inferno, and, of course, murder is involved.

"How are things at the restaurant?" I asked. "Were you able to leave on time today?"

"Yes, I did. Bob's coming over for dinner. I've got a ham in the oven."

"How are Miche and Jeffrey doing?"

"I didn't see either of them this morning. They probably came in after I left at three."

"They weren't there for lunch?" Lunch was a busy time at St. Cloud's, especially on Fridays.

"No, Donna was in charge." Donna Ballard was the most experienced waitress at the restaurant. A short, pretty blonde in her early 40s who had three school-age boys at home, Donna worked the lunch rush on Tuesdays through Fridays. She didn't suffer fools gladly, and the other waiters and waitresses respected and liked her.

"Well, I hope they're okay. Give them my condolences when you see them."

"I will. Maybe I'll see them tomorrow morning. I'm going in early, at five, so I can finish baking and be at the train station to pick up Elizabeth Crisp and Royal Jefferson at 12:30."

"I really appreciate you doing that for me, Abby. Usually Andy does it, but the agents didn't want him driving alone. And if he'd shown up with an agent, it would have been suspicious."

"Of course it's no trouble. Bob and I are just going to have to go to bed early. He called me before and said he's exhausted. He'll probably sleep in while I go to work in the morning. He loves staying at my place on weekends, says he sleeps better, isn't that sweet?" She paused and I nodded. Which of course she couldn't see through the phone. So I murmured something like "awww" and she went on, faster. "But, oh, he told me some good news. Danielle Schacht's paperwork is going through smoothly. Zoe is already staying with Danielle as her foster parent, and the adoption paperwork is down in Trenton already."

"That's wonderful. She must have a good lawyer."

"Ben Lanningan's handling it for her. Isn't it great? I think they're going to have their happy ending."

"I sure hope so. They both deserve it." We were both silent for a moment, but I could tell we were smiling in unison.

"Well listen, honey, on that happy note I better go. I want to get this laundry put away before Bob gets here."

"Thanks again for tomorrow." I started to sign off, then remembered something. "Wait a minute. Abby?"

"Yes?"

"I told Royal you have a key to my place. If they want to freshen up before they come to the store, would you mind bringing them here so they can do so? Andy always suggests it to the authors, and sometimes they take him up on it, sometimes not. It's on the way."

"Sure, not a problem. I'll make the offer."

"There will be agents outside, but they'll be in their cars, so Elizabeth and Royal will never see them. Don't worry."

"I'm not. I'm looking forward to it."

"Me too."

"Good night!"

"Get some sleep," I replied, and went back to join William.

Before we knew it, Andy was walking in the door, the day's mail in one hand. He came over and kissed me on the top of my head and ruffled William's hair. We were near the climactic end of the movie, he could tell.

"I'll go in the kitchen and read the mail," he said. "Who's in there?"

"David Jorgensen."

"Cool."

Not five minutes later, he was back. He took a deep breath and shuddered, "Is it over yet?"

"Dad, you can see that it isn't. Stop talking, please!"

Andy slumped down beside me. He leaned over and whispered in my ear, "I have to talk to you."

I nodded, and pointed at the screen, hoping he'd understand that I would talk to him after the movie was over. He nodded, and waited. It was only a few minutes.

"Awesome as usual," crowed William when the credits rolled.

Andy reached for the remote and turned off the television and DVD player. Then he said to William, "Why don't you go upstairs and work on that new Star Wars Legos ship that Grandpa got you? We'll call you when dinner is ready."

William looked at me, and I nodded in assent. So off he went.

"What's the matter?" I asked as soon as I knew William was upstairs and out of earshot.

"Come into the kitchen."

I followed a somber Andy into the kitchen. Rick Harris, Louie Nicholas, and David Jorgensen were all seated at the kitchen table. I had heard more people come into the house while we were watching the movie.

Louie was on his cell phone, and got up and walked down the hall when we came in. Rick said, "Hi, Bonnie, how are you?"

"It was a busy day, and tomorrow will be even busier, but I'm fine," I said with hesitation, looking from Rick to Andy to David. "What's going on?"

"You received some mail that we think is suspicious. It's a hand-addressed envelope without a return address." He held up a dirty, dusty envelope that bore my name and address in thick black ink from a marker. "We've dusted it for prints, and there aren't any." I noticed the fingerprint dust and brush on the table.

"Before we open it, we all have to put on masks. In case there's Anthrax or some other substance inside."

David handed each of us a mask.

"Dear Lord," I said, "I hope William stays upstairs for a while."

"I think we have a few minutes," said Andy. "But let's get to it."

After we had all quickly donned our masks I looked around my pretty kitchen table. We looked like a scene from a horror movie. Rick asked, "Do I have your permission to open the envelope?"

"Of course," I gulped.

Except for the rain pounding outside and the distant grumbling of our basement sump pump, there was silence. Rick put on white gloves. Then he carefully held up the envelope in his right hand and gripped it so hard that the muscles in his forearm rippled a little.

This is frightening, I thought, glad Andy was there. Louie came back into the room and stood across from him. He reached for a mask and put it on. He nodded to David. David nodded back, and handed Rick a metal letter opener. I took a deep breath and took Andy's hand under the table, resting our joined hands on his thigh.

Without a word, or even a sigh, Rick opened the envelope. *Nerves of steel*, I thought. Wish I had them.

He drew a single sheet of paper out of the envelope. It was a piece of lined paper from a yellow legal notepad folded in thirds. He carefully laid it on the table. Using the tip of the letter opener, he slowly unfolded the top, then the bottom.

Whew. No powder. Nothing inside. Andy and I both sighed involuntarily, but the others were still silent. Reading.

Scrawled in what looked like ink from a black Sharpie, the same as the envelope, were the words "I KNOW YOU KNOW WHAT HAPPENED." All in caps.

That's all. No signature. No "Dear Bonnie," no scribbles, doodads, smiley faces or peace signs. Just those six words. Six. Terrifying. Words.

Without a word to us, Louie turned around and left the room, his cell phone to his ear. I could hear him saying something in the hallway, but couldn't make out the words.

"Oh my God." Was that my voice? I didn't know who said it. Me? Andy? Certainly not cool, calm, and collected Rick Harris and David Jorgensen.

Andy let go of my hand and said to Rick, "What do you think it means?"

Rick frowned and said, "I think Ginger Harrison's killer sent it, and that he thinks Bonnie saw something that day. That is one of the scenarios we've been considering. Maybe he was nearby when Bonnie found her body, and thinks that Bonnie saw him."

I stared at him. "Are you serious?" I asked.

His wide-eyed, challenging expression in return told me that he was.

Louie came back, all business, as always. "I'll take it to the lab," he said sternly.

Rick opened a black briefcase that I hadn't noticed on the end of the table, and put the letter inside. We were all still wearing masks. "Let's take the masks off now," he said.

After we did, he piled them up and nested them in a large zip-lock plastic bag which he then put inside the briefcase. Then he put the letter opener in a small Zip-Lock plastic bag, and placed that in the briefcase too. He clicked it closed and handed it to Louie.

A minute later Louie, the letter, the envelope, the opener and our masks were gone.

"The lab?" Andy asked, breaking the silence while the packing up was going on. "Where's that?"

Louie looked at Andy and said evenly, "Newark," then turned to Rick and said, "I called Quinn and Baker."

"Good," replied Rick.

"What happens now?" Andy asked Rick.

"Now we keep going about our business. Our plan is working; he's starting to reveal himself. We haven't drawn him out completely yet, but we're getting there. Frankly, I was hoping his next move would be to call you."

I shuddered. "I'm glad he didn't."

We heard footsteps on the stairs, and a few seconds later William had bounded into the room. "Is dinner ready yet?" He looked around at us. "What's going on?"

"We're just talking about tomorrow," I lied, and went over to check the timer. The chicken would be ready in two minutes.

"William, please set the table."

"No prob, Mom. Are they having dinner with us?" He nodded toward the agents. "No, not tonight," said Rick, "but thanks for the offer."

William smiled and went to the drawer, found three sets of silverware, grabbed three napkins from the basket, and set them down at the kitchen table.

"Water, too, please," I said. By now I was getting the chicken out of the oven.

Andy, Rick, and David got up from their seats and went into the living room, Andy hollering "Be right back" over his shoulder.

When he came back his expression was grim, but he was going to try to hide it from William, I knew. I would try to be cheerful too, for William's sake. And patient, although that was not one of my virtues. I sure hoped the power wouldn't go out, someone wouldn't try to break in or shoot us through one of the windows, or call and frighten us. It was, after all, a dark and stormy night.

My imagination was going full speed, and conjured a few other equally terrible events that could happen. Lord, I thought, let us make it through to tomorrow, and get through Cookbooktoberfest with everyone unharmed and happy.

I carved the chicken and listened to my husband and son's banter after William said, "So, Dad, how was work today?"

I don't know if it was the sound of the heavy rain slamming the windows and the ground outside, or my anxiety about Cookbooktoberfest, but I barely slept. Andy, William, and I played a game of Monopoly after dinner, and turned in a little early. I felt like a child the night before school started. As I lay in bed looking up and out the window, I thought I saw movement in the tree limbs that swayed with the storm. Oh, would morning ever come?

It finally did, and safely, without any more incidents. The sun rose in a bright clear crisp sky. The grass would be wet for a while, but at least the sun was shining and the rain had stopped. The plan was for Andy (and whatever agent was guarding him) to bring William to his friend Alex's at noon, where he would spend the afternoon. The agents didn't want him to be at Cookbooktoberfest. They felt they'd have enough to do watching me. And Andy, of course. William had been crushed when we first told him. He had been to every Cookbooktoberfest since the first. Then Rick Harris offered to take him to a shooting range and show him how to shoot, and that — almost — made up for it. I had looked over at Andy in alarm, and he had quickly said he'd go with them, so I kept quiet in agreement. Alex had gotten a new XBox game for his birthday, and they were planning on spending the afternoon breaking it in. By the time Saturday morning dawned, William was comfortable with the arrangement. My boy was growing up.

When I got out of bed (I guess I had finally fallen asleep at some point, and Andy let me sleep in), Andy was already up, showered, dressed, and downstairs. I could hear his voice, William's, and two others I couldn't immediately identify. I quickly showered and dressed in a pumpkin skirt with gold ribbon swirl appliqué embellishments and a pumpkin sweater set that matched the orange in the skirt. I put on textured stockings and my tan one-inch pumps with pointy toes. I brushed and combed my hair and decided to wear it loose, but wondered if I'd be too hot. I stuck a hair clip in my skirt pocket just in case I would need it later. I put on small diamond earrings that my parents had given me when I got married. I added my gold locket that held a picture of Andy as a boy on one side, and William as a baby on the other. I wanted to look nice on this special day. At the store I'd be wearing my blue and yellow Village Cooks apron, as usual.

As I walked down the stairs I repeated my morning mantra to myself "Everything's going to go beautifully. It's going to be a perfect day." Rachel Johnson was in the kitchen, wearing jeans and a navy blue turtleneck. Louie Nicholas was there, too, dressed casually in khakis and a red cotton button-down shirt with a small Polo symbol on the left side.

Andy was eating a bowl of Cheerios and William was devouring a blueberry muffin and a container of strawberry yogurt. Not a bad breakfast, I thought. That'll work. I was always amazed when they managed to feed themselves breakfast without me, because when I was there they seemed utterly dependent on my serving them. Not so today. William was chattering cheerfully to Rachel about school and his latest math test, on which he had gotten a B.

"Good morning, everyone!" I said as cheerfully as I could muster.

"Hi, Mom, are you nervous?" asked William.

Andy chuckled.

"Not at all, honey, I'm enthusiastic!" More chuckles, this time from Rachel and Louie, too.

The phone rang. I answered it.

"Hi, Sally."

"How are you this morning, dear? I know we're opening at 1 today for Cookbooktoberfest. Do you need me to go over to the store early?"

"Everything's fine. Thanks for asking. I think if we meet there at 12:30 we'll have plenty of time to pour the cider. There's nothing else to do, other than put on our aprons." I laughed, and so did she.

"And keep the throngs away," I added. Although 20 people were signed up and had been told not to bring their food till 1 p.m., sometimes there were people outside waiting when we opened the store for Cookbooktoberfest.

She laughed, and we signed off. We were all set. Everything was going to be fine.

But I had three more hours of morning to get through until then, and I didn't have the faintest idea what I was going to do.

"What time am I going to Alex's?" William asked after I hung up the phone.

"Not till noon."

"Can I go over to Max's house this morning, first? He called before, and guess what, Mom? Their cat had kittens while I was away. Can I go over and see them, please?"

I looked at Andy, who looked at Louie and Rachel for assurance. They nodded and Rachel said, "Your parents will have to go with you, and we'll be outside."

"Can we, Dad?" Ah, he was asking his father this time. I hadn't answered.

Andy reached out and put his arm around William's neck playfully. "Sure, let's. How many kittens are there?"

"Five. I can't wait to see them! They're so young, their eyes are still closed!"

"Call Max and tell them we'll be over in half an hour."

"Cool, thanks!" he cried and was off.

I got a hard-boiled egg out of the refrigerator, some coffee from the pot Andy had made, Vanilla Silk from the fridge, a muffin from the counter and sat down at the table. I always liked to start my day with some protein.

With William gone, the room was silent. Andy sipped his coffee and read the paper. I grabbed a section, and read as I ate. Rachel and Louie sat opposite us, both working the text functions of their iPhones.

Twenty-five minutes later, William, Andy, and I walked down the block the distance of four houses to the Barretts. Louie and Rachel sat in a car outside our house, and there was already a car parked in front of the Barretts with God knows who inside.

My stomach jumped as I retraced our steps of that fateful day. I hadn't walked on our road since then. Today was sunny and crisp enough to wear a sweater or light jacket; that Sunday it had rained buckets. Just like last night. That day we had innocently walked to and from Max's birthday party, without a care in the world. Today Andy and I wore the knowledge that our lives were in danger. And might never be the same. Maybe the note didn't mean that the killer was getting closer to showing himself; maybe there'd be more notes. And phone calls in the middle of the night. Maybe he'd continue to harass our family *ad infinitum*. Just because Rick Harris said the killer was getting braver didn't necessarily mean it was so. He was working from a profile, but killers didn't always fit the profile. I had watched enough "Law & Order" episodes to know that.

The kittens sure were precious little munchkins. Jack and Dianne had portioned off a corner of the living room with a file cabinet and an old baby gate. Behind this barrier the mother sat curled up in a wicker dog's bed with a green plaid flannel pillow. Her tiger fur was matted in spots where the kittens had licked her. There was a large bath towel surrounding the dog's bed.

Dianne told William, "You may not reach inside. They don't know you yet, and will be frightened. And, remember, they can't see yet. But they can feel you. Stand there, and I will get one of the kittens and give it to you to hold. Which one do you want?"

"That one!" William pointed at a calico kitten with a white belly. The kitten was licking his foot.

"I like him, too," said Max eagerly.

Dianne slowly moved to reach inside and carefully pulled out the calico kitten by the scruff of the back of her neck. There was a hushed silence, broken by the soft "Mew" of the kitten as Dianne lifted her up.

William held out his arms and Dianne dropped the squirming ball of fur into them. The kitten immediately settled down, lay on her back like a baby, showing her white tummy.

"Look, Mom, Dad, I know she can't see me yet, but I think she likes me!"

"Or he," Jack said.

"I think it's a girl. Hello, little girl," William cooed.

"Mom, Dad, look at her little face!"

The kitten quietly lay back in his arms. Then she leaned over a little bit, rested her chin on his arm, and seemed to go to sleep.

Max said, "Look, William, she's sleeping."

She was.

"She just finished nursing and now she's ready for her nap," explained Dianne.

As soon as she said the word "nap" the mother cat meowed and startled everyone. We all laughed.

"Guess Mother knows best," said Jack, grinning.

The kitten stayed like that for another moment, then squirmed. Dianne reached over and silently took her — or him — from William, who nodded, hushed. Dianne put the kitten down next to her mother, where she snuggled under the curve of one of her front legs.

"What are you going to do with the kittens?" William asked her.

"Three of them already have homes spoken for, but the other two — including the one you held — don't have homes yet. We'll see what happens with them."

William looked at me, then Andy, with that expectant look of hope we had come to know. Andy spoke, so I didn't have to, thank God. "We'll talk about it, sport."

"Really?"

"But not now."

"If you're interested, let us know by the end of the week," Dianne said, grinning.

"We will. Thanks," I said, turning to go.

"Bye, kittens!" called William. He knew better than to push his luck, and was on his best behavior. "Thank you, Mr. and Mrs. Barrett. Bye, Max!"

"I'll see you later. I didn't make anything, but I'm going to drop by Cookbooktoberfest," said Dianne.

"Great, see you then!"

We walked back to our house, the car still guarding out front. It was only four houses down, but there was land between the houses, so it was about a quarter of a mile from the Barretts' house to our house.

We walked in silence. William was thinking about whether or not we would let him have a kitten, and Andy was probably trying to think of a good way to say No. I felt guilty that I had forgotten my cell phone. What if Elizabeth and Royal's train was delayed? What if Abby called? I was losing it.

I was distracted from my reverie by the sight and sound of a car going by. It was slowing down as it got to our house. I looked up, but then something caught my eye over in the woods, by the stream, where I had found Ginger.

The yellow crime scene tape was gone. What had I seen? I looked around, trying not to be too obvious. Then I saw it. A branch hung from a tree a few feet back from the stream. It hung in a funny unnatural way, like an arm bent at the elbow. Something must have knocked into it with some power to bend the branch like that. What could it have been?

Once again I was distracted from my reverie, but it was by Andy's voice this time.

"Come on, Bonnie, let's go inside. It's almost time for William to go to Alex's. I'm going to drive him over, then I'll meet you at the store."

"Who's going with you?"

"Adam Swift."

"I like him."

"Me too. He's funny, but on the ball."

"Let's have a quick lunch first. We have a few minutes."

I went into the kitchen and found some frozen quesadillas in the freezer. That would do. We'd be having lots of good stuff at the store, but I wanted to quell my jumpy stomach and make sure that William was properly fed before he went to Alex's.

I put three of them into the toaster oven. While they were heating I dug out some Mexican chips from the pantry, and some salsa and sour cream from the refrigerator. Also some guacamole, but I had to spoon off some of the brown stuff to the good green underneath.

Ten minutes later, we ate at the kitchen table. Miraculously, my phone didn't ring. It felt like the calm before the storm. Like so many weekend afternoon quick lunches we'd had before on busy days. But for me, this was the busiest day of the year.

Twenty minutes later Andy, William, and Adam were on their way to Alex's house on the other side of town. I had cleaned up the dishes, so I went into the bathroom and brushed my teeth and combed my hair. I looked in the mirror and tried to project a look of confidence, and of cheer. Truth was, my heart just wasn't in it this year. I was too worried about Ginger and maybe Tony's killer coming after us.

"I KNOW YOU KNOW WHAT HAPPENED."

It was like a mantra rhythmically repeating in my brain. I didn't know what happened. Did I? Was the broken tree limb a clue? I wouldn't be able to go out there and look around today, that was for sure. And the police had combed the area carefully, and hadn't told us of anything they'd found. Maybe the limb had broken before Ginger was killed. I wouldn't have noticed it one way or the other. Or it could have broken last night, during the storm. Now, I had no way of knowing whether it was significant or not. Now I had to focus on being charming and keeping things running smoothly at Cookbooktoberfest. I took a breath, smiled at myself in the mirror, and went out and told Rachel I was ready to go.

Chapter 13

The store was quiet when Rachel and I got there. Abby hadn't called, so I assumed all was going well picking up Elizabeth and Royal from the train station. I unlocked the door to Village Cooks, and walked to the back to turn off the alarm. Rachel walked off, and was checking every aisle.

Mrs. Beeton waddled up to me and rubbed up against me.

"Your feeding time is a little late today, isn't it?" I said.

I went in back and set out fresh food and water for Mrs. Beeton.

"Today's the big day!" I told her.

Then the doorbell jingled and a woman I recognized as Elizabeth Crisp and a handsome gentleman in a salt and pepper beard and neatly trimmed but longish silver hair ambled in, followed by Abby, and the photographer, Kathy Post, with her camera bag in tow. Royal, true to his word, was wearing a white suit and a deep orange tie, and he carried a walking stick. I could tell that the suit was fine quality by its cut, and imagined that it was probably a lovely gabardine wool. A tall, gangly man, he carried himself with fine Southern posture and displayed true masculine elegance.

Elizabeth was equally — no, more — magnificent. Her wavy auburn hair shimmered around her shoulders, her thick eyebrows accent marks over deep-set almond eyes. Her pale skin glowed as it never did on television. She looked like a porcelain doll come to life. Famous people, in my experience, were usually shorter than expected when you met them in "real life." Elizabeth was tall, statuesque, lovely in a chocolate brown knit sweater dress with long bell sleeves. She had a black, brown and white hounds-tooth knitted wrap draped around her shoulders and then thrown over her left, with plenty hanging down behind her back. She wore brown tights and brown suede boots that came almost to her knees.

"Lovely to meet you!" she greeted me warmly while Royal silently grinned behind her.

I reached out and shook her hand. "Welcome!" I beamed. "Thank you so much for coming."

"Bonnie invented Cookbooktoberfest, you know," said Royal. I reached out and hugged him. He responded the best he could while holding his cane. I gathered that he needed it, it wasn't just for effect, so I backed away, but not before he had warmly patted my back and kissed my cheek.

"Good to meet you, girl," he said. "You're younger and prettier than I expected. Over the phone you sound like an old biddie!"

I was stunned. "What?"

"Just kidding, just kidding."

Elizabeth broke in. "I love your store! Especially all of the cookbooks!"

"Thanks," I replied. "What are your favorites? Where do you get your inspiration?"

"You'll laugh if I tell you," she chuckled.

"What do you mean?" I leaned closer to her, sensing a wonderful secret about to be revealed.

"I read old cookbooks. I collect them. Especially from the 1800's, when a lot of them were really about household management, you know, the whole home — cleaning, organizing, sewing — not just cooking. Some of them are very funny. I've modernized some of the recipes for my books."

"That is very interesting," I said, thinking of the enlarged section of used cookbooks I was planning. "Tell me more, I'm captivated."

"Well there's one that I love that has a wonderful title. It's called *The Cook Not Mad.* Isn't that great? I might steal that title one day. It was published in the early eighteen hundreds, by 'Anonymous.'"

"Ah, that prolific author, 'Anonymous,'" Royal teased.

"Back then women authors were not accepted in society the way they are today, so many of them published anonymously," Elizabeth said.

I nodded and put in, "Some published under a first initial too, I've noticed."

Rachel appeared and joined our little group. "Even today they do that," she smiled graciously at Royal and Elizabeth and added, "Look at J.K. Rowling."

I introduced them to Rachel, and told them, "She's a friend who's helping out for the day." They nodded, no questions. So far so good.

I could tell Elizabeth was still excited about *The Cook Not Mad*. She continued, "There's a recipe in there that is one of the earliest known in American cookbooks, and it comes from a sea captain named Captain Riley. Isn't that just delicious!"

As we laughed at that and I was about to tell her about Mrs. Beeton, because I was sure she would know all about our cat's namesake, Kathy Post joined us. She had already stashed her bag behind the counter and her camera was in her hand. I made more introductions.

Elizabeth was lovely and delightful and Royal was a charming gentleman. I felt lucky to have met them. I was starting to breathe. Kathy got busy directing them to pose near the sunflowers.

Elizabeth continued the conversation. "I love the names of some of the old recipes, especially the British ones. Everyone's heard of 'spotted dick' today but many people don't know about 'Roly-Poly,' for instance."

"Elizabeth is well-known for the fanciful names of her recipes." Royal put in.

"I know. I love them —" I started, but the doorbell jingled and Sally rushed in, followed by an ambling Andy, and then Adam.

"Elizabeth Crisp, what an honor!" Sally exclaimed. She rushed up to Elizabeth and grasped both of her hands in hers. "I've been so looking forward to meeting you!" she chirped. And they descended into British chatter like two old best friends.

Andy gave me a kiss and whispered, "How's it going?"

"So far so good," I replied, and then noticed that Royal was standing there looking a little lost. I introduced him to Andy and Adam ("a family friend," I told him), then motioned Royal over to the book table that Sally and I had set up yesterday. Forty copies of Elizabeth's book, *Holiday Delights*, were stacked in piles of ten. Another twenty were in the back room, just in case we needed more.

"Here's where Elizabeth will sit. Would you like a chair next to hers?"

"I'd like to wander around, if I may."

"Sounds good. She'll probably end up doing that for most of the time, too. Most authors only sit at the table to sign books at the end."

Rachel brought out two gallons of cider from the back room. "Time to pour the cider?"

I looked at my watch. It was eight minutes to one. Yikes. "Yes, ma'am!" I crooned.

"I'll supervise," said Royal, and sat down in the author's chair.

Andy chuckled.

Then the feature writer and photographer from New Jersey Country Magazine arrived.

"Make yourselves at home," I told them, and they wandered over to meet Elizabeth.

I laid out paper cups while Rachel poured. We worked in rhythm. Through the window I noticed a line of people outside. Some were holding insulated food bags; a few held disposable aluminum pans in their arms, covered with tin foil. I smiled out at them. Elizabeth and Sally were over in the pots and pans section, and it sounded like they were laughing about baking parchment paper. I couldn't imagine what could be funny about parchment paper, but I didn't have time to find out.

Rachel finished pouring and I fluttered around the table. Just as I was wiping a few stray sunflower petals off the tablecloth, Sally and Elizabeth came over to join us. "I think it's time!" said Sally.

"Indeed it is."

I nodded, and Elizabeth sat down behind the table. Royal stood behind her. A regal pair.

I looked around. Sally and Rachel stood on each side of me, the three of us a cheerful trio in our blue Village Cooks aprons. I cocked my head to Elizabeth and Royal, Andy and Kathy. I smiled at Sally and Rachel, took a deep breath, clutched my clipboard and pen to my chest, and opened the door.

Twenty people had signed up to bring dishes, but there were at least thirty people outside. There were always some nonparticipants who came to join in the fun. I saw Ian walk across the street from his parking spot and join the line at the end.

"Welcome to Cookbooktoberfest!" I exclaimed to the crowd, and Sally repeated my words in her lovely accent.

I stationed myself by the door and checked each contest participant off the list, and gave them a pre-printed name tag which listed their name and their dish. Sally went around and showed them where to place their dishes on the T-shaped tables.

Sue Russo came in, alone — where was Dennis? — bearing Apple Crumble in an aluminum pan. "I made it three times!" she said, then stopped, mouth open, when she saw Elizabeth.

"Oh!" she called, and rushed over to meet Elizabeth. By now Elizabeth was out from behind the table, ooing and aahing over the dishes as they were laid out.

Royal was right. Her book included recipes with some of the most wonderful names I'd ever seen, and our customers had made quite a few of them. Ella Scott, from Willow Lane Inn, had made "Lovely Buns." Zuzu Rubin, from Zuzu's Travels, had made "Yes it's Bunny," a rabbit curry.

"Where did you get the rabbit?" Sue asked her.

"From the far ends of the earth." Zuzu grinned devilishly and waved her black fingernails and large silver cuff bracelets on each arm. Her hair was cut in a short Buster Brown bob with a red streak in the bangs over her left eye, and today she was all in black — a turtleneck and black pants, with a large silver mesh belt wrapped around her slender hips. I suspected that some people felt that Zuzu (real name "Sue") Rubin was a bit too exotic for our part of New Jersey. But it was New Jersey, after all, and only an hour from Manhattan. And I liked her. She was single and I found her, like Abby, to be a breath of fresh air among the soccer moms. Of which I was one.

"How are you doing, dear?" Kay gave me a peck on the cheek as she came in to the store.

"So far so good," I whispered. "I'm glad you're here."

"I closed up my shop for two hours, like I always do, for Cookbooktoberfest." She raised her arm and waved it around, as if to encompass the whole crowd.

Ian was right behind her. "You don't have to make a dish to vote in the contest, do you?" he asked heartily. "Can you merely 'eat'?"

"No, you don't have to bring a dish. Everyone who wants to can try the dishes and vote. Of course if you eat, you have to vote." I laughed.

"Whew!" He wiped his forehead in feigned relief.

Others came in bearing "Beef Maharaja," "Pink Avalanche," "Cha Cha Turkey," "Custard Hearts," and "Santa Pie."

I leaned down and pecked Zoe's cheek when she came in with Danielle, their arms loaded with covered pans. "Well, hello there, honey," I cooed. I nodded hello to Danielle. I knew what they had brought, because it was on my list, but I asked anyway. "What did you make for Cookbooktoberfest?"

"Turkey with gingerbread stuffing!"

"Yum."

Danielle said, "It turned out so well that we're going to make it again for Thanksgiving, aren't we, honey?"

Zoe beamed. "Then we'll make mashed potatoes and green beans too. But not today. It was enough making all of this."

I chuckled.

Sally came over, gave Danielle's arm a squeeze and asked Zoe, "Would you like to meet Elizabeth Crisp?"

"Me?"

"Sure, come with me. Let's put your food down over there near her."

She led her over to a corner of the table, where they laid down a large pan containing the turkey and a smaller one that held the stuffing. Danielle followed.

After Sally introduced them, Elizabeth said, "Can I see?"

Zoe looked at Danielle, who nodded approval. Then Elizabeth carefully lifted up the tinfoil from the golden turkey and exclaimed, "It's absolutely brilliant!"

Zoe beamed.

Then Danielle unveiled the gingerbread stuffing on its red ceramic platter and placed it next to the turkey.

Royal came over and grandly piped in, "May I carve the turkey?"

"Why, sure," agreed Danielle, a bit confused until Sally said, "Dr. Danielle Schacht, this is Royal Jefferson, Elizabeth's publicist."

"Lovely to meet you."

"Likewise."

Abigail Frost from Abigail's English Tea Room came bearing "Abundant Mince Pies."

"I've been making mince pies for thirty years, so these better be good," she told me as I checked her name off the list. "Her recipe is very close to my own."

"But you made Elizabeth's version?"

"Of course," she snipped.

She was nearly pushed aside by the person behind her, Jim Leonard, co-owned Wilmington Books with his partner, Evan Powers. Together they were carrying a large tray. I quickly checked the list. "Jim Leonard, Evan Powers. 'Roast Goose in Splendor.'" As usual, Jim's curtain of straight chestnut brown hair fell in his eyes, and since his hands were full, he could not tuck it behind his ear.

Sally was there in a flash. "Over here," she motioned to a large open space at the end of the table.

When Jim removed the foil from the top of the goose, nearly everyone in the shop let out a collective "wow." The poor goose, legs splayed, surrounded by a circle of apples, lay face down but head-less, on a white ceramic platter.

Kathy Post took a picture of it, as she had been doing of each entry. When she was done, Jim asked, "Okay to carve now?" and she said he could. I didn't envy him that job. Royal had almost finished carving Danielle and Zoe's turkey, with Zoe's assistance placing every piece "just so" on the platter.

A moment later Jeffrey and Miche came into the store. Miche kissed me on both cheeks, but Jeffrey merely muttered "Hello." I shot Miche an inquisitive look, and she nodded her head. He looked fine, I thought, but as he passed I smelled alcohol. Uh-oh.

"We came to meet Elizabeth Crisp," Miche said cheerily. "Wow, she's beautiful," she added quietly, after she saw her. Elizabeth was sipping cider and talking to Abigail and Sally, the other Brits in the store. Miche and Jeffrey made their way over to join them.

Soon it would be time to begin judging the recipes.

The idea of *Holiday Delights* was that it included everyday recipes that would make each day seem special, like a holiday. There were the expected chapters on holidays throughout the year, plus some extra chapters that were meant to, well, delight, such as a chapter on whipped cream, one on pies, and one on chocolate cakes. Andy had teased me that I selected this cookbook for Cookbooktoberfest because it had a whole chapter on chocolate cakes, and he wasn't far off. That was certainly a draw, but I loved the cheerful celebratory nature of the book, and to me it represented home and hearth the way only the best cookbooks could. I tried not to show favoritism, or drool, when Lisa Rounds from Vintage Ladybug came in bearing Elizabeth's "Old World Chocolate Cake" and Steve Schramm and his wife Molly (from Schramm's Hardware & Furniture Restoration) brought "Casbah Cake," which was a chocolate and cinnamon cake. One of them would probably get my vote.

The store was filling up, and by the time I had checked off 18 of the 20 dishes, it was starting to get loud. I signaled to Rachel.

"Would you mind going in back and turning up the air conditioner? It's going to get hot in here if one more person walks in."

"Sure, no problem." She smiled. "Thank God you know everyone who's come in so far."

I nodded. "I would have signaled to you if not."

There were quite a few other Secret Service agents in the store, but no one from the police department. They would have been recognized too easily. I had suggested that Michael Quinn come as a civilian just so that he could try some of the recipes, but he had politely declined. That guy needed to loosen up. He was across the street watching from a window above A House in Provence. He had people in other local shops so that they would be close by if needed. Baker Security was out in full force too. Terry was down the block "shopping" in Sunset Shoes. I didn't know exactly where Charlie and Greg were, but I knew they weren't far. Maybe they were in the empty store across the street. Probably a good place to set up surveillance. Because Cookbook-toberfest was a public event, none of our protectors — Baker Security; the Wilmington, New Jersey, police force; or the United States Secret Service — were taking any chances.

The final two submissions arrived, and Sally helped Karen O'Keefe ("More than Muffins") and Maggie Murphy from Maggie's Irish Imports ("Heaven's Cream Pie") find room on the table. Kathy quickly snapped pictures of them, then gave me a thumbs up. Her signal meant that all 20 dishes had been photographed.

Now we could start. I nodded to Sally. She went over and told Elizabeth and Royal that we were ready. I watched while Elizabeth took her seat, then Sally and I got in position with our backs to the front door.

"Ladies and gentlemen," I called out. Then again, louder, "Ladies and gentlemen."

People stopped talking and looked at me expectantly. Excitement sizzled in the room.

"Welcome to our seventh annual Cookbooktoberfest. Thank you for joining us."

I paused, and there were a few murmurs of appreciation. I looked around the shop. About 40 sets of expectant eyes met mine. In this uncertain world, it was satisfying to know that I, and my crazy invention, Cookbooktoberfest, could bring a respite of homey comfort to at least a small group of people, for one crisp autumn afternoon in Wilmington, New Jersey, each October.

"This year I chose one of my all-time favorite cookbooks, *Holiday Delights*, and we are honored to have its author, Elizabeth Crisp, here with us today, to break bread — and also chocolate cake — with us."

The crowd turned toward her, and applauded. She stood, and bowed graciously. I went on, "Elizabeth is accompanied by her publicist, Royal Jefferson." Royal stood up and bowed grandly.

"*Holiday Delights* is Elizabeth's fifth cookbook. I am glad I waited till this one was published to choose one of her books, although I was tempted by *How to be a Kitchen Queen*, but I knew those shoes were too big for us to try to fill."

A few chuckles here and there punctuated the air.

I looked at Andy, and was encouraged by his gentle smile.

"I am glad I waited because *Holiday Delights* is a book that celebrates tradition, and for me, whether it be a daily ritual of egg-in-a-hole cooked perfectly in a copper pan every morning, or coffee beans ground and brewed in a Cuisinart — whether it be Hannukah latkes, Christmas cookies, or my son's favorite chocolate cake made for his birthday each year — tradition is where we celebrate our connection and love for one another, and the recipes in *Holiday Delights* enable us to do just that."

I went on. "That's the emotional reason I chose this book. I also chose it because I absolutely love the names of so many of the recipes." A few more laughs, Royal's the loudest.

"As those of you who have been here before know, at this time I always read the names of the recipes and their maker aloud. But you have never before heard names the likes of 'Hot Cream Bath.' Or 'Potato not

Poison.' Or my favorite name, 'Apples in Warm Sweaters.' You folks have selected some great ones, but I can assure you, there are more in the book."

"How about 'Bucharest Baklava,'" Jim Leonard called out. "I made that last weekend." He paused, and added, "It didn't turn out too well."

Everyone laughed — with him, not at him. These were home cooks who understood all too well.

"There are so many terrific recipes in this book, and Elizabeth's introductions to each one are wonderful bonuses," I continued, then looked down at my clipboard. "Here are the ones entered in today's contest." I read the names of the recipes and the contestants.

What a nice group of people in our town. As I read each name, I could see from the corner of my eye that others would nod and smile at the person named. It was a competition, but a friendly one.

When I finished with the list, I went over the rules. They had been given to each participant when they registered, but I went over them anyway, since there were quite a few guests.

"Now we'll go around and everyone will have the opportunity to fill their plates and try some of each dish. Afterward you can use your ballots to vote. Does anyone need a ballot?" Silence. "Okay, great. The ballots go in this box." I pointed to an antique recipe box with a hinged lid that my mother had given me.

"There is enough for each person here to try a bit of each dish, but you may have to go back for a second plateful in order to sample every dish. We encourage that!" I exclaimed to more laughter.

Now it was time. "Enjoy!" I said, feeling as if I had called the beginning of a horse race. People managed to get in line to get their sturdy paper plates and plastic ware, then make their way around the "T" and fit a bit of each dish on their plate.

We had set up a dozen folding chairs around the shop wherever there was an open spot, and people gathered in small clusters around the lucky one who got a seat. As I did each year at Cookbooktoberfest, I filled my plate, then brought my plate to the back room to devour quickly. I didn't want the participants to see me react to their dishes, and I always found that I needed a few moments to decompress. Not meaning to be partial to sweet Zoe, and to Danielle, I knew that I would vote for her "Turkey with Gingerbread Stuffing." The turkey was very good, but it was turkey. It didn't have a crazy name like others in the cookbook, but the gingerbread stuffing was divine. I filled out my ballot.

I finished up, tossed my plate, silverware, and napkin in the trash, and placed my ballot in the ballot box. Then I found myself in the cooking tools section where Miche and Jeffrey were talking to Jim and to Evan, who was sitting in a folding chair balancing his plate on his lap.

"Did you like our goose?" Evan asked as I approached them.

"You know I can't say, and neither should you!" I teasingly admonished him.

"Well of course we're going to vote for our own dish, so we know it will get at least two votes," joked Jim.

"We'll have to go to the gym afterward to work off all of these calories," the ever-buff Evan answered. Then he turned to Jeffrey, whose eyes were closed in satisfaction as he finished off some "Chelsea Morning Jam" slathered on "Strawberry Scones Forever."

"Haven't seen you at the stables too much lately. Have you been riding on Sunday mornings, like you used to?" Evan asked.

Jeffrey squirmed a bit in his collar, and turned his head from side to side, oddly.

"I was there just the other day," he replied, and started tapping his finger on the bookshelf next to him.

"Huh?" Evan said. "Steve told me he hadn't seen you in weeks. In fact, he told me he hadn't seen you since you went out a couple of weeks ago, the day Honey got hurt. Her flank was all scratched up. He said at first it was nothing but it got infected a few days later and he was treating it."

"How's she doing now?" Jim asked Jeffrey.

"Who?" Jeffrey turned his head from side to side, looking distracted and confused. His eyes bugged.

Evan looked puzzled. "I was talking about your horse, Honey. Didn't you hear me? Weren't you going to take Tony's girlfriend out riding that day? I think it was a Sunday —"

Then he gasped as realization spread over his face.

Ginger Harrison.

In a fraction of a second I remembered: Tony told me that Ginger was learning to ride. "She always wanted to learn how to ride, so I got a friend to give her riding lessons at Morris Farms," was the last thing he had said to me in the only conversation Tony and I had ever had. Now they were both dead and...

Jeffrey looked pleadingly at Miche, who didn't say anything. Her eyes were on Evan, unmoving.

Jeffrey whipped his head toward me and stared. I was afraid to move or turn away. I stared back, but I didn't breathe. I tried to relax and look "normal," as if I hadn't just figured it all out in that moment when Evan casually asked him about his horse.

And Abby had ridden Honey the very next day, when he offered Abby and me his horses. Why had he done that? He had wanted us to think he was too busy to take them out, that they needed exercise, when in fact he and Ginger had ridden them the day before. Which he obviously didn't want anyone to know.

I didn't want him to know I knew.

I KNOW YOU KNOW WHAT HAPPENED.

I didn't before, but I knew now. Oh my God.

Transfixed by this realization, I was startled from my reverie when Jeffrey reached and grabbed an 8" Henckels chef's knife from the display behind him. He pulled me to him, and held it to my neck. In about two seconds flat.

What?

I gasped in shock and horror. Jeffrey reached for the apron tie behind my back, and pulled at it with his left hand. The apron tightened around me as he pulled the tie, and I felt his grip tighten on the knife. He was breathing hard, but he didn't speak. Neither did I.

"He's got a knife!" Sue Russo, who stood at the end of the aisle, facing us, screamed. Miche, Evan, and Jim were frozen in stunned silence.

"What?" I heard Rachel's voice, then Andy's.

"What?"

People rushed over, and I saw Andy push his way through.

"Let her go!" he hollered.

Seconds later Rachel Johnson and Rick Harris were standing at the end of the aisle, guns drawn.

"Shit," muttered Jeffrey under his breath. I could smell his sweat now, mixed in with the alcohol.

It was Andy's voice I heard next. I felt strange, like I had separated from my body, but I didn't know where I was.

His voice was even, calm. "Jeffrey, there is no reason to hurt Bonnie. Let her go, and we can go on with things. Bonnie has to make sure that everyone has voted. She has to count the votes. Let her go, so she can do it. It's important. This is Cookbooktoberfest. All of these people have worked very hard to make this food."

"I worked hard, too," Jeffrey growled. "I got out of Philly after Cinny died, I went to Florida, I made money, I came here, built the restaurant..."

Rick Harris spoke, evenly. "Who is Cinny?"

"What?" Jeffrey seemed to notice him for the first time, and the others. And their guns. He turned his head quickly, like a bird alerted to a new sound. I could feel his breath on my neck. Was he going to cut me? I tried not to move. I could feel the corners of the apron fabric cut into my armpits.

"Cinny died. In Philly. She was a chemistry genius. She mixed up the drugs, and we were gonna get rich. I sold a lot, and we were gonna go to Florida."

He stared ahead, seeing nothing. "I went without her."

By now the entire shop was silent. I wondered where everyone was. Sue was gone from the end of the aisle. There was Andy, in front of the spatulas, not moving a muscle. Next to him were Rachel and Rick. Their guns were trained on Jeffrey. From the way Jeffrey had my head turned I couldn't see Miche, or Jim, or Evan. But I knew they were inches away. Everything was still.

"What happened to her?" asked Rick. He had clearly taken charge. Thank God.

"She had an allergic reaction. She kept rubbing her hands on her thighs, back and forth, back and forth. She couldn't control her tongue. I brought her to the hospital. They couldn't save her. My Cinnamon..."

"Cinnamon?" asked Rick, calmly. He was trying to get him to keep talking.

"Yeah, Cinnamon Harrison, Ginger's sister. Their mother liked spices." He snickered, and tensed.

"Ha!" he sneered.

The knife nicked me. I felt my blood trickling down my neck.

"I'm sorry, Miche. I tried, I really tried," he murmured. There were tears in his eyes.

"Jeffrey, no!" she begged.

He drove the knife further into my neck. I heard a loud pop. Then I felt an uncontrollable urge to vomit. Which I did, a little. Then Jeffrey let go of me, his fingers tangled in the apron strings.

Cinnamon. In my head I heard Neil Young singing, "I wanna live with a cinnamon girl." The song Ginger had sung to Zoe must have been a song for the sister she had lost.

Then the singing stopped, and I was falling. I saw stars, which I always did when I vomited. Hundreds of pretty little stars…

Andy caught me.

There was a big commotion.

I heard Rick's voice. "We got him."

But that was Andy's shoulder, Andy's shirt. In front of my eyes, close. He was holding me tight. Squeezing me. I was safe. Something was pressing on my neck. I turned my head. It was Rachel, pressing something into my neck. Out of the corner of my eye I could see that it was a checked kitchen towel from the display.

More shouting. Now I was loose from Andy, and some other arms were moving me. Andy's voice, far away now, "It's all right, Bonnie, you're going to be fine."

Chapter 14

I opened my eyes. Andy was above me, looking down at me, smiling tenderly. I was lying in a bed and there was a white sheet over me. I blinked. I tried to move my hand, to touch him, but my arm was attached to a tube. An IV.

An IV? Was I in the hospital?

"Andy?" I squeaked.

"Bonnie, it's all right. You're okay, honey, you're fine." His voice choked, but I understood him. I was fine, everything was okay, and I loved him. So much.

"You lost a lot of blood, and you passed out. He missed the carotid artery. They're giving you blood. And painkillers. Dr. Ruskin is taking care of you. You're going to be fine. You can go home tomorrow."

"Tomorrow?" What day was it? Oh my God — Cookbooktoberfest! Elizabeth Crisp! Royal!

I tried to sit up, but there was something big on my neck. I reached for it. A large cushy bandage. Ugh.

"Everything's okay," Andy said, again. "They are giving you blood now, and some fluids, and you'll stay here tonight."

"What time is it?" I asked.

"Almost six."

"William?" I asked.

"He's fine. He's still at Alex's. It's dinner time now. I told him I'd pick him up later. I just talked to him. They're watching a movie. He's fine. I told him there was a little accident and you were in the hospital but you were fine and you'd be home tomorrow. We'll pick you up together and bring you home."

"Okay. What about the contest, and Elizabeth…" I said.

"After the police released them, Abby took Elizabeth and Royal to the train station. I talked to her a few minutes ago. She's on her way over. She said that after we left in the ambulance, the police herded everyone into the empty store across the street from Village Cooks. After the police interviewed them and the commotion died down, Elizabeth, Royal, and Sally took over the rest of the contest."

"Really? How nice!" I was feeling very peaceful, and very happy. Andy looked so handsome.

Then Abby appeared in the doorway, and rushed into the room.

"Abby, hi…" I managed. She had tears in her eyes as she rushed over to me. Andy was holding one hand, and she gently grabbed the other, the one with the IV.

"I'm so glad you're okay," she croaked.

The three of us fought back tears for a moment. I think I felt better than they did, probably due to the painkillers I was on, and recovered my emotions first.

"Cookbooktoberfest?" I asked.

"Oh Bonnie, it was wild." Abby said, and sat down in a chair next to the bed. "The police moved us all across the street into that empty store. We were all hanging around, absolutely miserable. Then they took us, one by one, into the back room, and interviewed us. It seemed like it was going to take forever, and everyone was upset. The police wouldn't let us leave, we had to all stay there. So Elizabeth and Royal took over. I think they were trying to cheer us up. Royal took charge of everything, like an MC. He stood there with his booming voice and banged his cane on the wall to get everyone quiet. He told us all to sit down on the floor. A lot of people were already doing that, but some were milling about. Then he said that you would want us to continue, and that we should do so in your honor. That you had worked very hard on Cookbooktoberfest and developed a wonderful annual event. He said your business was an asset to the community and that it brought people together."

"Really? How sweet of him," I said.

She continued her story. "He calmed everyone down, then he asked if everyone had voted. Apparently Sally had the ballot box in her hands when the commotion started, and was still holding onto it when we went across the street. So a few came forward and slipped their ballots in. Then he sent Sally and me to a corner to count the votes. When Sally and I started to walk to an empty corner to count them, people cheered and applauded."

"Wow," said Andy, shaking his head.

She patted my hand, then let go. Andy was holding my other hand.

She continued. "We were off counting and Michael Quinn came in and told us that they were finished interviewing the people they needed to, and we could go, but they'd be in touch. Everyone clapped again. Then they looked at us. Sally and I had finished counting, and we had a winner. Sally held up the ballot box, and everyone cheered."

"Wow," said Andy. "What a crazy scene."

Abby grinned and went on. "So we brought the box over to Royal and Elizabeth, and Sally whispered the names of the winners to them."

"Who won?" I asked.

"Danielle Schacht and Zoe Harrison!"

"Ah!" I burst out.

"That's great!" exclaimed Andy.

"Elizabeth "judged" the vote and said she accepted the results after she announced Danielle and Zoe's names. It was touching, poignant, really, when you think of that sweet little girl, her mother and all that happened… especially today…" She choked a little, and cleared her throat.

Andy finished her sentence. "Linking it all together," he said. I slowly turned my head, which wasn't easy to do with the bandage on my neck, and looked over at him, my wonderful insightful husband. He had blood on his shirt, a lot of it on his shoulder spilling down on to his chest.

"Your shirt!" I yelped.

"It's all right. It's only a shirt."

"Who took second place? The goose?" Andy asked, getting the discussion away from the shirt and back where it started.

Big presentation dishes like the turkey or the goose often won first prize. But that gingerbread stuffing had been absolutely delicious.

"Yes, Jim and Evan won with their Roast Goose in Splendor and all of their sauerkraut and apples. It was very good."

"No desserts?" I asked.

"Don't worry. Third prize was the Old World Chocolate Cake."

"Oh, Lisa Rounds won!" I was pleased. I liked her, and I loved the clothes in her shop, Vintage Ladybug. "It's a great recipe," I said. "I've made it twice. Good for her."

Then I remembered. "We have to give them their gift certificates!"

"Yes, and the nutmeg grater gifts for the participants. Elizabeth said you would give them out at a later date, and she got choked up when she said that. I think she was worried about you, although Michael Quinn had announced that you'd be fine. Elizabeth was so nice during that awful time when the interviews were going on. She talked to everyone at length, trying to distract them. Not just about the food. She asked them what they did, where they lived, how long they had been cooking, about their children, that sort of thing. She was absolutely charming. So was Royal."

I shook my head in disbelief.

Abby shook hers, mimicking me. "We almost forgot what had happened, it was so much fun and they did such a good job rallying us and distracting us. After all, it had been pretty grisly."

Jeffrey! I remembered. Evan innocently chatting about Honey, Jeffrey's horse, being scratched up. THAT Sunday. Jeffrey suddenly grabbing me. The knife. Miche's face looking at me with such sadness and fear. Then Andy's shoulder, cradling me.

"Dear Lord, what about Jeffrey?" I asked.

Andy stood up and looked down at me intently. He said, "He's here in the hospital. Under guard."

"Is he hurt?" I asked.

"Rick Harris shot him right after he stabbed you. In the shoulder just above the heart. It's touch and go."

The pop. I had heard the sound, but I didn't know what it was. It sounded fuzzy, certainly not like a gunshot. But then again, I had just been stabbed, and my senses weren't working at full alert.

"Did Jeffrey kill Ginger?" I asked.

Andy's voice was quiet and very serious. "Miche rode with him in the ambulance. Before he lost consciousness he told her he didn't mean to hit Ginger, but they were arguing, she wanted money, and she accused him of killing her sister, Cinnamon. So he lost it and yelled at her and maybe swung at her — he wasn't clear — and she fell off the horse and hit her head. It must have happened just as we were walking home, because he told Miche, 'Bonnie saw me on the horse. She knew.'"

He took my hand again.

He went on. "I talked to Michael Quinn. We don't know for sure about all of it, of course, because he lost consciousness after he spoke to Miche, and when he got here they brought him right into surgery. He's in recovery now. Michael thinks it's probable that Jeffrey slashed your tires at the cemetery, hired someone to shoot the store window, and sent you that note. By the time of the note, he had been drinking a lot and had been getting paranoid. Miche said he was a mess all week, drinking heavily, worse than she'd ever seen him. She thought it was because of Tony's death. Which was part of it, of course."

"Did he kill Tony?"

"Don't know. Miche thinks he was jealous of Dennis and Tony starting the school. He knew they had inherited Christopher Russo's fortune and would use that for the school. He wanted to be part of it, but they wouldn't let him."

Andy asked, "Why not?"

"I don't know. I'll have to ask Dennis if he knows."

"Where is Miche?" I asked.

Andy answered, "She was at the police station when I spoke to Michael, oh, half an hour ago."

There was a flash of movement in the doorway and we all looked up.

"Bonnie!" cried both of my parents in unison.

"Oh, sweetie," crooned my mother as she reached over the bed and put her arms around me. She hugged me for what seemed like a long time. There was silence in the room. I realized I was crying, safe in my mother's arms. She was crying, too. After all my parents had been through with my sister, I too hadn't been safe.

I had been stabbed, but I would survive.

Slowly she let go and stood back, moved away from the bed. My father took his turn. "Bonnie!" he cried, his lips quivering as he reached to give me a hug. He recovered more quickly than my mother had, and pulled up a chair.

"How are you?"

"I feel wonderful. It's wonderful to see you. You didn't have to come, but I'm glad you did. I feel wonderful." I beamed.

"She's on morphine," Andy told my parents.

"Oh," they nodded in unison.

"We spoke to the doctor outside," my father said. "He said you're lucky to be alive."

My mother's face cracked, and she burst into a sob.

"I'm okay, Mom, I am. Dad, I'm good." I tried to reassure them. I watched as my father put my mother's hand in his, then patted hers with his other hand, cupping her hand in both of his.

"Well, it looks like this episode is finally over," Dad said.

Andy said, "I agree."

"Thank God," added Abby.

"It turns out that Jeffrey Sloane was involved in the accidental drug death of Ginger Harrison's sister, Cinnamon," Dad explained.

"We suspected that," I said.

He went on. "Apparently Ginger asked him for money. I don't know if it was a bribe. Ginger wanted to buy a house in Florida."

"Florida?" asked Andy. I was surprised, too.

"The police found real estate literature in her room. They found a computer printout from Realtor.com of a deli with an apartment upstairs in Palm Beach County."

"Awww," I heard myself say. I was imagining Ginger planning a new life with Tony and Zoe in Florida. He could cook Italian specialities, she could wait on people in the deli. They could live upstairs. Zoe could go to school. Compared to what they had been through, it would have been wonderful…

Dad continued. "She had $4,600 in the bank. Tony had $3,500. The deli was $110,000. With their background, it's doubtful they could have gotten financing."

Andy said, "And that all happened before Christopher Russo died and left Dennis and Tony millions. Ginger wouldn't have needed to ask Jeffrey for money if she'd waited one more week."

He sighed and looked around grimly. "When you put that together with what Miche told the police, it sounds like Ginger asked Jeffrey to

take her riding, and used the opportunity to ask him for financial help —
while trading on her knowledge of his role in her sister's death to pressure
him."

"The restaurant has a big mortgage," Abby put in. "He might have
been able to co-sign for her, but Jeffrey didn't have extra cash lying
around."

"He didn't?" I asked, remembering the black cashmere sweater he had
worn to Cookbooktoberfest. Undoubtedly a bloody mess now, and torn to
shreds.

Abby sighed. "The economy has affected business. People still go out
to eat on weekends, but not as much as they used to during the week. Even
around here. Jeffrey was paying the bills, but just barely. He was very
anxious about it. That's why he was pushing Miche about developing the
catering business."

"So he couldn't help Ginger," Mom said.

Abby continued. "Knowing him, the way he always flailed his arms
around when he was excited, he was probably telling her that. Maybe they
had a fight and he pushed her, or maybe he accidentally knocked her off
the horse."

"Honey," I said.

"What?" Dad asked.

"Honey was the name of his horse. His other horse was Gulliver," I
said. "Remember, Abby? I rode Gulliver, and you rode Honey. We didn't
notice that he was hurt."

"But he was slower than Gulliver, remember?"

"Yeah, I do."

"If only horses could talk," I mused, then giggled, thinking of Mister
Ed. "A horse is a horse of course of course and no one can talk to a horse
of course…" I sang.

"Bonnie!" scolded my mother.

But Dad's eyes twinkled. He remembered my childhood Nick at Nite
rerun favorite. We had watched it together.

I straightened up the best I could, and recovered.

"If horses could talk," I stated, "Honey would have told us what
happened to Ginger."

"Gotta love morphine," said Andy.

Dr. Ruskin woke me up at seven the next morning. She reviewed my chart and said I could go home.

"But please take it easy," she admonished. "Stay home and rest for a few days. The nurse will bring you some bandages with your discharge instructions. Change the bandage every day, and come back for a wound check on Tuesday. I'll be in the ER in the morning, so if you come then, I'll look at it myself."

"Will do," I agreed. She nodded, and was gone. A nurse came in and removed my IV, then got me a washcloth and towel. I was just finishing washing up the best I could without turning my head, and was heading out of the bathroom, when Andy and William arrived.

"Mommy!" William squealed and leaped toward me. His embrace nearly knocked me over. Andy joined him. For a long moment we stood there. Dr. Ruskin had told my parents I was lucky to be alive. I felt like the luckiest woman in the world.

Andy and William went to the waiting room while I changed into the clothes Andy had brought me from home. Andy had wisely brought me my brown loafers, navy blue sweat pants, and a yellow oxford button-up blouse I didn't have to put over my head to get into. The outfit didn't go together, but I didn't care. Leaning forward to put the sweatpants on was harder than I expected it to be. I slid into the loafers, took a deep breath, and settled into the visitor chair beside the bed and waited for them to come back.

They did, a moment later, and to my surprise, Danielle and Zoe were with them.

"Dr. Schacht works at this hospital, too," William explained to me. "She has an office, but she comes here to check on her patients."

I looked up at Danielle, who was beaming at me. So was Zoe.

"Some of them are so sick they have to stay here on the weekend," added Zoe. "So we had to come and check on them, right?"

Danielle nodded. "My two patients who are here today are going to be fine. They'll probably go home tomorrow."

"Are you going to go back to Village Cooks?" Zoe asked me, shyly.

"Yes, I am. After the doctor checks my bandage on Tuesday," I told her. "I'm going to stay home and rest until then."

"Oh, I'm so glad!" Zoe exclaimed.

"You are?"

"I have a favor to ask you." She drummed her hand on the white sheet on the bed, and twisted her leg in that coquettish pose I remembered from the first time I met her.

"What is it?"

"Will you have children's cooking lessons at your store?"

I laughed too loud, and my neck hurt.

"What a great idea. We have never had them, but there's no reason why we shouldn't. What do you think we should make in the first class?"

"Christmas cookies?" William eagerly suggested.

"Not quite." Zoe gave me her most impish, precious smile, then shouted, "Gingerbread!"

www.ingramcontent.com/pod-product-compliance
Lightning Source LLC
Chambersburg PA
CBHW021232130626
46554CB00004B/1446